THE LAWS OF DYING

The Laws of Dying

Louise Walsh

Carreg Gwalch

First published in 2025

ISBN: 978-1-84527-960-8

Published with the financial support of the Books Council of Wales

Cover design: Eleri Owen

Published by Gwasg Carreg Gwalch
www.carreg-gwalch.cymru

Printed and published in Wales

For my family

Acknowledgements

Firstly, thank you to Belinda Bauer and Sharon Bolton, together with my fellow attendees, for their feedback during 'Lost the Plot?' – a Ty Newydd crime writing holiday in 2022, where I began to shape this story.

Thank you to Jacqueline Harrett for the useful beta reader comments on an early draft. Thanks also to Catrin Kean for reviewing my opening pages with an expert eye.

Mentioning Catrin brings me to my other Writers at Work friends that my creative heart can't live without: Rhian Elizabeth, Zillah Bowes, Mark Blaney, Clare Potter, Rebecca Parfitt, Phil Jones, Ben Wildsmith and the rest of the W@W gang. A string of blowing-a-kiss emjois to Tiffany Murray and Literature Wales, for bringing us all together at the Hay Festival in 2016.

Thanks to Martin Shipton for championing me always, beta reading my draft manuscripts and finding typos everywhere when I'm convinced there are none.

I count my IC1 female blessings to have the formidable knowledge of Paul Howlett in all matters police procedural. If I could dust my draft manuscript for corrective fingerprints, his ex-Senior Investigating Officer's loops, ridges and whorls would show up in every interview scene. The fictional Detective Inspector in this book, Cerys Lennon, thanks him too.

Gratitude goes to Professor Penney Lewis and Professor Richard Huxtable for guiding me towards their published research material which was so pertinent to the plot.

Finally, enormous thanks to Myrddin ap Dafydd, the Gwasg Carreg Gwalch team and the Welsh Books Council, for giving this book a chance. It was in a drawer, gathering dust, until a surprise email arrived. There's more in the drawer, if you want them!

Huge thanks to my brother, Tommy Walsh, for his interesting/shocking rugby tales.

Thank you all so much.

Chapter 1

It wasn't every day a great sporting hero wanted to die, but Harriet Erskine's future at Eiriol Law depended on it.

The former international rugby player's case had landed on her boss's desk the previous Monday. Already engaged in a two-day London hearing that second week in October, Rowan Tudor had instructed her to put together the background in Kennedy Jones' assisted dying challenge. Harriet seized this rare opportunity, knowing the high-profile instruction had the potential to dominate news headlines and spark a national debate.

The previous afternoon, she'd set up Kennedy Jones as a client on the system. Though a proud Welshman, Kennedy's friends and family had, long ago, nicknamed him 'JFK' and therefore she and Rowan had adopted the same shorthand.

JFK's nurse, Boyd Evans, had acknowledged safe receipt of the firm's formal letter of engagement, which Harriet had finalised in Rowan's absence using his digi-signature.

Though Harriet revelled in her promotion, her desk, at a right angle to Rowan's impressive oak expanse, reminded her of a ticket sales table or coat check at pub events. All she needed was a money tin full of change, a raffle ticket book and a rack of hangers on a clothes rail behind her.

Harriet suspected Rowan's father Nigel, who set up Eiriol Law, also wanted a spy. Rowan had managed to embarrass the company at the Welsh law awards during his first week at the firm by drinking too much red wine. From the way she'd heard it, he'd leered over female solicitors, teeth stained in Bordeaux grape and his shirtfront spillage looking like he'd taken a knife to the heart.

Catching the faint whiff of Rowan's tequila breath in the room from the previous Friday afternoon, Harriet looked at the silver, ornamental letter opener on Rowan's desk and knew just where she'd like to plunge it.

Nigel Tudor had instructed the two of them to 'make it work' and, since then, they had, although she only really relaxed when she had the room to herself. At such times, Harriet gravitated to the window where she pressed her fingertips to the cold glass. She was drawn to that glimpse of Bristol Channel between the prison-like, smoked-glass structures of the corporate buildings opposite.

Today, however, there was little to see.

Beyond the floor-to-ceiling windows on their fifth-floor office, such rain fell on Cardiff that city and sombre sky softened behind a pale mist. Drops tapped at the glass. It was late enough in the morning for the streetlamps to be off and the inclement gloom, brightened only by the head and taillights of bumper-to-bumper morning traffic had, for Harriet, a melancholy feel.

She knuckled down to finish her two-part report, cross-referencing the background notes she'd compiled from JFK's past interviews and the resources of Eiriol Law's library on the seventh floor.

The first section outlined what Kennedy Jones had endured physically and mentally since his accident in the Six Nations. The second required a neat paraphrasing of the three most instructive judicial review assisted dying cases of *Purdy*, *Petty* and *Nicklinson*.

This was a world away from the mindless audio typing of attendance notes, alongside her old secretarial colleagues.

For a moment, Harriet lost herself in Kennedy Jones' passport picture. So handsome, she thought, leaning on an elbow and pinching the frame of her glasses between finger and thumb. She sighed at the scanned on-screen image, wondering how long before the incident it had been taken.

Kennedy's cartoon-cowboy jawline, his muscular shoulders and his mangled cauli-ears told of countless battles on the international rugby field, yet his face had a presidential symmetry. His blue eyes, framed by pale lashes, had the pride and determination of a man not asking what his country could do for him, but what he could do for his country – via his kicking game and scoring of tries.

Heartbreaking, she thought.

There was so much to learn. Lawyers remained detached, but how could anyone remain objective about Wales' beloved JFK wanting to end his life when there were others, like her boss, who didn't deserve or appreciate the charmed life they had?

Interrupted by the admin assistant delivering post, Harriet grabbed the green-handled scissors from her mesh pen pot and snipped through the brown parcel tape sealing a small, padded Jiffy bag. The package was addressed to Rowan 'care of' her, which Harriet liked because it meant Rowan was deputising to her in his absence, just as he should.

The envelope's damp and grubby exterior, along with an odd odour of raw meat packaging, put Harriet off touching it any more than she had to. Grimacing, and unable to quite make out the contents wedged within, she turned the envelope upside down and gave it a shake.

When a gold ring fell onto the desk with a coin-like metallic clunk, followed by a severed finger, which landed on Kennedy Jones' open client file, she shot up from her desk and recoiled with a sickened groan.

If this was a joke, it was a cruel and unforgivable one. It looked so real. Prosthetic effects like that – the joints, the perfectly formed nail – demonstrated impeccable make-up artistry. Would her boss, Rowan Tudor, really enact such a disgusting, early Halloween prank – after everything that had happened last Friday afternoon?

Maybe the gruesome fakery was Rowan's unconventional way of acknowledging he'd never put his hands on her again, but this idea didn't square.

Harriet recognised the signet ring, a gift from his father, because Rowan wore it daily. And the finger, well, the likeness was uncanny.

To prevent anyone bursting into their office before she'd processed what she was looking at, Harriet closed the door and appraised the items from the other side of her desk.

No, it *was real.*

Kneading her hands, she clenched her jaw to stop her teeth chattering. It was as though someone had turned the aircon down ten degrees. Physical sense of her own body ebbed and her head floated, like the silver foil helium balloons they'd bought Rowan's father, Nigel, for his 60th birthday.

She forced herself to pick up the envelope and look inside. A slip of folded paper bore the name Nigel Tudor. Had someone kidnapped Rowan to blackmail his father and senior partner at Eiriol Law? It hardly seemed credible.

Hoping he'd answer on the first ring, Harriet called Rowan. She visualised him answering and anticipated mixed feelings if he did, but the call went to answerphone. She left a message full of vague ramblings, asking him to urgently get in touch.

Harriet didn't want Rowan hurt, of course, and the effect the severed finger would have on Nigel distressed her, but there was a good chance Rowan would survive and hopefully return a chastened individual, with more empathy for others. Someone wanted to teach him a lesson and there was little she could do about that.

She'd wanted to teach him one herself.

She'd even got herself a nice little spin-off, side-hustle off the back of it. People could relate. Everyone had fallen foul of a lousy boss at one time or another.

With a white, plastic ruler, she manoeuvred her boss's little finger off her keyboard and encouraged it back into the envelope. Next, she hooked the ring on a pencil and flicked that too, back into the narrow mouth of the Jiffy bag.

The police needed to be contacted, but not without Karen's authorisation as her direct line manager. Harriet phoned her, but Karen didn't answer.

For the second time, Rowan's number went to voicemail.

She had to find Karen.

At the office manager's empty desk, a personal injury lawyer helped himself to a lens-wipe sachet from the box next to her monitor, topped up often because of Karen's compulsion about clean specs.

Debbie, a secretary in dispute resolution, watched the lawyer walk away, before turning to Harriet.

'Are you okay?' Debbie asked, wrinkling her nose. 'You look dreadful.'

'Can you tell Karen I need her urgently – in Rowan's room.'

'Sure, can I be your secretary too? Run and fetch you coffee? Let me know if you put any dictations on the BigHand system.'

Harriet sagged against Karen's desk and put her hand to her sticky forehead. It was support she needed, not sarcasm.

'I was only joking,' Debbie said. Her tone translated to *Jeez, you're sensitive.*

'Yeah,' Harriet said, breathless and distant, conflicted as to whether to return to their room or continue her search for Karen.

'Honest, you look like shit. Do you need to go home?'

'When Karen comes back,' Harriet said, 'tell her I'm in Rowan's room and she needs to come. Please tell her it's urgent.'

Another ten minutes passed. Her foot tapping with impatience, Harriet leant against the wall staring at the envelope as if half-expecting the finger to creep out like Thing, from *The Addams Family*.

Finally, Karen turned up, teasing volume into her short highlighted, hairspray-hard hair.

'What's going on?' she asked, concern ringing in her voice. 'Debbie said you were in some kind of state. Are you sick?'

'We need to speak to Nigel about that envelope,' Harriet said, pointing to her desk. 'And probably call the police.'

From the corridor came the flat, hurried footsteps of Nigel. His frown suggested he was aggrieved his son had missed their morning meeting.

'Where the hell's he got to?' Nigel said.

Harriet's heartrate increased like paid-by-the-word typists approaching home time.

'Harriet says we need to call the police,' Karen said, her voice squeaky, holding her hands wide. 'I think your Rowan's had something dodgy delivered to the office.'

'What are you talking about?' Nigel said.

'Karen, can I have a quick word with you?' Harriet asked, pleading with her eyes. 'In *private*.'

'Where is it?' Nigel asked, arms folded, head back.

Harriet stood in the way of her desk. If only she could explain to Karen and get her to break the shock to Nigel with a little compassion.

'Karen?' Harriet said, wide-eyed, desperate to communicate a need for caution. 'I really need to talk to you alone first.'

'Give him the envelope, Harriet,' Karen said, tucking her teal blouse back into the green waistband of her skirt. 'For goodness' sake. If Rowan's had it delivered here, it's office property.'

Fine, Harriet thought, surrendering with a side-step.

'There it is,' she said. How innocent the small Jiffy looked, belying the horrific things it contained.

Harriet's expression must have betrayed her thoughts because Nigel, allowed to proceed, now showed sudden hesitation. For what seemed like an age, the three Eiriol Law staff stood there in the silence of the room, staring at each other.

'Is it drugs?' Nigel asked, moving a step closer, but still not picking up the envelope. 'How dare you call the police about my son without speaking to me first. You, of all people, should know the toxic relationship I have with South Wales Police.'

At last, Nigel picked up the envelope and looked inside. Then he took it over to the window and angled it, throwing natural light on the contents, scowling as he did so. When he withdrew the slip of paper with his name on, Harriet bit her lip and turned away.

'I'm sorry,' she whispered.

He held up the paper for them to read.

We've got your son. Don't involve the police. We're watching.

Nigel tipped the package so Karen could also see inside.

The office manager grabbed Harriet's shoulder, knees buckling. Harriet held her, drawing unexpected comfort from Karen's warmth.

'It can't be real,' Karen whispered, letting go of Harriet. 'This has to be a sick joke, Nigel?'

Harriet's sense of smell was suddenly intense: the stale cigarette smoke from Karen's pre-work ciggie and her Carmella perfume. They at least overpowered the smell of the envelope which had clung to her since she'd opened it.

'That's what I thought, at first,' Harriet said.

'That's not my son's,' Nigel said, full of heated conviction, throwing the envelope onto Rowan's desk in disgust. 'I don't know who that damn thing belongs to, but it's not Rowan.'

'Then why would ...?' Harriet began.

Nigel took his mobile from his pocket and called Rowan, first on his work phone, then on his personal mobile.

'You think I wouldn't recognise a part of my son's hand? I'm his father. I didn't become the lawyer I am today by accepting anyone's old say-so. No. Show me some evidence first, then we'll talk.'

When a further call to his son went unanswered, Nigel covered his mouth with both hands. Harriet had never seen Eiriol's senior partner so hesitant and conflicted.

'It's the signet ring too,' Harriet whispered, trying to help him accept the situation, ignoring Karen who shook her head in warning.

'Karen. Make her see sense,' Nigel said, waving in her direction.

The two women looked at each other.

'Yes,' Karen said, after a revealing hesitation where, arms crossed, face waxy, she gave Nigel a sideways glance. 'We ... can't jump to conclusions. If anyone, anyone knows Rowan ... it's Nigel.'

'Anyone can steal a gold ring,' Nigel said, flapping his fingers at Harriet as though they were adorned with jewellery. 'Ten-a-penny. I want proof. Get the fucking DNA match off that thing. Then we'll talk.'

While Harriet admired the man's conviction in the sanctity of legal fact, she hoped he didn't mean she was supposed to arrange a DNA match. Her mouth gold-fished for a moment and she pointed to herself. Me?

'Not you, Harriet,' Karen said, placing a supportive hand on Nigel's shoulder. She was there for him, the gesture said. 'We'll instruct an outside agency if we have to.'

Rowan's desk phone rang and Harriet picked up, half expecting to hear Rowan on the other end, laughing at their collective gullibility.

‘Hello?’ she said. ‘Harriet Erskine of Eiriol Law speaking.’

A distorted, artificially deep voice said, ‘Is he there?’ Harriet blanched and held out the phone to Nigel.

Chapter 2

'Yes?' Nigel said, snapping his fingers for one of them to hand him a pen. Harriet snatched the Biro off her desk and passed it to him. He clamped the black top between his teeth, spitting it to the floor as he scribbled.

His handwriting, Harriet noted, bore a resemblance to his son's.

'Now, you listen to me,' Nigel growled into the receiver, 'whoever the fuck you are. This monstrosity you've delivered doesn't convince me. Could be anyone's. Likewise, the ring. So, you can wait until we've got a positive DNA match ... No, not using the police. I've got my own clinical contacts for the DNA. Yeah, however long it takes. Yeah, yeah, yeah – it's *always* imperative. First rule of scamming is to get the clock ticking over my head. In my world, evidence is king. Tough shit. Yeah, is that right? Once we've established it's not some eighty-year-old hobbo who got hit by a valleys' train, we'll talk.'

The kidnappers set out their instructions, while Nigel pushed back on some things and agreed with others, taking notes.

There's nothing the man can't negotiate, Harriet thought. She just hoped his playing for time didn't result in an index finger or thumb arriving by 1pm guaranteed Royal Mail special delivery.

'As long as we're agreed that we're not moving until we've established provenance?' Nigel said, eyes fixed on the ceiling as the kidnapper on the other end agreed and gave instructions. 'Good,' he concluded.

'This is what we're going to do,' Nigel said, after he'd hung up and paced a few lengths. 'I'm going to call the Chief Super at South Wales Police and do my best to bury the hatchet.'

'Is that wise?' Karen said, 'given everything?'

'Yes,' Nigel said, nodding. 'It is. Harriet, would you bring a jug of water in here, with some glasses. On your way, ask Clare to give you my first aid kit. If she's not there, it's in the bottom drawer of my desk, left hand side. Tell her to clear my diary for the rest of the day. And let Petra know to hold all client calls to my office or coming through here.'

Away from her desk, in the main office and on the floors above and below, Eiriol lawyers continued their work for the large firm. The contrast struck Harriet as surreal. Metres away from a living nightmare, lawyers made coffee, answered calls, drafted emails and got on with the essential business of law. How would they react when they found out, she wondered.

She experienced a surge of elation. Usually, lawyers were the ones with power: the kings and queens of the jungle. It was easy to forget there were bigger predators out there – until some monster had snatched one of their number.

Their collective, continued ignorance, while they set up Teams calls with clients and emailed their secretaries, cast them in a new and vulnerable light, ill-equipped for the evils of this world. When it came down to it, their underbellies were as soft and helpless as infants in a crèche.

Nigel's PA, Clare, had worked for him for seventeen years, though she looked twenty-one, with her Cleopatra hair and dewy, Botoxed skin.

Unlike Harriet, who shared Rowan's office, Clare sat to the left of Nigel's door, but her white desk and the side-by-side black-framed Banksy police prints above her head spoke to her seniority. The first image depicted a police officer patting down a little girl. In the second, a crouching cop snorted a line of coke.

In Nigel's room, opposite the Tudor family portrait, hung a larger canvas where a sulking policeman gave the viewer the middle finger.

Early on in his career, Nigel had won, in short succession, a string of major miscarriages of justice and personal injury claims against South Wales Police. The work was lucrative enough for him to open his own office before turning thirty. Nigel's cases often attracted widespread publicity, which led to a fearsome reputation as an expert in his field.

It was therefore in connection with a potential action against the police that Nigel had promised Harriet a second chance. As an indebted law school dropout, she'd just needed to talk her reluctant parents into providing witness statements against South Wales Police, following the murder of their friend, Roddy Roberts.

Clare responded to Harriet's request for Nigel's first aid kit with a shrug, running a tongue over the shimmering gloss of her top lip. She disappeared into Nigel's room, where Harriet caught the faint strains of Baroque music played on an acoustic guitar. Nigel believed Bach, Vivaldi or their fellow composers in the background clarified his thought process. All the Eiriol lawyers had tried it out at one time or another. Clare switched the music off and closed Nigel's door behind her, carrying a half-full bottle of Penderyn Welsh whisky.

'One first aid kit,' Clare said, handing over the bottle.

Harriet's already overwhelmed system recognised it as the one her parents had sent Nigel as a gift. Then she remembered theirs had been 'Legend', while this one was 'Madeira Finish'.

Despite her protests that it wasn't the way things were done, her parents, Lottie and Louie, had also sent Rowan a bottle of Jose Cuervo tequila when she'd been made his legal assistant. The irony wasn't lost on either Harriet or Rowan. He'd pronounced the gesture 'kind' and her parents 'sweet' in such a patronising tone that it could only mean parochial. The way he said it made her want to snatch the gift back and keep it for herself.

When Harriet returned with the bottle, the water and three tumblers, Nigel stopped pacing to pour them all a good measure, which he diluted with a splash of water.

To be included in the round and not dismissed from the room touched Harriet. She'd remained in the inner circle, which spoke to Nigel's continuing trust in her.

On speakerphone, a woman came on the line, apologised for the wait and asked him if he was happy to hold, to which Nigel barked, 'yes'.

'Chief Superintendent Wallis,' a clipped voice said.

'Mark, it's Nigel Tudor. I need your help. My son's life is on the line. I really need for us to set aside our differences.'

A pause. 'What's going on?'

'It's my son, Rowan. You've probably read about him joining Eiriol. He may've been kidnapped. I've been sent a goddamn finger through the post, with his ring. They just called.'

'They've made contact?'

'Yeah, just now. They want a million in cash.'

'Cash?'

'Yeah.'

'Hmm.'

'What is it?'

'Sounds amateur.'

'That's what they've asked for. I can't raise anything that quickly, so I've stalled. I said I'm not doing anything until we've run a DNA test to prove the finger's his. I mean, it might not be. What worries me is that no-one can reach him. Nobody's heard from him since yesterday.'

'You've done the right thing contacting us.'

'Thank you. Because it's never been personal,' Nigel said. 'I appreciate it doesn't always feel like it, but it's not.'

'Water under the bridge, Nigel.'

That water might be icier than it looked, Harriet thought. Even if the Chief Super was prepared to let bygones be bygones, he surely couldn't speak for rank and file. Urban myth had it that images of Nigel's face were used by South Wales Police during firearms training.

'Are we still covert?' the Chief Super asked.

'You mean, do they know I'm contacting you?' Nigel said, staring into his whisky. 'No. I'm sure they think I wouldn't approach you given our history. But when my son's life is at stake, there's nothing I won't do.'

'Quite right.'

'So, what would you suggest?'

'I'll have to hand this over to CID, Detective Inspector Cerys Lennon. She'll want to meet you, away from the office.'

'Okay. I'll have to bring someone called Harriet.'

'Wait. What?' Harriet said, forgetful of the speakerphone.

'Who's she? What's her involvement?' the police chief said.

'Harriet Erskine,' Nigel said, silencing Harriet with a glare. 'Rowan's legal assistant.'

'You should only involve other Eiriol employees if absolutely necessary,' the Chief Superintendent warned. 'DI Lennon will be in touch. Expect a phone call and try not to worry.'

'Thank you,' Nigel said, before hanging up. 'I appreciate it.'

'Sorry,' Harriet said, 'I didn't expect my name to come up.'

'Not my choice,' Nigel said, reading through the notes he'd made while on the phone to the kidnappers. 'The original envelope was sent to you. The people who've got him also want you to make the drop.'

'That doesn't make sense. Why me?' Harriet said, massaging out the tension in her neck.

Nigel looked up from his notes and flicked the pad with the back of his hand.

'Those are the instructions.'

Harriet chewed her lip. Something wasn't right about any of this.

'I don't know,' Harriet said. Remembering the alcohol in her glass, she knocked it back. It scalded her throat and she refilled her glass with water to cleanse her palette. Her mum's favourite drink was an Old Fashioned, but even then she exchanged the whisky for bourbon and added a spoon of brown sugar. 'I don't get why they'd want me to do it.'

'You don't *get it*?' Nigel said, putting his middle finger to his temple and tapping three times. 'Just do as you're told. You think I'm enjoying this?'

Such condescension hurt and Harriet looked away, her face tingling with humiliation.

Nigel wasn't finished.

'After everything this firm's done for you?' he said.

'Let's see if it's him first,' Harriet said. 'It might not be Rowan. You said it yourself.'

'Promoted to legal assistant. Offered CILEX,' Nigel continued, voice raised, counting off her opportunities on his fingers.

‘It’s not that I’m not grateful,’ Harriet said. She was, up to a point. The job she was grateful for. Her promotion and the offer of Chartered Legal Executive training, however, didn’t come without a few misgivings.

After the third tequila incident, Harriet had tentatively tapped on Nigel’s door in the hope of an intervention due to Rowan’s harassment. Nigel promised to take his wayward son in hand.

The next day, Nigel called Harriet back to his office.

‘I’ve warned him to utilise you the right way,’ Nigel said, after an authoritative clearing of his throat. ‘He really needs your support. I can’t say too much, but he confided in me – shared some information that sheds light on his behaviour.’

‘What did he say?’ Harriet asked, relieved that she wasn’t being fired for complaining – and too intrigued to keep up the poker face. If Nigel Tudor had the key to his son’s instability, then the information was more valuable to her than an extra day’s pay. The puzzle of it sometimes kept her awake.

‘It’s a deeply private matter,’ Nigel Tudor said, milking each of his last three words for their two respective syllables. ‘It’s possible he’ll tell you himself but, in the meantime, you’re going to have to harmonise. If things carry on the way they are, Rowan risks not meeting his ambitious billing targets. He’ll have a problem with the firm’s other senior partners to add to his difficulties. To that end, he did have one good suggestion.’

‘Which was?’

‘A promotion. He needs a legal assistant. You did have ambitions in law, right? There’s more than one route to qualification. If the pair of you can make it work, I’ll see you’re enrolled for CILEX next year and pay the fees myself. It’s not the LPC, but a Chartered Executive course amounts to nearly the same thing – and you won’t have to pay a penny.’

Harriet brightened.

‘At his last firm, Rowan tells me he mentored a secretary,’ Nigel continued, ‘in her route to legal qualification. Social mobility is something he’s passionate about.’

‘I had no idea,’ Harriet said, wondering why Rowan so often aped stereotypical class-snobbery if he felt that way.

‘He doesn’t want it made common knowledge,’ Nigel said. ‘We can’t pay for everyone’s education, you understand. There are secretaries who should undoubtedly *stay* secretaries.’

Harriet smiled, thinking of her colleagues, Debbie and Ffion.

Yes, it was an obvious pay-off, but Harriet recalled the numerous times she’d soft-sold CILEX training to Karen and the ‘tough love’ advice she’d received the last time she’d mentioned it.

‘You’ll never be one of them, Harriet,’ Karen had said with a regretful smile. ‘Nobody’s doubting your intelligence, but it’s a question of character. Lawyers are kids who grow up certain they’ll win every argument, even when they’re wrong. You dropped out of law at Cardiff Uni two terms in – and that says doubt to me. I know you had a tough time, after the death of your family friend, but still.’

Like ripples in a pond, the trauma of Roddy’s murder had seen her walk away from law school after just two semesters. Instead, she and her poet boyfriend, Carwyn, had travelled to the US on her university maintenance loan and credit cards.

Now, she couldn’t even remember half of it. Just snippets. Her and Carwyn in a hipster café, jetlagged and eating a breakfast of ricotta and strawberry jam on brioche toast; a man on the New York subway getting on with a shopping trolley and playing with his Zippo lighter until the whole carriage smelled like petrol; getting lost and wandering into a no-go homeless area; taking the overnight bus to Vegas and watching a cacophony of electronic signs announcing that a child had been abducted in a white Chevy; waking up to a Hollywood sky in California, a 1950s beauty parlour of breeze-blown translucent powder and blush; a man in gospel robes asking them if they wanted him to pray for them; US skies of the softest blue, like aged denim, and cities that twinkled at night like the low-lit window displays of expensive jewellers.

Running away had cost her a small fortune.

The legal assistant role was a chance to prove Karen wrong and get her career goals back on track. It amounted, finally, to redemption.

From then on, Harriet tried to view Rowan's occasional harassment as an occupational hazard and, as a budding Chartered Exec, challenged herself to not only resist but find a workable recourse. She'd already taken certain measures. On the likely tequila days – such as those when Rowan returned from London – she retreated behind a conservative, somewhat androgynous uniform of angular geometric-print blazers, black ankle grazers and patent penny loafers. Her long blonde hair was scraped into a ballerina bun. Contact lenses were dropped in favour of cat's eye reading glasses.

'Karen,' Nigel said, drawing Harriet back to the present, 'tell her how many complaints we got about favouritism for giving her these opportunities.'

'There were a few objections,' Karen agreed, wincing as though under duress. 'Secretaries who've been here longer. Secretaries who've got a better grasp of legal work.'

Harriet gasped. Who on earth were they talking about? No secretary at Eiriol had more legal ambition and commitment than her.

'Are you really going to refuse me this, Harriet?' Nigel said, sitting at his son's desk, examining every object as though it held a personal and emotive memory. He ran his fingers over the illegible scribbles on Rowan's old-fashioned desk blotter.

This compulsory item, together with the transparent plastic carpet protectors under the wheels of their chairs were, Harriet thought, Nigel's way of reminding his son who had the final say at Eiriol. There was something infantilising about it, which was perhaps why Rowan covered his blotter in cartoon sharks. They swam in and out of the numbers and reminders. There were great whites and hammerheads, tiger sharks with inked-in stripes and dorsal fins cutting through serrated wave-crests.

'You, no,' Harriet said, 'but these people are sadistic.'

'If we do it their way, it'll be fine.'

Harriet stared at Nigel, unable to commit.

Infuriated by her reticence, Nigel stood and pointed at the door.

'If you're not going to help,' he roared, bringing his fist down on Rowan's desk so hard the handset jumped off the desk phone, 'leave and never come back. Tell your parents I helped their child, but you didn't help mine.'

'Nigel,' Karen said, taking a step forward, hands outstretched in appeal. 'You can't ...'

Though scared, Harriet couldn't see a way out.

Nigel lowered his head and began to cry. He covered his eyes with his hands and his shoulders juddered.

It felt mean of Harriet to even think it, but there was something inauthentic about it. Not that he wasn't desperately worried about his son, but Nigel's weeping seemed more for her benefit – a manipulation. She took a step closer, hoping to see glistening tears that would prove her wrong. Unable to tell either way, she parked her cynicism.

When Nigel stopped with a sigh, he dried his hands on his clothes like a little boy.

'No, I mean it, Karen.' Nigel said, with a sniff. He came out from behind Rowan's desk, the muscles on the left side of his jaw twitching. 'She's told both of us how she wants to be a lawyer, and this is a negotiation for my son's life. Harriet, that's the extreme definition of what we do. Litigation lawyers are level-headed mediators, the go-between in a dispute where, without that experienced middleman, wars break out. And they've picked you. Not me. Maybe they asked Rowan who is best placed.'

Nigel had a point. Harriet could see that.

'I still don't believe it's Rowan's finger,' Nigel continued, crossing the room to the window, brushing down the lapels of his jacket. 'But if it were to be ...'

'I'll do it,' she said. 'I'm sorry. It's hard to think straight. It's just the shock.' Harriet pointed at the envelope. 'Whatever you need.'

'Thank you,' Nigel said with a weary sigh. 'I'm sure DI Lennon will ensure you're fully prepared. I'm on your side, Harriet. You do believe me, don't you?'

Nigel rubbed his hands over his cheeks and under his nose before turning to the window. Two gulls flew past and turned south, towards the sea.

‘Yes, I do,’ Harriet said to the senior partner’s broad, sober, chalk-striped back.

‘Do you know why I called this firm Eiriol Law?’ Nigel asked.

‘No,’ she said, though she’d heard it was the name of his dead wife so she was loath to bring it up.

‘It’s from the old Welsh – to advocate,’ he said, without turning around. ‘And I need your advocacy now.’

Chapter 3

After two Teams calls, Nigel and Harriet met DI Lennon at a location the police termed the 'red centre' – an anonymous, budget hotel room in the south of the city, where they could await the kidnappers' next call undisturbed.

Nigel's combative history of litigation against the police went unmentioned. DI Lennon reassured Nigel that getting Rowan home safely was her sole focus.

Such professional courtesy and generosity of spirit surprised Harriet. Karen had long shared tales of letters dictated to police lawyers that were so vitriolic the other partners had appealed to Nigel to lay off stock inflammatory language like 'fascists' and 'criminals in uniform'.

Harriet shivered as she imagined Rowan, bound and beaten half-unconscious, dragging himself across some filthy garage floor in an impotent attempt at escape, one mutilated hand swathed in blood-stained bandages.

Hours went by as Harriet fielded endless questions from the police about her mental fortitude and potential capability of delivering a ransom. She glanced at Nigel, concerned he might reference her initial resistance back at Eiriol.

Every so often, between bursts of texting his oldest son, Leighton, or on the phone to the bank or his accountant, Nigel sat on the edge of the bed gazing out the window over the city. The grey light gave him the look of a statesman, cast in marble.

Perhaps sensing Harriet's gaze, Nigel turned to the police and acknowledged, 'She's more than capable.'

Nigel's composure and faith in her gave Harriet confidence. Yes, the idea of walking to a lonely spot carrying a gym bag containing one million, in £50 notes, made her feel faint and dry-mouthed, but she would do her utmost to embody the cool-headed lawyer that Nigel had talked of. Rowan would return and she, Harriet, would stand out amongst her peers as having dealt with the ultimate arbitration challenge – the negotiation for a man's life.

'Trust me. I'll get it done,' Harriet promised, looking from the detectives to Nigel and back again. 'I'm not going to overthink it or lose my head. I'll give them the money and bring all this to an end.'

When DI Lennon appeared satisfied, a swell of pride took the edge off Harriet's fear. Lifting her chin and giving an easy shrug, she declared, 'I've got this.'

Later in the evening, the police allowed Harriet to return to her flat under the strict condition she kept her phone on and didn't speak to a soul. The feigned trust aroused her suspicions. The police, she feared, were watching and listening.

They suspected Harriet's involvement, that much was clear. The DI suggested twice, with unjudgmental encouragement, that Harriet might even know the kidnappers, suggesting potential connections through her parents' pub, The Poet's Arms. Maybe, Harriet countered, Rowan had given the kidnappers her name under duress, as Nigel himself had suggested.

Scared it was already too late, Harriet withdrew her 'Let's Kill All the Lawyers merchandise' – primarily T-shirts, notebooks, tote-bags and mugs – from the Etsy marketplace. It had been Carwyn's idea that she do something arty with her revenge fantasies, but suddenly it didn't seem such a good idea.

Before Rowan's recent remodelling, his desk had been positioned in front of the floor-to-ceiling window, silhouetting him against a backdrop of sky, distant glimmering sea and the sharp, mirrored glass towers of Eiriol's neighbours.

If the reflections of clouds slipping across the black, glassy surface of the opposite buildings drew Harriet's gaze, Rowan teased her for ogling him, cutting her off when she tried to explain. He played on an old stereotype, that comprehensive girls learned to type with the sole and cynical aim of finding an office job just long enough to snag a middle-class husband.

The more Rowan provoked her, the more Harriet mused on the fact that a thin, albeit toughened wall of glass was all that stood between Rowan and a fall of five storeys.

She often daydreamed about the window shattering as Rowan leaned back in his chair, arms flailing, before disappearing with a girlish scream. She'd edge to the gaping hole as wind whistled in from the sea, blowing the papers from their desks. Below her Rowan lay spreadeagled on the pavement – a small, lifeless heap among the twisted metal and torn memory foam of his executive chair.

When Rowan had the room decorated, he'd repositioned his desk away from the window and against the wall, as though he'd sensed where her imagination was going.

His designer had also covered the wall behind Harriet with cream fabric panels, broken up by four thin, horizontal strips of rose-gold tinted mirror. As well as making the room look larger, brighter and adding a touch of 1980s opulence, the mirrors gave the room an unintentional, delicate pink hue in late afternoon. Rowan's office design, Harriet liked to think, signalled its feminine solidarity with her, blushing on her behalf at times and rooting for her like a mute witness.

But imagining Rowan plunging down a lift shaft or choking on an oyster in the Eiriol Law bistro, on the top floor, only brought Harriet so much satisfaction.

The marketing idea, taking the quote from William Shakespeare's *Henry VI, Part II,* had been her ex-boyfriend's parting gift.

Her commitment to the concept had more to do with winning Carwyn back – he was the creative one, after all, not her – but it proved cathartic. He was right, she needed an outlet somewhere until she earned her qualification and could leave Eiriol for a better job in law. Carwyn knew loads of creatives who had put her in touch with the raw materials needed.

All she'd done was have a little fun with a cheeky product line. Now, however, each tote sold spoke to motive. Innocent coincidence wouldn't be allowed for. The police might deduce Rowan's kidnapping and mutilation was conceived as part of a brand marketing campaign.

Oh God, Harriet thought.

Surrounded by boxes of surplus stock she'd probably never now sell, Harriet was unable to sleep. Instead, she listened to the rain and gale force winds, which arrived as the weather presenters had predicted.

The industrial bins shunted around in the car park and metal road signs sang spectral songs, like wind-chimes.

When Harriet awoke after a fitful couple of hours, the world was still in a soft darkness and the storm had passed. The digital clock on her bookcase read 5:54.

Going to get a glass of water, Harriet stopped by the lounge window to see if it was still raining. The grey paving under windswept, fallen leaves looked dry. It took Harriet a moment to notice a man standing against the back wall of the car park, camouflaged by patchy ivy growth.

Harriet reared back from the window. Something triggered a security light at the flats opposite. The orange glow shone through the dipping branches of the trees bordering the property and threw dancing shapes across the wall behind her. Fearful that the illumination would reveal her presence, Harriet ducked out of view.

When she peeked again, her surveillance had gone.

Dawn arrived with a brooding sky the colour of cold breakfast tea.

As advised by the police, Harriet dug out the most colourful coat she owned, an orange and black check, along with a burnt orange wool hat. The more she stood out, the easier she'd be for surveillance to keep safe.

At 9am, Harriet got a taxi back to the hotel.

By the time contact from the kidnappers came, the severed finger had been DNA tested and it was confirmed, beyond a shadow of a doubt, that it belonged to Rowan. Nigel, before he had the chance to ask for it, received proof of life – a close-up of Rowan with that day's *Sun*, and a grim shadow of certainty settled over him.

Twice, Nigel left the hotel for meetings to arrange the money and a confined frustration descended on Harriet. Her lack of sleep and previous day of hyper-anxiety, followed by a morning of hanging around waiting, left her fatigued. She suppressed bouts of yawning, fearing the police in the room would find such lethargic behaviour inappropriate.

And then, just before 3pm, everything went to breakneck. Harriet found herself whizzing along in Nigel's midnight blue BMW, heading for the Bay with a million pounds on her lap. He drove as though trying to lose any officers tailing them.

'Please slow down,' Harriet said, clutching her seatbelt and the door handle, knuckles white.

Any moment, some poor, elderly pedestrian might loom out into the road on Lloyd George Avenue and somersault over the windshield of Nigel's car.

Harriet was just old enough to remember the promises of the Cardiff Bay redevelopment. People bought flats but, after a year or so, many moved back to the north, east and west of the city centre. The lure of coastal life wore off in winter when howling storms turned landward and horizontal rain drove in off the sea.

Rowan, where are they holding you, she wondered?

A line from Kate Bush's 'Wuthering Heights' came to mind. But it wasn't true. She didn't hate him or love him.

'I appreciate this, but I'm going to need your help in other ways too,' Nigel said, depressing the brake and slowing a little. 'The police aren't stupid and they can't be trusted. They want Rowan's desktop, laptop and his mobile phone for examination. I've told them they're not taking anything that could breach client confidentiality until I've spoken with the Solicitors Regulation Authority for guidance. God knows, Rowan and I had begun laying the groundwork for a major inquiry against them. There's no way they're accessing that. While I'm stalling, they'll probably try to get information through you. Don't tell them anything.'

Nigel barely suppressed the word 'fascists' by biting his lower lip.

'I won't,' Harriet said, swallowing hard.

She had her own reasons for not wanting Rowan's computer examined by the police.

Rowan, after each tequila incident, usually apologised in person and via email. The vagueness of his self-loathing, written apologies would only raise more questions. Harriet would become a person of interest, if not an outright suspect.

That the police had called the demand for cash amateur also bothered Harriet, knowing this added to their suspicion she might be involved. To break the tension, she asked Nigel about it.

'Why what?' he said.

'Why not an online money transfer?' Harriet repeated.

'It might be easily traced, I suppose.'

More easily than bank notes? Harriet thought, puzzled.

Thinking of things tracked brought Gethin Price, Eiriol Law's own private investigator, to mind. Did Nigel have him on the case too? It occurred to Harriet that the publicity around Rowan's career move to Eiriol might have attracted the attention of these criminals. Gethin must have contacts in the underworld he could use.

Gethin had served as a police officer himself until he spent a short time in jail for assault. Harriet didn't know the specifics, but it hadn't dented Gethin's popularity outside South Wales Police. The man had bona fide charm, a gift for getting a laugh, and he and Nigel went way back. Inside the Force, however, Gethin's association with Nigel and Eiriol Law, was seen as a double betrayal.

The wind teased the promotional banners on the fencing around the inner bay, where a single blue and white vessel was moored up. Two fishermen, heads down, navigated the rocks carrying rods and tackle boxes. Harriet remembered her ex-boyfriend's dad giving her two large mackerel, having caught them sea angling off the Bay Barrage.

Filled with dread at this new idea – that someone she knew might recognise her during her mission and get in the way – she slid down in her seat. Being recognised was an occupational hazard when your parents owned a pub.

They sped past the Norwegian Church, outside which three Salvation Army band members, post recital, stood chatting in their dark coats with red epaulettes.

Straightening her legs in the footwell of the BMW, Harriet's gaze followed the chain-link fence that snaked in front of the industrial estate- style warehouses before considering the bag of money on her lap. Nigel had put the money in Rowan's own brown retro Adidas gym bag.

At lunchtimes, when he had time, Rowan would race off to smash out a 20:20:20 routine: twenty minutes each on a rower, a static bike and a treadmill at the nearby corporate gym. A moderately handsome man, who awarded himself a straight ten out of ten, Rowan liked to keep in shape.

He'll have a difficult time coming to terms with a disfigured hand, Harriet thought.

Nigel slowed to pass a group of dog walkers.

To Harriet, everyone seemed preoccupied, as if they were also weighed down with troubles they hoped the sea air would lift – some personal or national buried trauma.

Speculating as to what the kidnappers would look and sound like, Harriet decided her background of working-class pub and professional law firm provided maximum code-switching potential. Whatever their background, she'd charm them into a smooth, seamless exchange.

Nigel swung his BMW into the empty Aqua Park car park. The event itself had closed for the season and the giant inflatables had been removed from the bladderwrack-tangled water. Only the Portakabins, signage and footfall-damaged tufts of scrubby grass growing out of littered sand remained.

'What now?' Harriet asked.

'We're early, so we wait.'

Harriet looked at Nigel Tudor and wondered. The engine ticked as it cooled.

'What was Rowan like as a kid?' Harriet asked, unable to imagine a junior-school sized Rowan sluicing down an Aqua Park slide and equally unable to sit looking at the clock in silence.

Nigel lost a little tension around his mouth.

'Up until the age of about seven or eight,' Nigel said, 'he was a happy, carefree little boy, independent and lively. But then life happened, and we moved from Llantwit to Cardiff. Unlike Leighton – who's two years older – Rowan struggled to make friends. He's got an oddball sense of humour, as you've seen yourself. Found himself being bullied in school, that kind of thing.'

'Must have been hard for him,' Harriet managed to say. Was the choice of revelation Nigel's oblique way of excusing Rowan's behaviour towards her? The idea, while disappointing, didn't come as a great surprise.

'How's Leighton taking it?' she asked.

'He's holding up. I've asked him to handle Eiriol while I'm dealing with this. He always said it was a mistake for Rowan to join us at the firm.'

'Why?'

'Rowan's always been, as Leighton says, "too much of himself".'

He is *that*, Harriet thought.

'How's Natasha?' Harriet asked, shocked that, with the turn of events, she hadn't thought of her earlier.

'Who's Natasha?'

'Rowan's on-off girlfriend,' Harriet said.

'Rowan isn't seeing anyone,' Nigel said, shooting her an incredulous look. 'And he's certainly never mentioned anyone called Natasha.'

They sat in silence for a minute and Harriet tried to spot covert or concealed police officers while she mulled over why Rowan hadn't mentioned his girlfriend to his father.

The sky brightened slowly in gradients of paler greys and an icy sea breeze nudged damp litter into the gutters.

'Time to go,' Nigel said, on some invisible cue. 'Are you ready?'

'Yes,' Harriet said, tightening her grip on the holdall.

Chapter 4

Harriet's instructions were to walk to the canvas sail structure a little way along the barrage and wait.

'You'll be okay, I promise,' Nigel said. 'I'm grateful. We all are. I'll never forget this.'

Harriet swallowed, nodded and got out of the car. When she shut the car door, the soft, weighted closure had the finality of an airlock or a hatch on a submarine. Her new environment was unknown, unmapped and dangerous.

Since childhood, Harriet always experienced a minute or two of micro-macro adjustment at the seaside. Her singular perspective zoomed straight up, like Google Earth, panning out wider and wider, reminding her that earth was a planet in an expanding universe and she merely an insignificant spec within it, among billions of other insignificant specs.

This notion had come from a profound experience she'd had as a kid, on a day trip with her parents to Llantwit Major. Harriet had floated on her back in the sea in her pink daisy costume, while the sounds of other swimmers larking around carried over the swoosh of the waves.

Her upward gaze followed the spiralling gulls until the stub of blackboard chalk moon registered in the afternoon sky. She drew a breath in, like cold-water shock. The sun was up, but moon was up. These astral bodies couldn't co-exist in the same sky.

The end of the world was nigh.

Her amused parents reassured her that it *was* possible to see the moon and sun in the day, depending on the lunar cycle. Most kids her age, her mum said, were more scared of the drifting blooms of moon jellyfish, but, forevermore, the sea reminded her of her own fragile mortality in the empty, vastness of space.

Feeling insignificantly human, Harriet began to walk, self-conscious in her bright, Halloween colours. She was grateful to see that the barrage wasn't entirely deserted. There were dog walkers around, and the odd runner and cyclist. Walking seemed to help her nerves.

Harriet dabbed her tired, wind-watering eyes with a tissue as Penarth become visible at the other end of the barrage. Its densely packed slope was jammed with properties jostling for a view when summer came.

How long ago had the kidnappers started scheming? Maybe they'd been monitoring Rowan's comings and goings for months.

With the white noise of the wind roaring in her ears, she followed the sweep of the rocky barrage, with its ochre tideline of lichen-covered rocks, littered with driftwood and tangled strips of plastic net. The ocean scent of salt water and seaweed was stronger now.

Gulls cried mournfully in the sky and a duck quacked on the water.

Every so often, she swapped the bag to her opposite hand and jammed her frozen fingers into her coat pocket.

The sail structure wasn't on the road itself, but on a path a little way across the boulders to the landward, Bay side. Picking her way across the rocks, Harriet put down the bag.

In position, scanning this way and that, she shook with cold and nerves. Then, coming from the direction of the Norwegian Church, two men appeared. As they neared, she recognised them as the fishermen they'd passed on the road earlier. Over in the distance, in the direction of Penarth, a dog walker ambled after a boisterous retriever.

The wind pierced the fibres of her wool hat and iced the tips of her ears. Shivers ran in currents across her shoulders.

The fishermen wore dark waterproofs, camo trousers and boots. The man on the left carried two rods. The other, a dark plastic tackle box in one hand and a phone in the other. In no apparent hurry, they strolled her way and, twice, stopped to scan the road behind them.

'Are you alright, over there?' one of them shouted from the road.

Swallowing hard, Harriet knew this was it. The ground under her feet seemed to shift, as though she were swaying on the deck of a boat.

'Yes, thanks,' she shouted back, her words coming out in a mumble. 'Waiting for someone.'

The two men looked around, prospecting for other arrivals.

'Want some company while you wait?'

Harriet found herself mute, knees shaking. She still hadn't seen or heard any sign of the police. This won't do at all, she told herself. She pulled her shoulders back and lifted her chin as they started over the rocks towards her.

The tallest looked like a middleweight boxer running to fat in middle age. The other was younger, shorter and meaner, though Harriet couldn't have explained how or why she knew this: the ruthless expression perhaps in his small, sharp eyes.

'Are you alone?' the middleweight asked, putting the tackle box down next to the money. His partner kept hold of the fishing rods.

'Yes.'

'No wire?'

'No.'

'Mind if we check?'

Resistance would only compound their mistrust.

'Do I have a choice?' she said holding her hands up.

Satisfied they were unobserved from the road, the men instructed Harriet to open her coat, the larger one vocally and the smaller man with a gesture. Struggling at first to undo the tight-fitting, plastic buttons with her numb fingers, she complied and raised her arms higher still. The taller man slipped the backs of his hands underneath her coat and blazer rubbing his hands lightly over the fabric of her blouse. A sticking plaster on his neck, she guessed, covered an identifying tattoo. A woman's name most likely – a good detail to remember for the police.

Feeling manhandled, she allowed the guy to slide his hands across her back, up over her shoulders. The action caused the material to bunch, bearing her midriff to the biting wind. Knowing her chest and legs were still to come, she resisted, despite wanting the ordeal over with.

'Where d'you think you're going?' the smaller guy said, stepping in behind her.

'Please, just take the money,' she said, looking from one to the other.

'We're not doing anything until we've checked things out. See that white boat, way out on the horizon?'

Their menacing figures took up too much of the landscape and Harriet, in the circumstances, didn't have the concentration required to pick out one small vessel in the tarnished, uniform silver of the sea, but she nodded.

'Tudor Junior is out there on that vessel, trussed up like a chicken. One phone call from me and the man I work for feeds him to the fishes.'

It's fine, she repeated to herself as her heart rate spiked. But it wasn't fine. Why had she put herself in mortal danger? And if she bolted in panic, she'd have a lot of explaining to do to the police and to Nigel. Harriet drew in a big gulp of air and got her flight instincts under control, but stress hormones compounded her trembling.

'I'm not perving, love. I'm using the backs of my hands, see?' the man searching her said, holding up the calloused, hairy hands and dirty nails. She was right about the history of contact sport. His knuckles had toughened. Another good detail for the police.

Closing her eyes didn't help as the man rubbed his freezing fingers over her bra, around her pants and finally down her legs, mercifully over the fabric of her trousers. Her face tingled with shame and anger. She'd been through all this with Rowan and now, also because of him, she was suffering a humiliating pat-down at the hands of dangerous men.

Before she opened her eyes, fighting tears that threatened to squeeze between her lashes, Rowan's desk-blotter drawings of sharks came to mind.

She wanted to sit down, recover, get her breath, but it wasn't over yet.

'There,' she said, opening her eyes when the fumbling and digging through her pockets had stopped. 'No wire. Nothing. Now take the bag.'

The retriever barked madly and a tall woman swinging a leash, wearing skinny jeans and Dr Martens called after her dog. 'Honey,' she called. 'Honey.'

The dog stopped barking and lolloped towards Harriet and the men before looking over its shoulder at the fourth call. It trotted back over the rocks in a wide circle to the road and waited, panting.

The smaller man grabbed Harriet by the scruff of the neck, fingers digging. She gave out a gasp of fright. Stronger than he looked, the arm that snaked around her waist was vice-like.

'Do you know that woman?' the meaner guy asked, his voice hissing in her ear. 'Is she police?'

'No,' Harriet said, struggling to talk with the pain of the man's grip and the dread that this was an excuse to kill her and take the money. 'It's just a dog walker.'

'There's another one,' the taller guy said, nudging his friend, watching a black-clad rider on a bike. 'What's this dickhead up to?'

The iron-like clamps at her neck and waist tightened and, with her sense of claustrophobia, the wide sky was a hessian hood over her head.

'You recognise him though, don't you? This place is crawling with fucking cops.'

'No, you're wrong,' Harriet said, wriggling in pain. 'The police have no idea. Nigel would never go to them and they wouldn't help if he did. Please, just take the money.'

Once she'd said it, she couldn't stop saying it. The phrase became a panicked mantra that got louder until it emitted from her as a shriek. 'Take the money. Take the bag. Just take it.'

Her words carried on the wind, as did the terror in her voice.

The dog walker stopped and turned in their direction. The cyclist, about to zip past the dog walker, heard it too, because he slowed to a rolling glide, stood out of the saddle and stared.

The middleweight grabbed Harriet by the throat and raised his fist. Instead of a knockout blow, a shove landed Harriet on the rocks. Pain shot through her right hand and hip.

The dog walker shouted, 'Hey,' and put a mobile to her ear.

‘Deal’s off, bitch,’ the bigger guy said, slicing the air with a hand. ‘It’s a set up. We’re out of here.’

Only when Harriet saw they’d left the Adidas bag containing the cash did she remember her primary objective. What had happened to her acting like a lawyer? Instead, she’d gone to pieces and now ... what?

She’d felt the same helpless dread only once before – in the early hours after Roddy’s death, after the police had woken her and her parents, and she’d pieced together her part in it.

The kidnappers were already at the road, sprinting back in the direction of the Norwegian Church. Where were the police to intercept them?

Above the waves and the gulls, Harriet heard the faint burr of an outboard motor. She stood, picked up the bag of ransom money and stumbled across the stones and boulders to get as close to the water’s edge for a better view.

Ignoring the dog walker and the cyclist, who kept asking if she was alright and reassuring her the police were on their way, Harriet spotted the white boat. It looked tiny – a speedboat perhaps. As she watched, a dark, heavy object was shoved overboard and Harriet screamed into the wind, raising the holdall up over her head with both hands, as though a trade for Rowan’s life might not be too late.

Chapter 5
Kennedy Jones

From over in the doorway, Dr Stockton and Augusta stand watching Boyd administer your pills.

The smell of wet paint and the occasional working-class whistle of a builder in the corridor behind them, without his radio, remind you how new this all is.

'All the facilities at the Afternity Clinic,' Augusta said, that first day, in that empathetic American wellness-way of hers, 'are on the house – from our treatment programme to our first-class hospitality. No expense spared. If anyone can get results, we can. No time limit. Dr Philip Stockton is a master in his field.'

Augusta stepped back, tucking a strand of poker-straight strawberry blonde hair behind her ear.

You were relieved to hear it. For two months, the NHS committed everything they had, but rehab was slow and you are so used to the quick gains of professional sport.

Daily, you remind yourself you didn't get as far as you did in international rugby by accepting limitations put on you by others. The investments you have made in your fitness and physicality are what separates you from the ordinary people overcoming odds like yours.

There's only one outcome you'll accept: maximum recovery, improvement to a point that satisfies you. And then you will return to your friends and family in Wales.

To turn from them and focus one hundred percent on training or rehab is the only way to achieve. It's the way you have always approached things.

Augusta and Dr Stockton are also sure of the validity. Otherwise, this broken, sub-optimal ex-rugby player is who your loved ones will remember. The elite sportsman you were only a year ago will exist only in celluloid.

Boyd uses warm but chiding arguments against.

'Kennedy,' he says, both hands crossed to his chest, fingertips touching the pearl and gold vintage nurse's watch that hangs from his breast pocket, 'your family and friends love you no matter what and they don't understand this.'

He comes from a long line of Welsh Valleys nurses and the watch was his grandmother's.

'They'll think you're freezing them out. Those people love you unconditionally.'

Yes, you're driving loved ones away left and right but, in the psychological equation, it's A hurts B, who hurts C, who then takes it out on D. You don't need a psychologist to tell you that. You just need time to see what's recoverable, how permanent the damage is.

As long as Boyd's here with you, you'll be okay, though you fear Augusta and Dr Stockton are looking for ways to purge their clinic of him.

Now you've had your pills, Dr Stockton and Augusta leave and Boyd can sort breakfast.

Not five minutes later, with the inexplicable fatigue creeping up again, the smell of burnt toast filters down the corridor from the kitchen at the end of the hall. You can, in the silence of the clinic, just make out the snap of Boyd's tea towel, ushering away the smoke before it triggers the alarm or appears on one of the countless CCTV screens Augusta installed to ensure patient safety.

'Shit, shit, shit,' you hear him mutter, each curse more panicked than the last.

The tension of whether the alarm over the door will sound worsens the match-day-airhorns that blast your brain from time to time since your injury.

Come on, Boyd, lad. Don't let the side down.

Within days of Boyd joining the rehab team in Cardiff, you worked out you had history. Apparently, he was on shift the day of the accident. He remembers you being brought in on the stretcher, medics in a conflab.

Sure, Boyd can't put two slices of bread in a toaster without causing an evacuation, but he's a Welsh boy and he listens if you're getting something off your chest. You sense he doesn't like that you're both here, though he never talks about himself. That's loyalty for you. He brings you Welsh memorabilia instead, tries to make you homesick.

Last week's arrival of Scorch the Dragon reminds you of all the similar, plush scarlet WRU Scorches you've given away to kids over the years. And that makes you recollect all the rugby balls signed and jerseys framed.

A dragon's eye of ruby light begins to blink, followed by a piercing siren that washes the room with warning. Escape from danger, it says. Fire and smoke, it says. Seek a place of safety.

But you can't run.

Can't even cover your ears to the sirens outside and the ten-quid street-hawker's bugles sounding between your ears.

Boyd appears at the door, his freckled face flushed and twisted in helpless apology. How on earth does he expect you to put the situation right?

You can't do anything, can you Ken, but press one side of your head against the pillow and hope they don't use this as the final excuse to send Boyd back to Cymru.

Chapter 6

As the police drove Harriet away from the scene, a police helicopter swept through the indigo dusk above two RNLI boats. The small inflatable inshore and its three crew members looked toy tiny as they chopped through the waves.

The bigger, all-weather lifeboat threw up sprays of milky foam and a searchlight sliced across the green-grey water like a scalpel. A land-based RNLI volunteer and a member of the coastguard operated a drone.

Visibility was disappearing fast in the gloom, leaving her frustrated.

Nigel, at the roadside, stared after Harriet, holding a Styrofoam cup of hot tea, cloaked in a space blanket which buckled in the wind, reflecting the sapphire strobes and silver torchlight.

Harriet bit her lip. Nigel's vacant gaze scared her. For now, he was broken, but he'd recover himself and then she'd have to watch out. She'd failed him.

Nobody wanted Nigel as an enemy.

At Cardiff Bay Police Station, DI Cerys Lennon gave Harriet's arm a supportive squeeze and showed her into a bare, bright interview room without a window. Harriet had expected something moody and ill-lit, with closed charcoal blinds – recreating the atmosphere of all good TV cop shows – but the room had all the drama of a former stationery cupboard.

Under the compression bandage applied by the station's first aider, Harriet's sprained wrist throbbed. Her hip had fared better. Although a hydrangea-size bruise was blossoming, there was no serious damage. Harriet swallowed a couple of pain killers with a mouthful of bottled water, before drinking the rest in one go, the thin plastic crackling as it buckled in her left hand.

'You mustn't blame yourself,' DI Lennon said. 'But things obviously didn't go to plan. Perhaps there are details you can tell us that will help put things right. Is it possible, for instance, that you unwittingly signalled our presence to the kidnappers?'

'No way. I didn't see any sign of you. I wasn't sure you *were* actually there,' Harriet said, her lips tight and numb, and her hands and legs shaking. Her body hadn't time to register she was back indoors. 'Have they found him yet?'

'They're still searching. So, what happened?'

'Did you catch the men?'

'Unfortunately not.'

Harriet frowned and licked her dry lips, which had begun to tingle as she warmed up. The tip of DI Lennon's nose was still red with cold.

'There were difficult choices to make,' DI Lennon explained. 'They probably dumped Rowan overboard to focus our resources on rescuing him. Preserving life is our priority, way before evidence and prosecution. But let's get to all that later. Would you take us through what happened?'

'I still can't believe you didn't catch them,' Harriet said, thinking that they shouldn't move on that fast. 'They were right there.'

DI Lennon looked at her sergeant, deliberating. Then the DI explained that, against her better judgement, Nigel had agreed with Chief Superintendent Wallis, at the eleventh hour, that the police should back off.

The truth, Harriet guessed, lay somewhere in between. Nigel had probably asked the police to keep further back, out of sight. The police would have obliged without quibbling and, not without a little schadenfreude, watched the criminals escape.

Aware of the camera, Harriet wondered who else was watching on the other end of the video stream. As far as the investigating officers were concerned, she had done nothing wrong, so she considered herself vindicated. Yes, her genuine anxiety under pressure hadn't helped Rowan, but surely the fact that the kidnappers abandoned the money had to prove she had nothing to do with its planning? Why sabotage the heist if she were amongst those who would financially gain? DI Lennon must be able to see that.

'I knew it would be hard,' Harriet said. 'But making the drop was something else.'

'I know, it must have been quite an ordeal. After we've taken your statement, we'll have you sit with a Facial Imaging Officer to create an E-fit of the men. But is there anything specific you can tell me about them?'

Harriet relayed the details she'd observed.

'Height?'

'The lead guy was about 5' 10", the other was just a bit taller than me. 5' 7" maybe.'

'This is helpful. We'll come onto their conversation next. Anything else? Did either have a particular smell? What of their accents?'

That DI Lennon wasn't treating Harriet like a suspect supported her theory. She was assisting the police, nothing more, and this brought her comfort. As the shock wore off, she remembered details with more clarity and her confidence grew. She elaborated on her observations about the neck plaster, knowing that if her information led to a conviction, her innocence would be established beyond doubt.

'The big guy had a Cardiff accent,' Harriet said. 'No scent I can remember. The smaller guy – now you mention it – there was a slight, very slight, Bristol-twang, which makes me think Newport. And there was a trace of stale smoke on his clothes. Not like he smokes himself, but more like he lives with a smoker. Like his clothes air in the same room.'

DI Lennon nodded, her expression engaged, as though finding Harriet's answers acceptable and helpful.

'Thank you, Harriet. This is all useful. So, let's go through the actual exchange.'

On Harriet's third run-through of events, a frown replaced DI Lennon's previous open and attentive expression. When Harriet remembered something else, she hoped this would appease the troubled detective.

‘Sorry – it’s just occurred to me – the main man said his boss had Rowan on the boat, trussed up like a chicken and he threatened to feed him to the fishes, but I could swear the guy put on a bit of an East London accent when he did an impression of his boss. I don’t think their boss is from Wales.’

Sitting back in her chair, DI Lennon considered this. ‘That doesn’t narrow it down hugely,’ the detective said, tapping the side of the table with her fingers, ‘but it might prove useful.’

‘Could you just check,’ Harriet said, as an image of her boss came to her, spitting up spumey bubbles of seawater, hacking into the churning water as he floundered in the freezing Bristol Channel, ‘if there’s any news about Rowan?’

‘Rest assured, we’ve got the most experienced search teams out there you could ask for.’

‘I just want him found,’ Harriet said, thinking how utterly fascinating it would be to have Rowan back now, in a mindset forever grateful to be alive. If this didn’t alter his character for the better, nothing would.

‘We all do. But you have vital background information. I want to go back to the last time you saw Rowan alive.’

‘Okay,’ Harriet said, shivering again.

‘You were Rowan’s secretary, until you were promoted to his legal assistant. Were you aware of any changes in his behaviour that may have suggested he felt threatened?’

‘Um, no, I don’t think so,’ she said. Nigel’s words sprang to Harriet’s mind. Rowan had confided in his father and shared some secret information. Whatever he’d divulged, it was for Nigel himself to share it with the police.

‘Tell us about the gift Rowan received on the Friday afternoon. I believe that’s when you saw him in person last?’

‘The tequila?’ Harriet asked, caught off guard. ‘Is that relevant?’

‘We recovered the packaging from the gift of tequila from Petra’s bin and the printed address details are identical to that on the envelope containing Rowan’s signet ring, ransom note and finger.’

Harriet buried her mouth in the joint between her thumb and

index finger, trying to recall the address label on the envelope and wondering what on earth it meant. She hadn't noticed the address details on the tequila, but then she and Petra had unwrapped it, thrown the wrapping in the bin and handed the bottle to Rowan.

'The receptionist gave the parcel straight to Rowan,' Harriet said. 'He unwrapped it and opened it.'

'You mean he opened the box?'

'He opened the box and then the bottle itself.'

'What did he do with the tequila?'

'Like I said, he opened it.'

'I mean, did he taste it?'

'Yes, he poured it straight into his mug.'

'Did he say who it was from?'

'He knew who it was from.'

'Who?' DI Lennon asked, leaning forward.

'He didn't tell me. He just said it was a peace offering or something. Tequila's his favourite tipple, you see. And I'd commented that there didn't seem to be a card with it. He said he knew exactly who'd sent it. He sent me home early because he wanted to phone the person in private and thank them. It wasn't that early a finish – only 30 minutes or so in the end – but I was happy to get away.'

Between the handful of facts Harriet had given of her last encounter with Rowan, so much went unsaid. That she'd been happy to get away was an understatement.

'And he'd already started drinking it?'

'Yes. He offered me a mug. He was in good spirits.'

'Did you accept?'

'No, I was in work.'

'Was it unusual for him to drink in the office?'

'I'm not sure what this has to do with his kidnapping,' Harriet said, sounding more obstructive than intended. But, if they found her merch, she'd need a lawyer.

DI Lennon narrowed her eyes and gave Harriet a small serious nod to continue.

'He'd come back from the occasional client lunch a bit worse for wear,' Harriet said, 'but this was the first time I'd seen him overtly drinking in work.'

That was true, at least.

'Ever a problem, his drinking? Did you ever fall out over it?'

Her thoughts went to the previous February when the weather had warmed a few degrees and Rowan's post-New Year sobriety allowed Harriet to relax. In doing so, she discovered that she had more problems at Eiriol Law than just him.

When confronted by Debbie about a rumour, likely started by Debbie herself, that Harriet and Rowan were 'at it', her denial only made things worse. This, Debbie said, turning puce with anger, was 'treating them all like they were stupid'.

Harriet therefore had lunch alone at her desk of Rowan's office, eating a couple of homemade tuna sandwiches, desperate to take some sort of action.

At 3.10pm, Rowan returned drunk and attempted to straddle and snog her. Harriet had recoiled, not just from him but at the aloe vera, peppery fumes of tequila mixed with his musky aftershave. When she pushed him off with a yelp of fear and disgust, Rowan had lost his balance and then straightened up, red with embarrassment.

Brushing himself down, he denounced her as frigid, but a noise in the corridor – which turned out to be nothing but a false alarm – brought him up straight, as though he'd received the very slap she'd wanted to give him.

The bottom line was she'd successfully pushed back and he'd complied.

Harriet shifted position, scratched an eyebrow. She looked around the room, searching for an appropriate answer.

'No. It was nothing I couldn't handle,' she said, again thinking of the painful way he'd grabbed her wrist the last time she'd seen him. 'He wanted to make a call. So, he sent me home.'

DI Lennon took a big breath in and paused for a second.

'The next morning,' she said, 'the parcel that arrived with Rowan's finger had your name on it. Is that right?'

'It was addressed to Rowan,' she said, 'but "care of" myself.'

Too easily, Harriet thought, their working relationship could sound closer than it was. She hoped the police weren't going to speak to Debbie and Ffion. God only knew what *they'd* tell them.

'Rowan never spoke of her, but somehow Debbie and Ffion found out he had a girlfriend called Natasha. I wondered if she'd sent the tequila. They argued sometimes. But when I asked Nigel about her, he knew nothing about it.'

Now Harriet thought about it, she'd never heard the name Natasha from Rowan. It had come from Debbie and Ffion and their gossip wasn't always on point. There was the time they heard a member of the IT staff was stealing laptops. They'd spread the word and baited the thief, moving three spare laptops from a locked room to open shelves. They shared breathless stories about workplace embezzlement and how it started small.

'Check your purses, everybody,' they'd said, with the bright eyes of born-again vigilantes.

Three days later, the office rife with paranoia, an introductory email had gone around. Eiriol Law had been joined by an employment lawyer, working from home – who'd just taken on an interesting case of workplace theft at a factory in Swansea.

Those idiots, Harriet thought. There was no Natasha. But she was sure there'd been someone.

Meanwhile, DI Lennon wrote down the name Natasha, followed by a question mark.

'Actually, I might be wrong there,' Harriet said. 'Maybe it's baseless office gossip.'

'We'll look into it, but is a girlfriend of his likely to address it "care of" you, in any event?'

'Good point,' Harriet said, relieved that they weren't running with her inadvertent Natasha red herring. 'Probably not.'

'Do you get a lot of parcels like that?'

'Not really.'

'On the days leading up to these deliveries, had you seen anyone suspicious in the area of your office? Anyone asking you strange questions?'

'No. Nobody.' Harriet had already considered this.

'On the morning the finger was delivered, what time did you arrive for work?' DI Lennon asked.

Harriet began to go through the mundane details but tailed off.

'Look,' she said, 'would you mind checking if Rowan's been found? I mean, that would solve everything, right, because they abandoned the money?'

'We can't rule out that the primary crime wasn't about that.'

Harriet had a flashback to her lurching about in the front seat of Nigel's BMW, holding the Adidas bag containing the bank notes.

'How is this not about money?' she asked.

'For one, the money might be a red herring, because things aren't adding up. On the one hand, your evidence suggests organised crime. But these gangs don't ask for cash in a bag and send two goons to collect it. They're far more sophisticated.'

'Okay,' Harriet said, not sure she agreed.

'And these guys you met, you said they were paranoid about police officers nearby, they lost their heads and called off the deal. Do you know how long they were there with you?'

'Ages.'

'A grand total of three minutes.'

'No way,' Harriet said, crossing her arms.

'Your exchange lasted exactly three minutes, almost like it was timed.'

'I don't get it.'

'Possibly rehearsed.'

A prickle of annoyance ran though Harriet. If they were monitoring the situation that closely, they should have caught the two men.

'But why?' she asked.

'Like I said, maybe money isn't the motive.'

Harriet sat still and swallowed hard as she felt the finger of suspicion moving closer.

'Maybe someone wanted to kill him,' DI Lennon said, 'and the kidnapping is a decoy, to throw us off the scent.'

‘Please could I have some water?’ Harriet whispered.

‘We’ll get you some water in a second. But can you think of anyone who might have wished Rowan harm? Problem clients? Problem colleagues? Anyone who might want to stop him joining Eiriol Law to work with his father?’

‘For a start,’ Harriet said, thinking DI Lennon wasn’t the only one who could turn the tables, ‘there’s you guys. I mean, it was public knowledge wasn’t it. That’s why Rowan came back. Members of the Welsh Senedd approached Nigel about a judicial inquiry into miscarriage of justice cases. All of them linked to South Wales Police. And that’s what Rowan does, judicial reviews.’

Harriet’s bravado ran out there, but they all knew what she meant, even though they wouldn’t thank her for saying it. Nigel’s inquiry would consider whether South Wales Police had a culture that tolerated dishonest practices; whether ‘suspect-led’ policing contributed to manipulation of evidence; and whether certain interview techniques had led to false statements from witnesses and false confessions from suspects.

South Wales Police needed to put themselves at the top of the suspect list.

Chapter 7

Harriet had so wanted to use her legal career to escape The Poet's Arms, with its pub drama and small-time violence. And here she was, back in the lounge with its Cardiff karaoke clientele, sticky red carpets, grey nets, spindle chairs and wooden tables stabilised by creased Guinness coasters.

She pondered how to begin summarising the day's events for her parents: how her boss had been abducted by criminals, how he'd lost a finger and was unlikely to survive freezing water temperatures, and that the motive was either money or murder.

She'd tell them after they'd closed the pub. Then, she'd stay over. But first, she had to speak to Mike Powell.

A giant print of Landseer's *Alpine Mastiff Reanimating a Distressed Traveller* – depicting a St Bernard with a miniature brandy barrel on its collar – had always hung in The Poet's Arms. Harriet had grown up thinking it had a connection to her parents' pub.

Now, instead of the wan, snow-submerged adventurer in the painting. Harriet saw Rowan washed up on a rocky shore, breathing his last, rasping breaths.

Brandy, Harriet decided, was exactly what she needed now.

Her mum, Lottie, with a questioning stare, poured Harriet a single measure, while her dad, Louie, continued serving customers. Before handing over the balloon glass, Lottie raised it in a toast at the grainy, framed A5 photo of Roddy above the bar.

Weary exhaustion followed the warmth of the French liquor. The sounds of the pub soothed her, the familiar chatter in the foreground and, from the games room, the echoey clunk of pool balls colliding or dropping into the pocket and rolling to their cradle.

Occasionally, the skyward explosions of early bonfire night fireworks reflected red and green in the Landseer's glass, like an emergency flare sent up in a call for aid by sinking sailors.

The drink stirred up something sentimental. Looking at her mum and dad behind the bar, further trauma in her life seemed inevitable and she'd already had enough of it.

When Mike, a Mensa group member who ran his own IT company, walked in, Harriet put her forearms on the table and sighed with relief.

The Mensa group was a male-dominated, high IQ, weekly gathering. Her parents had tried to civilise The Poet's by encouraging working-class intellectuals. They'd created a world of pub quizzes, with Mensa meetings on Mondays and episodes of *The Chase* streamed daily on the wall-mounted TV. On Sunday afternoons, they hosted open mic nights for poets and writers, which was how Harriet and her ex, Carwyn, had first met.

In the corner was a *Who Wants to be a Millionair*e arcade game, flashing purple and blasting out the show's jingle in the same way Harriet thought her dad would have liked to advertise his own intellect to punters. A brain with bells and whistles, that's what he wanted. She couldn't blame him. After all, she'd not been able to persuade anyone other than Nigel and Rowan that she was underachieving at Eiriol Law.

Mike was in his 30s and sometimes asked Harriet over for dinner, but never pushed when she declined. Now, she was taking advantage of him by seeking out his free advice. She hadn't known anyone else with the right IT skills to trust.

Mike observed a strict vegan diet and most of his income went on either crypto currency or his head-to-toe biker wardrobe of convincing non-leather products.

When Rowan's harassment had started, Harriet's first counter was to draft a grievance. Though useless, its composition gave her the lawyerly feeling of someone who pre-planned arguments. Its flaw lay in a complete lack of unbiased reviewers. Policy and procedure necessitated addressing it to Nigel Tudor. He was hardly likely to take her side against his son.

While her grievance underwent amendments, deletions, revisions and additions, Harriet, her frustration increasing, tried out a few futile, office-based pranks before getting more technical, with tips from Mike.

Using CTRL + ALT + ↓, she'd twice managed to set Rowan's desktop screen settings upside down. Once, she'd changed his screensaver to a screenshot of the blue error 'System updating' message.

Eiriol's IT department righted everything for Rowan without question. Perhaps they'd known Harriet was behind it and, out of non-lawyer solidarity, allowed her to have her occasional joke.

However, with her 'Let's Kill All the Lawyers' merchandise, Harriet moved into the revenge big league. She'd called on Mike to create for her an anonymous email address and simple trade website, which could be linked to Etsy and eBay. Who could have predicted that a fountain pen, dripping blood beneath the Shakespearean quote, would take off the way it had? Now Rowan had been kidnapped, the risk of it backfiring multiplied tenfold.

'Thanks for coming,' Harriet said, as Mike took the seat opposite. 'I need your help again. Rowan's in deep shit and so am I.'

'That arsehole deserves everything he gets,' Mike said, watching his pint settle. 'Karma's a bitch.'

'No, this is serious. Deadly serious. Really bad. We need to remove any link from me to my 'Let's Kill All the Lawyers' products. I mean, none of it can show up on any browser, under any search.'

Mike touched her arm. 'What's going on? Has someone found out?'

'Rowan's been kidnapped,' Harriet said, pulling away. 'If they've done what they said they would, he's dead already.'

'Jesus.'

'I know. 'They took a finger,' Harriet said, wiggling her pinkie. 'They posted it back to work. They said they'd exchange money for Rowan's safe return, but it went wrong.'

'God, Harriet,' Mike said. 'Can't you see what this is? I mean, the damn thing is prescient. It'll put you on the map.'

Mike's enthusiasm made Harriet flinch and lean away, aghast.

‘Are you for real? If the police find out, they’ll think I had something to do with it.’

‘What’s wrong with you? You’re not thinking big enough. I can help you set up a YouTube channel to hunt those responsible. Do you still have his password? The armchair detectives can help. They’ll eat this up.’

‘Mike, I’m not kidding. Promise you won’t tell anyone. We’ll both be in the shit.’

‘I’m hardly to blame. He wasn’t my boss and I don’t read Shakespeare or know any lawyers.’

‘Well, do you know anyone with a van? I’ve got surplus stock at my flat. I need it taken away and destroyed as soon as possible, burnt or something.’

‘A couple of weeks ago, death was too good for him. Now, you want to self-sabotage your own successful e-commerce.’

Hadn’t she just told him Rowan might die and her actions could be misinterpreted as motive? Did he not believe her? Mike had such an affinity with animals and, in contrast, zero empathy for people. She couldn’t trust him to keep quiet.

‘I need you to nuke it all to protect me – not him. Don’t you understand?’

‘Then put it on ice, but you mustn’t destroy your business. You’ll regret it.’

‘I’ve already shut it down,’ Harriet said, leaning forward, ‘But would you please check there’s nothing online to connect me to it? I thought I’d done the job, but a product link still came up when I did a search. And there’s a ton of stuff at my place.’

‘If the police suspect you and put their tech bods on this, I’m afraid you’re screwed. Information stays out there. It’s sold all the time. Look at Facebook. They made 500 million users’ information free to download. And trace information can still be found using the Wayback Machine.’

‘Look, I need you to do your best,’ Harriet said, scared and frustrated by Mike’s obstructive IT babble.

‘My advice is to lean into it. You might be approached to make it into a book or, even better, a TV special. True life crime is huge,' Mike said, fingers to each thumb, holding up a fan of imagined bank notes in each hand.

'Mike, that's where I went wrong,' she said, finishing her brandy and sliding off the chair. 'I was happy to continue as I was – emptying all the office hole punches and pouring the clippings into his coat pockets.'

Rowan had failed to ever mention Harriet's home-made confetti.

'He had no right to treat you like he did,' Mike said. 'And look at the result. You're making good money. Hey, where are you going? I'm giving you a compliment.'

Intending to trade seats rather than leave the pub completely, Harriet still snatched up her coat as though she were heading out the door. Mike had failed to take her seriously, so she'd had to make her point in stronger terms.

'Hey, don't be like that,' Mike said. 'You haven't actually told me where the prick is now.'

'It's on the news,' she whispered, with a nod of her head in the wall-mounted TV's direction.

The 10 o'clock bulletin started with the usual Westminster scandal but included a highlight of the forthcoming Welsh news.

The presenter, a woman with a long face and chestnut bob, announced a well-known figure in the legal world was missing at sea in life-threatening circumstances.

Mike and Harriet looked at each other.

The news anchor worked hard to keep her hair from fanning across her face. Behind her, the Bay disappeared into an unlit void.

'What's going on?' Louie said, motioning to Lottie and lifting the hinged bar top. They joined their daughter.

Harriet remained transfixed on the national news.

'Harriet, love, what's happened? You've gone white. Is this what you were going to talk to us about later?'

'I've been trying to find the words,' Harriet said, trance-like, 'but it's so surreal.'

'What's going on?' Louie asked Mike.

‘Something happened with her boss today,’ Mike said, shaking his head as though the precise details were anyone’s guess, ‘and then she saw this on the news. They’re searching for someone lost at sea.’

‘It’s Rowan. Down Cardiff Bay,’ Harriet said, dazed.

‘Rowan? God-alive. I’m closing the pub,’ her mum said, ringing the brass bell at the side of Roddy’s picture.

‘I shouldn’t have panicked,’ Harriet said, beginning to weep. Her face itched as tears streaked her salt-dried cheeks. In getting back at Rowan through her sales line, she’d also betrayed his father and all other lawyers out there. ‘Nigel’s never going to forgive me.’

Only later did Harriet realise her conversation with Mike had failed to resolve how to remove the online or physical evidence linking her to Rowan’s possible murder.

Chapter 8

Harriet lay awake in her childhood bedroom, more recently The Poet's Arms' office, reliving the kidnap drama of the last couple of days and questioning her decision to stay with her parents instead of going back to her flat. Ultimately, she hadn't wanted to stare at those plastic wrapped piles of T-shirts and boxes of notepads.

The old bed she remembered as soft and yielding proved less so for an adult body now accustomed to IKEA memory foam. The springs dug in and the mattress, sunken in the middle, gave her backache. She smelt dust in the ancient crumbs of sponge that packed the candy-stripe, brushed-cotton pillowcases.

The lace silhouette projected across the walls, created by the nets and the sodium light spilling from the streetlamp directly outside the pub, had once terrified her. As she grew older, it brought comfort.

In addition to her old sprung bed and the dated 80s wallpaper was a computer her parents had bought fourteen years before. Above it, mismatched lever arch files and filing trays of unpaid invoices threatened the meagre weight capacity of shelves that had once contained Harriet's Ladybird storybooks.

Every few minutes, she checked her phone for news of Rowan.

She'd lied to Mike when she said she'd have been happy to continue with her low-level subversive acts. This had been true for a while, but then things had changed. But the police surely couldn't take what she'd done *that* seriously. She hadn't made much money – more like broke even. And Harriet herself was training to be a lawyer.

A small moan escaped from Harriet as she, at last, fell into a mud-green half-dream, where, from a sandy, ridged ocean floor, she watched Rowan sinking towards her. Wriggling, he freed one arm from his restraints, but not the other. His briny cries streamed upward as oxygen bubbles. When near enough to claw at her with his damaged hand, Rowan anchored himself by grasping her shoulder. And then, in the darkness behind him, a looming shadow grew, an outline of a sweeping tail and proud dorsal fin.

'Harriet? Harriet?'

Her mother's voice.

She opened dry, sticky eyes. Her head was feeling heavy. Her mum stood over her in a white nightdress, pink dressing gown and fluffy slippers.

Morning had broken behind the discoloured nets.

'Have they found him?' Harriet asked, sitting up.

'Yes and no. Some of his clothes have washed up at Llantwit Major. A fisherman spotted them. Don't know exactly what they've found, but it doesn't look good.'

Harriet watched the news until 7am, when the newsreaders repeated what the family already knew for the third time with no updates.

They exchanged the living room for the kitchen and the TV for the radio while her mum finished part-baked rolls in the oven, fried bacon and scrambled a box of eggs. Harriet laid the table with three plates, spreadable butter, and HP and tomato sauce.

'I still can't believe the police didn't manage to arrest the men I spoke to', Harriet said, as her mum placed a crisp, golden-brown roll on each place with a pair of tongs. 'It's like they let them get away.'

Harriet's father nodded, patted his daughter's back with his bear-like paw before splitting his roll. Tendrils of steam evaporated as he spread the melting butter and layered on two pieces of crisp bacon. Harriet followed suit.

'We saw enough of that from the police after Roddy. Even with us doing half their job for them,' he said, taking a bite.

'I still can't believe they admitted they lost the evidence,' Lottie said, spooning steaming, creamy eggs.

'I can easily believe it,' Louie replied, chewing with relish, holding a polite hand in front of his mouth as he talked. 'Look at the Lynette White case – how those 227 boxes of papers to do with police corruption that the police claimed were destroyed turned up, mildewed, in some police lock-up at RAF St Athan.'

Harriet had often witnessed Nigel referencing Lynette White's murder as an example of why he wanted his son – an expert in judicial reviews –back in Wales.

The police investigation into the Butetown murder of Lynette, the 20-year-old stabbed over 50 times on Valentine's Day in 1988, was exactly the kind of miscarriage of justice case Nigel Tudor had a passion for.

Five subsequent random arrests led to a lengthy trial and three of the five received life imprisonment. The 'Cardiff Three' were wrongly convicted in 1990 with no evidence as to motive or scientific proof. They were only exonerated when the real killer of Lynette, Jeffrey Gafoor, was identified by DNA in 2003.

Subsequently confessing to Lynette's murder, Gafoor apologised to The Three and made it clear he had no connection with any of the five original suspects targeted by the police.

But if the Cardiff Three weren't guilty, how come one of them was recorded confessing to police and multiple eyewitnesses put them at the murder scene?

With systemic racism and corruption being suspected factors in the miscarriage of justice, it didn't help when the subsequent police corruption trial collapsed after evidence went missing, allegedly shredded in error. With the evidence unable to be tested in court, the police officers involved were acquitted.

No sooner had the case been mothballed, the 'destroyed' documents were magically rediscovered.

In 2012, the wrongly accused men sought a judicial review for a public enquiry into the collapse of the corruption case. The judicial review, called the Mouncher Investigation Report, was authored by Richard Horwell QC. The barrister found that because human failing, rather than corruption, was the deciding factor, a public enquiry was not necessary.

The Lynette White judicial review, to all intents and purposes, had failed in its objectives. However, that wasn't to say that similarly ambitious judicial reviews into police corruption, with Rowan's expertise, would go the same way if handled by Eiriol Law.

'I *can* believe they lost the evidence we gave them,' Lottie added. 'I just can't believe they *admitted* it.'

Everyone knew who Roddy's killer was and yet the police had been unable to prove a thing, despite help from the community. They'd long given up the idea that the misplaced CCTV footage might turn up.

The very idea that this situation might repeat yet again in Rowan's case was unthinkable.

'Anyway, did you honestly think the police would forget Nigel's history?' Louie said. 'No matter what promises they might make about being impartial.'

Harriet prayed the police would find the killer before they uncovered the true dynamic between her and Rowan. Then it occurred to her she could expedite that process. As Mike had reminded her, she had Rowan's computer password. And Nigel had, for the present, prevented the police from taking Rowan's computer.

A new plan took shape in Harriet's mind.

With her close working knowledge of Rowan and the access she had to his computer – his emails and his calendar – she'd recognise the clues better than South Wales Police. However, her window of opportunity would soon close. If the police considered the washed-up clothes as proof of Rowan's death, they'd veto Nigel's obstruction.

As soon as the police accessed Rowan's emails, the true, toxic nature of their working relationship would become apparent.

At the time, Harriet couldn't believe her luck when Rowan had given her his password. Each staff member was required to change their computer password every 28 days, with the result Rowan struggled to remember his own. He'd initially gone to IT for help, but when they started to joke about it, he claimed it too humiliating to ask them to help him reset again. Instead, Harriet would be his backup.

It had struck her as odd, suspiciously so. She'd wondered if it was a trap – a test of her trustworthiness.

And it was fortuitous she had it in her possession the following day when Rowan called her in a panic about a London meeting he needed to cancel at the last minute.

When she checked, he'd only had one appointment in a packed diary of general reminders – a lunch meeting at some brasserie with someone he'd abbreviated to AH, along with a mobile number.

'That's it,' Rowan said. 'Augusta Hertz. She's an American staying in London. Give her a call and postpone? She's not a client yet. I'm still waiting for her instructions so it should be fine. Tell her I'll be up on Friday. We'll fix something for then.'

'I'll call her now.'

'Thank you,' he said.

Harriet had called Augusta and was surprised to discover during the brief call that the American was somehow connected to the Kennedy Jones' assisted dying case, but there'd been a mix up. She hadn't any record of an arrangement to meet Rowan that day.

Recalling the brief exchange, something niggled at Harriet, but it didn't sharpen into focus.

It wasn't surprising. She realised that, at the time, the thought of legitimately accessing Rowan's computer had proved such a thrilling and daunting prospect that her subsequent call to Augusta was nothing more than an afterthought.

Chapter 9

Kennedy Jones

Why do you dream that same dream again? Thirteen years old, sitting in the south stand of Cardiff Arms Park. Skin blue white, mottled with cold as Ellis sucks the excess dribble off his gum shield. Ellis, with scrum-pox sores around his chin.

At the call of your name, you clatter down the yellow steps from the subs box and onto the pitch side, which is bisected with weak sunshine. The wind is fierce – stronger than when you arrived – and, even then, it tears at the Blues flag on top of the clubhouse.

Awaiting further instruction, you feel the teeth of it. No wonder the boys are struggling. The other team have the advantage with the wind at their backs. This will be a tough. Your chest is tight with nervous excitement.

The way the clouds and birds chase across the sky echoes your adrenaline build.

But then the assistant coach yells at you.

'Who called you, Jones? Nobody. Get back up on the bloody subs' seats.'

Somebody *had* shouted your name and you'd assumed you were on, is the truth of it. That's what happens when there are too many on the sidelines, pretending they're all in charge. Given half a chance, the dads would all be on in their flipflops too.

'Squeeze, squeeze,' Ellis shouts wetly at the running players as you return to the seat next to him. 'Chase, boys, chase.'

'You're a dirty fucking bastard, Ellis,' you say, slumping down, arms folded, glowering over your schoolboy error and glaring at the game in general.

When bright drizzle drives slantwise across the pitch, you tell yourself you had a lucky escape, but it doesn't warm you any. Instead, there's a glimmer of consolation in Ellis's misfortune. You've great skin. Always did. Clear, even, of the acne plaguing half the team.

'I've got some mousse and tablets, like,' Ellis says. 'It'll go in no time.'

He runs his dirty fingers over the weeping blisters.

'Stop fucking touching them, you dirty prick,' you say.

Swiftly, the scene changes and your dream cuts to the changing rooms, where you catch sight of yourself in the mirror. The face looking back at you is unrecognisable – hundreds of pustules on the verge of eruption and like partially healed scabs, like cigarette burns.

You awake, every time, with a start.

It means something, but what?

Chapter 10

'When's the Kennedy Jones' background likely to be ready?' Nigel asked, standing at the window of Rowan's office, coming out of his morose daydream with a nasal sigh.

'It's almost done,' Harriet said. 'I'll work on it over lunch.'

She guessed Nigel's thoughts were lost in that glimpse of dull, taupe sea between the buildings across the road. His son's body was out there somewhere, alone and half-naked, being dragged towards the shipping lanes by the currents. Harriet shivered at the thought of it and yet, she'd harboured her own vengeful fantasies for long enough.

If Rowan had just left her alone, she'd have proved herself a clear headed, laser-focused assistant and her work would have reached a higher standard. Now, she had to demonstrate her potential to Nigel instead.

The show must go on, she thought – and that was a good thing. With or without Rowan, everything had to settle down at some point. Maybe then she could still become a Chartered Legal Executive, which sounded, if anything, fancier than a plain old solicitor.

If her JFK research proved impressive enough, why not?

Anyone sports mad or Welsh thought they knew the Kennedy Jones story, but so much remained legally privileged and confidential.

His accident had played out on 19 March 2022 in front of JFK's dad, his older sister and his fiancée, Danielle – all of whom rose to their feet, reaching blindly for each other – and 74,000 other Six Nations fans nursing cold beer in plastic pints and jumbo hotdogs.

The pressure had been getting to the Irish, trying to force the game rather than let it play out. Twenty minutes to half time, with Wales ahead by 3 points, JFK made a cunning steal for the ball, dropped it and gathered again.

Immediately, he'd come in for a heavy tackle, barged into by the gargantuan Irish forward Darragh Murphy. When JFK hit the turf cradling the ball, he'd raised his head to shoulder out as various Celtic cousins and Welsh brothers lumped on top. Someone wrenched the ball from his grip – there were too many bodies to know who. Later, he recalled his neck had made a sound like snapping celery. A shock of electricity ran through him and all feeling drained from his arms and legs.

JFK knew instantly what the total loss of sensation meant, but everyone else had to catch up.

Though keen to finish her work, outside interruptions hampered Harriet's progress.

She stopped to read the firm-wide email from Nigel stating he wanted to protect Eiriol clients from the truth of his son's abduction. Anyone leaking information from within these four walls to the press, he said, would find themselves out of a job. This was short sighted, Harriet thought. Too many people already knew.

Business services staff, from credit control to IT, had been stopping by to grill Harriet about what she knew, the white-collar equivalent of war tourists.

The entire building, including Harriet, hungered for updates and information from any source who might have it.

An image of the sea of flowers outside Eiriol Law came to her, a collection to which she'd contributed herself, for appearances' sake.

Bundles of sharp, bare stalks stuck out from each bouquet, which she saw more as a cellophane cone of shame for Rowan. But candles were lit, vigils attended, prayers said – all mourning St Rowan.

To help her focus, Harriet made a temporary retreat to a meeting room, where she donned headphones to watch re-runs of Kennedy's final Six Nations game.

Harriet observed how the Principality Stadium, earlier deafening with airhorns, applause, harmonic snatches of 'Hymns and Arias' and the spontaneous call and refrain of 'Oggy, Oggy, Oggy' fell silent as the rugby international lay motionless on the ground.

Gentle but firm fingers formed cages around JFK's ears and packed rolled clothing about his neck.

Teammates surrounded JFK, kneeling to afford him privacy but, from the stands, most fans could see what the medics were doing on the pitch. Viewers at home, whether they wanted it or not, received unrestricted, live-streamed television coverage.

In the interminable time before the rigid stretcher materialised at his side, JFK's teammates were exposed to the full trauma. Some cried quietly, heads bowed, arms crossed. 'I'm sorry,' JFK told them. He didn't cry – that came later – but he did lose his bladder control, which is why one of the medics covered him with a blanket from the waist.

The team doctor fastened a neck collar with a lie of gentle reassurance in his smile. They strapped Kennedy Jones' broken, urine-soaked body to the board and carted him off to a concerned smattering of applause from the crowd.

Physically changed forever that ill-fated day, JFK's heart and mind suffered their own catastrophic trauma, which was how he ended up a client of Eiriol Law LLP.

Confident she'd been thorough, Harriet emailed her background report and accompanying research to Nigel and prayed it would distract him long enough for her to hack into his missing son's computer without being caught.

Come on, girl, she told herself, with a sigh that came all the way from her diaphragm. It's now or never. Did she want to spend the rest of her life wondering *what if*? Anything she found might also assist the police.

Turning on his monitor, Harriet typed in the password, expecting it to have been changed, perhaps by Rowan or by some remote Eiriol IT person.

It worked.

As she combed through his emails, the anxiety that had been pulsing in her chest, which she imagined would rise to an impossible crescendo, disappeared. An intense, liberated fascination took over as Harriet discovered she hadn't been the only one wishing Rowan Tudor ill.

Rowan had brought to Eiriol Law a handful of tail-end judicial reviews, with his previous firm's blessing. Two had ended badly and he'd saved the ensuing vitriolic email exchanges in folders labelled with the client's initials. Reading from the bottom in each, Harriet mapped how they'd escalated.

In the first case, a twenty-year-old Cambridge student, Jennifer McKinty, had purchased diet pills off the internet. Her family claimed her subsequent overdose was unintentional, that she'd only ever wanted to lose weight. The university, at the inquest, presented evidence of a student struggling with her economics coursework. Evidence of suicide threats to friends and fellow students were submitted. Concerns had been flagged to the faculty.

The family wanted a judicial review to re-examine the coroner's verdict of suicide. They were positive Jennifer's suicide threats were nothing more substantive than cries for help.

The second case involved Stewart Jessop, from Bristol, who'd been charged with the rape of a 16-year-old. Found not guilty at trial, the client's later application to become an adult literacy teacher was refused after an enhanced record check. Jessop wanted a judicial review to challenge the fact that a not-guilty acquittal doesn't appear in the DBS check results. This application to the court had also failed.

Having raised all the necessary money from family and friends, the McKinty and Jessop cases had both failed to get off the ground at the first application. Both parties threatened legal action and fundraised for professional negligence suits against Rowan via social media, in the hope, no doubt, that the threat of damage to Rowan's reputation might spur him into action and, presumably, result in a refund of his hefty fees.

Harriet noted down both complaints on her suspects list.

An email from Rowan's brother, Leighton, the day before his brother's disappearance also piqued Harriet's curiosity because the subject line was mysteriously blank. She'd never met Leighton in person. Unlike Rowan and Nigel who maintained an office presence, Leighton worked remotely and his office, two floors below, was often commandeered by dispute resolution for internal meetings.

In his email, Leighton confined himself to a single, curt sentence:

Whatever the hell you and dad are cooking up, leave me out of it.

Did he mean the judicial inquiry against South Wales Police or something else? Harriet chewed the end of her pen as she considered Leighton's words.

She turned to Rowan's private Outlook folders. Just like his father did with Members of the Senedd, Rowan exchanged heavy correspondence with various Westminster MPs. The contents were of minimal interest, often just arrangements to meet one or two of them at a time at L'Escargot for lunch whenever he was in London.

Rowan was particularly friendly with an MP called Nicholas Etheridge. Harriet already knew this because Etheridge had referred JFK to Eiriol Law.

Nicholas Etheridge campaigned hard on the crisis in social care and underfunded palliative care. He wanted people to have the best care and was open to everything from assisted dying to virtual wards where people could recover at home, monitored by their own mobile phones, the data from which could be reviewed by trained staff in a call centre.

Harriet shuddered at the thought. There'd been a popular Welsh documentary set in a call centre years before and, while entertaining, she wouldn't want any of *those* people responsible for keeping her beloved parents alive.

About to log out, Harriet spotted a folder called Thompson & Hurley, the London firm from which Rowan had come. The emails within concerned a secretary who'd complained of sexual harassment. Astonished, Harriet read email after email detailing how a PA, Sorelle, had lodged an Employment Tribunal claim following constructive dismissal. She'd cited Rowan as an individual respondent, as well as his firm.

Thompson & Hurley forced Rowan to personally pay a £10,000 contribution towards the agreed settlement figure.

While settlement agreements didn't confirm or deny guilt in sexual harassment claims, forcing an accused employee to bear half the costs of silencing an accuser was unusual. Thompson & Hurley, it seemed, had sanctioned Rowan themselves.

This new discovery spoke of motive. Thanks to the #MeToo legacy, even historic claims could damage, more so if they existed in clusters. And might not the victims, or their families, have sought revenge? More suspects.

Checking the monitor's digital clock, Harriet couldn't believe she'd been lost in her research for forty minutes, but thoughts of time vanished completely when she spotted a folder called 'HE'.

Chapter 11

Kennedy Jones

In the first few minutes of your Wales v Ireland game, with the final bars of 'Hen Wlad Fy Nhadau' in your ears and the tang of ammonia from the flares in your nostrils, comes a nothing incident.

That's all it is, a shoulder barge at the wrong angle. For a second, you're a surfer knocked off his board, unsure which way is up. Then your head clears of piercing tinnitus. Your boot studs root into the grass-covered soil. You're ready to get up and go again, to make inroads, smash the ball over the try line or run angles that open a hole for a teammate to sprint and score.

The medics decided there was no need for a head injury assessment, as per HIA protocols.

Your memories are mixed up because you're sure you played on, but now a pitch-side medic leads you down to the oatmeal-painted breeze block box below the stadium – an airless space vibrating with the noise of seventy thousand fans roaring above.

FOMO burns under the fluorescents.

It's Dr Stockton waiting in the first aid room with his clipboard, not your usual guys in green. You might be concussed, but this is a physical impossibility. You didn't meet him until *after* your SCI stopped you playing. Another thing that stands out is that this *isn't* the players' first aid room at the Principality Stadium.

Close, but no cigar.

'Sit yourself down, son,' Stockton says, as though addressing a stranger. 'Simple concussion test Q&A. Can you tell me who you're playing against today?'

'Dr Stockton, what are you doing here? Where's Mark, the paramedic? The usual team? And where am I?'

'As I've explained, I'll be performing your HIA today. Which half of the game is it? First or second?'

'I don't know. Where are the others?'

'The quicker you answer my questions, the quicker I can assess whether you're fit to get back out on the field. Tell me, who scored last?'

'Am I playing? I don't understand. I thought I was just remembering something.'

'Then what team did you play last? Can you tell me that?'

'When I got my injury? Six Nations. Wales against Ireland.'

'I'm going to repeat five words. Please repeat them back: *Death. Life. Assisted. Eternity. Release.*'

'Death. Life. Assisted. Eternity. Release.'

'Good lad. Now, I want you to hop down from the table and walk slowly towards the wall, tandem gait.'

'Why would you ask me to do something you know I can't?'

Dr Stockton makes a few notes.

'Do you have a headache?'

'Most of the time.'

'Dizziness?'

'Often.'

'Pressure in your head?'

'Always.'

'Nausea or vomiting?'

'Yes.'

'Blurred vision?'

Dr Stockton looks concerned at your hesitation.

'Blurred vision?' he says, this time louder.

'Sometimes.'

'Does light or noise bother you?'

'These lights are way too bright and I don't understand what you're doing here.'

'Do you feel like you're in a fog?'

'Since the spinal injury, my whole life is a fog.'

The lights get even brighter. The fog rolls in and consumes you.

When you next wake, Dr Stockton is bending over you with Augusta behind him. They say you failed to disclose that you had a head injury assessment for concussion earlier in the same Six Nations Wales v Ireland game. You don't remember, apparently, because the later spinal cord damage left memory blanks and overshadowed everything else.

The cost of your treatment over a lifetime, they explain, can run to millions. And that was before the cost of living and energy prices vaulted skyward. Now the insurance, thanks to the school-boy error of non-disclosure, won't cover further treatment at Afternity. Their advice is to sue the WRU officials for negligence and pay for private treatment that way.

'You *do not* want a lifetime of treatment on the NHS,' Augusta says.

'But didn't you promise,' you say, fearful that a terrible misunderstanding is coming to light. 'You said you'd take care of everything – all the costs?'

'We're just wondering whether you have any private income that might provide a top up? We always assumed your recovery would be more straightforward. These additional diagnostic costs were unforeseen.'

The shame you felt in the immediate aftermath of your accident as mum and dad rooted around in your finances, assigned Temporary Power of Attorney, returns tenfold.

Mum and dad tried to contain it, but it was evident enough they condemned your ill-judged extravagances. It scared them. Why hadn't you put more aside? Where was your rainy-day fund? Why such ridiculous spending: holidays, designer clothes, gambling, nights out?

You had to keep the adrenaline going for the next game, is the truth of it. That's what it was all about.

Your central Cardiff penthouse took months to sell amid a housing slump. Your racing-green Land Rover Discovery got returned to the dealership. They shipped off your furniture, designer clothes, athletic gear, electric bikes, paddleboard, artwork, wine fridge, music system and Sony entertainment system to Big Yellow Self Storage, along with your rugby kitbags, memorabilia and memories, trophies and rugby jerseys. Everything rugby-related was thrown, higgledy-piggledy, into 68 identical, unlabelled white archive boxes and clear Wilko cases with the kind of haste normally attributed, ironically, to people going on the run.

The wreckage of your old life is bunched up inside them.

For ten minutes straight, Augusta and Dr Stockton lounge on the Chesterfield, getting creative with your financial predicament.

'What about a sports bio?' Augusta asked.

You tell them trying to monetise through a book is a no-go. You'd burned those bridges a few months after your accident with the help of your then agent. Your ghost writer, a famous Fleet Street sports journo, had to be paid off, 55,000 words in. The first healthy instalment of three was returned.

You hadn't even wanted the book. That was dad's dream: his dear adopted son on the shelf alongside Alun Wynn Jones, Sam Warburton and Jamie Roberts.

Dan Lydiate's *Grand Slam Man* in the Quick Reads canon comes across like a textbook formula for a Hollywood sports screenplay. The guy breaks his neck in 2007, has a five-hour operation and still goes on to win the Grand Slam. Some guys – all the luck. Throw in an upbeat soundtrack and it's a Disney feelgood film with a 12 certificate.

'There's Nicholas Etheridge's campaign,' Dr Stockton says. 'I bet he'd be happy to assist with our costs if someone like Kennedy Jones were a poster boy.'

'What's the campaign?' you ask.

'D'you know, that's not such a terrible idea,' Augusta says.

'Let's not get ahead of ourselves,' Dr Stockton cautions. 'I'll sound the MP out on it first.'

Chapter 12

Harriet guessed the contents of the first email and was proven right: her witness statement in Nigel's case against South Wales Police.

'Harriet Erskine might make a useful assistant,' Nigel wrote in the body of his email to Rowan. 'She flunked out of law at Cardiff Uni after two terms, but I've attached the statement she put together herself in the case of Roddy Roberts. She's a reliable secretary. No sick days. Let me know what you think.'

It was some time since she'd provided her five-page witness statement, so Harriet couldn't remember all the detail within and was curious as to how Nigel had received it and subsequently framed it to his son. A flutter of anxiety in her chest reminded her of the pressure exerted on her at the time.

Having read it through, the structure still pleased her, but she congratulated herself on how much her writing skills had improved during her time as Rowan's legal assistant.

The statement opening set out the background, how Roddy, a law costs draftsman, friend of her parents and member of The Poet's Mensa group, had steered her A level choices.

'They set a high bar at Cardiff Uni if you want to study law,' Roddy had said. 'You'll need three As at A level. Get a B in one subject and you might find yourself out in the cold, on the phone to UCAS clearing.'

Though Harriet didn't know exactly what a law costs draftsman did, she didn't doubt Roddy's knowledge. Chin in hand, she considered the challenge ahead of her. Although on course for straight As at GCSE, to guarantee such stellar results at A level, she'd have to work a great deal harder.

Harriet imagined herself cramming in the upstairs bathroom, ears stuffed with tissues, while her parents belted out a duet version of 'Take Me Home, Country Roads' on karaoke night in their packed pub.

'So, what subjects should I be thinking about if I want to be a lawyer?' Harriet had asked.

'Most go for humanities,' Roddy explained. 'And that's sensible for the skills you'll need. English literature and history encourage extended writing and critical thinking. They're useful for getting students used to dissecting vast quantities of text, synthesising opposing viewpoints and arguments.'

Harriet smiled and nodded. English and history were Harriet's strongest subjects.

'Now,' Roddy continued, 'you could supplement these subjects with something like politics, but you're not going to far advance the skills you'll develop from English and history.'

'What about A level law?' Harriet asked.

'As far as I know, few sixth form colleges teach it and universities aren't impressed with the content when they do. University law tutors would rather you develop critical thinking through English Lit and then advance your legal knowledge at uni level. There's a far better way to stand out.'

'Which is?'

'How's your maths?'

'Okay. Better than average,' Harriet said, thinking A level maths had the same appeal as tending bar at The Poet's: competence didn't square with enjoyment.

'Law programmes are often impressed by technical STEM subjects. Few apply with these, even fewer when it comes to female students. A level maths demonstrates the ability to analyse and apply logic. But, more importantly, legal outcomes are financial: think estates, trusts, settlements, awards, compensation and legal costs. Employment law, for example, protects income, holiday pay, sickness benefit and looks to prevent inequalities that would unfairly affect the worker's wage packet or their ability to be productive.'

The information came to Harriet as a surprise. Maths had never come into her desire to be a lawyer. She'd had lofty notions of fighting for the underdog, impressed by dramatisations of John Grisham books and real-life tales portrayed in films like *Erin Brockovich*.

'Grade A in GCSE Maths is one thing,' Harriet said, 'but I'm not sure I could get an A grade at A level. Maybe I should speak to my maths teacher.'

'Look, if you're interested in taking maths at A level, I'm happy to tutor you on a weekly basis. I know how much you want this and what it means to your parents. And if you want work experience, it's there. My office manager can sort that out. Then you'll see how much calculating is involved. Give it a week, you'll never forget your six times table. And my clients are all law firms. I'll see if I can get you work experience with them.'

'That'd be fantastic,' Harriet said, keen to close the deal before Roddy found out how clueless she was about his actual job, why his clients were law firms or where the six times tables fitted in. 'I'd really appreciate it.'

Roddy had come through on all his promises. He'd even paid her for six weeks' work over the summer holidays, where she'd learned how to add up costs, calculator at hand, running her finger down the narratives of work done in six-minute billable increments on client files. She became acclimatised to the vocabulary: attendance notes, case management conferences, judicial mediation, preliminary hearings and pre-trial reviews.

It happened slowly, but Harriet came to enjoy studying maths as much as she enjoyed English. The two balanced each other. The lack of right and wrong answers in English sometimes frustrated her. She had a good maths teacher who administered feedback in its simplest form – a tick or a cross. It was unequivocal. When you were right, you knew it.

To have Roddy's guidance made her feel lucky and her parents couldn't do enough for him.

On a Tuesday night, a week before Harriet's maths A level, Roddy went through her final revision schedule. Before him on the table was a third of a pint of Guinness. In front of Harriet lay three maths textbooks, a jotter, pens, markers, sticky labels and a Diet Coke.

When Roddy next went to the bar, Harriet scanned the room.

Four painters and decorators at a table in the opposite corner were placating a fifth man whose black tracksuit with a white sports logo contrasted with their paint-spattered, white cotton overalls.

The old wall sconce above the table threw out a gloomy light, making shadows of the man's eyes and adding prominence to his heavy brow ridge. He's a Neanderthal, Harriet thought. His laugh was loud and dirty and, when his company failed to join in with his laughing, she wondered at the dynamic.

As Roddy sat down, the Neanderthal stood up. His height surprised Harriet. Over six foot and unsteady on his feet, he'd clearly grown up on a better than average hunter-gatherer diet. He veered in an unsteady course towards them, gave Harriet a smile and then, noticing the books, grimaced and barked:

'Don't you start! I'm hungover.'

Since Harriet had said nothing and hadn't even, as far as she was aware, given him any sort of judgemental look, she took the unprovoked defensiveness as a joke. Then she considered the idea that the decorators had perhaps given him a lecture, souring the man's mood.

In the opposite corner, the rest of the men stood and threw a hasty goodbye to her dad over their shoulders as they trooped out the door.

'You her teacher?' the guy in the tracksuit asked Roddy.

'I'm helping with maths revision. I'm a friend of her dad's,' Roddy said, tipping his head towards the bar, where her dad had put down the glass and was now watching the exchange.

Harriet arranged her A4 notes in front of her and opened a textbook as a cue for the knuckle-dragger to leave.

'Shall we get back to it?' she encouraged Roddy, who'd taken to staring into the dark depths of his Guinness.

'Teacher, ha. I know your game. Like 'em young, eh?'

Roddy cocked his jaw. The amused 'huh' that followed showed he wasn't falling for that game.

'Come again?' the man said.

'I didn't say anything,' Roddy said.

'You did pal. You mumbled something. If you've got something to say, come out and bloody say it.'

'I never said a word,' Roddy said.

'Right fucking night this is turning out to be,' the guy mumbled to himself, staring around the empty pub.

'Look, leave them alone, pal,' Louie said, 'or I'll have to ask you to leave.'

'Think you're so fucking clever, don't you?' The guy put his big browbone inches from Roddy's face.

'Leave them alone,' Louie warned.

Again, Harriet rearranged her books to create an impression that study was imperative.

'Wouldn't you rather have a drink with me, love?' the Neanderthal grunted.

'I need to study,' she replied, keeping her tone light and friendly but remaining firm in her boundaries.

'How about I sit at that table over there?' he said taking a seat a table away. 'Then you can choose. That old codger or me. Let me get you a drink.'

'I'm fine, thanks,' Harriet said.

The man tried a new tactic.

'Mate, what does your daughter drink?'

'She's got a drink, she says she's fine and I'm not your mate,' Louie said.

Rising from his table again, the man wiped his wet mouth and chin, and went to the bar where he stood watching them. 'I'll have a Diet Coke,' he said to Louie, over his shoulder.

Louie straightened up, took the payment and placed the soda on the wet bar towel. The Neanderthal returned to his table.

'This is for you, love,' the Neanderthal said, raising it in Harriet's direction before placing it down in front of an empty chair. 'Sorry if I've been bothering you.'

Catching Harriet's eye again, Louie spread his fingers and patted the air. Be cool, the gesture said. Ignore him.

They tried their best to continue. In their work on mathematical moments and torque, Roddy told Harriet he'd have liked to carry out a demonstration using the hinged bar top, had it not risked inviting further attention. Instead, Roddy asked Harriet to calculate the statistical probability of the fellow's behaviour escalating the more they ignored him.

Eventually, as if finally accepting Harriet wasn't about to join him, the man delivered the Diet Coke to their table, deliberately placing the frosted glass on one of the textbooks. Roddy lifted it off and slid a beer mat underneath the base.

'That's her fucking drink,' the guy said. 'Not yours. Hands off.'

Roddy suggested they should call it a day and continue tomorrow instead if Harriet were free.

'What the hell is your problem?' the guy demanded, gripping the edge of their table and flexing his arms in a way that reminded Harriet of an enraged gorilla.

Her dad, she trusted, would now intervene.

'That's it,' Louie said, coming out from behind the bar. 'If you can't leave them alone, I want you out of here, mate.'

'That wanker's got it coming,' the Neanderthal yelled, pointing at Roddy with a stubby digit, but he complied with Louie's order by returning to his table and lifting his glass to finish his pint. 'Thinks he's so fucking clever, doesn't he?' he mumbled into the rim.

When the guy finally left, Harriet wondered if his surly behaviour might be prompted by an inferiority complex. She wondered how the builders knew him. Maybe they didn't. She was still mulling things over when Roddy put on his coat, agreed to reconvene the following day and headed out into the night.

'Sorry about him,' Louie said, before he left.

'Not your fault,' Roddy said, giving a farewell salute. 'See you both tomorrow.'

Moments later, under a full moon rising and gusting clouds, Roddy was punched to the ground. Half conscious, he found himself dragged a few feet along Northcote Street by an assailant who'd appeared from Northcote Lane. Next and last, he suffered a savage and frenzied knife attack.

Running footsteps faded.

Roddy's blood leaked into the gutter.

The unblinking, inanimate eye of a working CCTV camera mounted on the wall of The Poet's observed all.

Chapter 13

Once Harriet had re-read the statement against the police she'd given after Roddy's murder, she noticed Rowan's 'HE' folder contained another seven emails.

Harriet went through them from bottom to top in date order so astonished and horrified that, for a few seconds, everything went dark and Rowan's screen appeared at the end of a long tunnel. Clenching her fists, she hated herself for her blind, unquestioning faith, her childish naivety.

Before she could decide what to do, Harriet heard footsteps approaching. She held down the power button on Rowan's PC, swearing under her breath. Diving back into her seat just in time, she typed loud, innocently industrious nonsense.

Nigel knocked and popped his head in.

'Ah, Harriet, just the person.'

Traitor, she thought, as she raised her chin in injured defiance. The man was just as much a shark as his son ever was.

Despite saying she was just the person he wanted, Nigel surprised her by asking her to leave the room.

'I need to look for something for HR,' he said, waving at the desk and the wall and shelves, where Rowan's practising certificate hung and a couple of thank you cards stood. 'I'll need privacy.'

Harriet rose from her desk in silence, unable to even look at him.

Your son was harassing me, she thought. You knew it at the time. You knew it was likely to escalate, but you gave him a free pass to continue.

There'd been any number of signs and less than acceptable situations she'd ignored at Eiriol Law.

'In any event,' Nigel continued, 'we can't leave you in here on your own. I've asked Karen to sort you a desk with the other secretaries. You might as well get settled in. It must be painful, working in here.'

'But what about the legal assistant work? What about CILEX?' she said.

'Have you forgotten, my son is missing, presumed dead?' Nigel said, turning to face her, eyes wide. 'Even if a miracle occurs and he's found alive, he'll be in no fit state to return any time soon. You argued for a promotion and now we've nowhere to put you.'

'But won't you hire someone else – a locum maybe – to take over his judicial review work?'

Planting his feet in front of her, Nigel put his hands in his pockets and leaned back. 'I'm taking over the Kennedy Jones case. That's why I needed your background notes. The rest, we'll refer onto other firms. Everyone here's struggling to keep their own caseloads on track as it is.'

Harriet dropped the subject, realising her out-of-character anger could appear both professionally and emotionally inappropriate under the circumstances.

Leaving the room loaded down with her personal items and stationery, Harriet consoled herself that evidence was still right there on Rowan's computer. She just had to return later and press print – as long as Nigel didn't get in the way.

In one email to Rowan, Nigel had warned his son to try and control himself with the advice, 'if you can't be good, be careful'. In another, Rowan had replied that his father shouldn't worry. Harriet wasn't half as clever as she thought she was.

Harriet's old desk, at the secretarial pods, had been reassigned to a temp. Karen pointed at an empty desk with a view of a blank wall. Her monitor, once facilities brought it from Rowan's office, would sit in full view of Karen, so that nothing during her working day would go unscrutinised.

Without a computer to work on, Harriet took an early lunch and wandered around the St David's 2 centre, window shopping and brooding on what she'd discovered.

In the stores' gleaming windows, mannequins were already

adorned in Christmas party-wear. Black sequin suits rubbed shoulders with scarlet satin dresses, cut on the bias.

It seemed unlikely Eiriol Law would have any festive celebrations this year and, even if they did, Harriet intended to boycott them.

She spent twenty minutes sitting on a bench in the arcade staring at her phone, hunting for Rowan's previous PA on LinkedIn. It transpired Sorelle was now working for a sports talent agency called Star One. Harriet wondered what Sorelle made of his disappearance and how she felt about it.

Then she carried out a little research on Jennifer McKinty and Stewart Jessop, Rowan's angry JR clients. Both had, given the news, ceased complaining about him on social media.

When Harriet returned to the office, Debbie scuffed towards her desk in her clumsy, careful way, ensuring her designer, but too-wide, sale shoes stayed put.

'Sorry about your old desk being taken,' she said, giving Harriet a thin, joyless smile of faux regret.

'That's okay. It's only temporary.'

'Have they given you someone else to work for then?'

'Not yet,' Harriet said.

'So, you're back with us minions then – picking up typing jobs from the BigHand system?'

'You'll want to pick a name for Secret Santa,' Ffion interrupted, with a forgiving smile. 'We're having our Christmas party on 2 December. We didn't invite you because we thought you'd be out with Rowan and them lot.'

'Feel free to join us,' Debbie said, 'if you're part of our lowly secretarial team again.'

'Yes, sure,' Harriet said, fighting the urge to walk out, 'count me in.'

Debbie was about to reply, but Karen interrupted to say 'they' were waiting for Debbie in the boardroom.

While Karen and Debbie headed off to their mystery meeting, Harriet snuck back into Rowan's room to find her desk gone. Faint imprints on the carpet tiles and a faded circular patch from her chair wheels remained. Dust suffused the room with a pale gold haze. How quick facilities could move when it suited them. Whenever *she* asked them to do anything, she usually had to wait a day or two.

It took Harriet a second to process the fact that Rowan's monitor had been unplugged and disconnected. The hard drive was missing. Likewise, his keyboard and mouse leads went nowhere.

Back in the main office, Harriet was still so outraged about her lost evidence against Rowan and Nigel that she didn't, at first, see the shocked faces around her. Some colleagues swore under their breath. Karen's mascara had tracked down her cheeks in charcoal streaks. Following the slam of a door, someone shouted, 'bastards'.

'What's going on?' Harriet asked, a fearful lump in her throat. 'Have they found him?'

'No,' Karen said, sniffing back tears while winding a tissue around her finger. She dabbed under her eyes, leaving a grey residue. 'The police are interviewing everyone. And they've taken Rowan's IT. Nigel's distraught. They're running around here like they own the place.'

When Debbie returned, she did so with a satisfied, loose-shoed swagger. 'The police asked all sorts about you, Harriet,' she said. 'How closely you worked with Rowan. Whether you saw each other outside work. How often you worked late. It was really *weird*.'

That explained it. Harriet had thought Nigel had taken his son's computer away, but its confiscation by the police meant the clock had started. The police would find Rowan's apologetic emails and then what? Now, she had days rather than weeks to find out who killed Rowan.

'They're ready for you now, Harriet,' Karen said, wiping her eyes and sniffing.

Nigel waited by the open boardroom door. Within, behind the vast, polished mahogany table, two detectives wore an air of public-facing professionals struggling to remain polite. Whatever Nigel had said to them hadn't gone down well.

The emails she'd seen between him and his son were bad enough, Harriet fumed. Why did he have to go and rile up the detectives right before her interview as well?

Karen turned on her heels and left.

‘Before you speak to Harriet,’ Nigel said to the detectives, ‘I need to speak to her alone – one moment. It’s a confidential HR matter.’

Harriet’s pulse fluttered in her chest as Nigel led her along the empty corridor. The events of the last few days had deepened the lines on Nigel’s harrowed face.

‘Thanks for sending over the Kennedy Jones research,’ he said. ‘I’ve gone through it and it’s everything I needed.’

‘Good,’ Harriet said, in a curt fashion.

‘I’ve asked so much of you. More than I should’ve asked of anyone. Once you’ve spoken to the detectives, I want you to go straight home. Take a couple of days off. Call it compassionate leave. It’s all cleared with HR. I’ll ask Karen to bring your coat and bag to the boardroom once you’re done. Take a few days to process everything that’s happened and come back fresh after the weekend.’

‘That’s kind, Nigel, but I’d honestly rather keep busy.’

‘I know. But HR are insisting. It’s an employee welfare thing.’

Maybe she was doing Nigel an injustice, but whenever he claimed he had her interests at heart, he was usually up to something. His previous words, *we’ve nowhere else to put you*, might well foreshadow redundancy planning.

‘Got it, thanks,’ Harriet said, cutting Nigel off from further conversation by stepping away, entering the boardroom and closing the door.

Taking a seat, Harriet became aware of the blast of freezing air con above her head and guessed that Nigel had knocked the boardroom temperature right down to inflict as much discomfort as possible on the detectives. She couldn’t decide if it was funny or childish. After all, she’d have to shiver with them.

The usual hospitality tray of sparkling glass tumblers, water jug, porcelain mugs, hot coffee urn and the locally baked mini bara brith biscuits had also been withheld.

‘Okay to talk?’ the detective with the retro 70s mullet asked, gesturing to the seats, rubbing his hands.

‘Yes,’ Harriet said, smiling and sitting down to avoid appearing guilty or complicit.

'We've spoken to a number of your colleagues,' the female detective said, 'and they mentioned something going on between you and Rowan. DI Lennon isn't happy. The situation, if true, ought to have been disclosed to us prior to your involvement in the ransom drop.'

'What did they tell you?' Harriet said, clinging to a faint hope that some staff knew of her problems with Rowan.

'I'm sorry to have to ask you this but were the pair of you engaged in some kind of sexual relationship?' the officer continued.

'Sexual relationship?' Harriet repeated, reeling. 'No chance. It was professional. Who's said otherwise?'

'A number of your colleagues went as far as saying you and Rowan were having an affair.'

'Now, that's just not true. It's dirty gossip.'

'It's best to be honest with us now.'

'This is me being honest.'

'They suggest you were up and down at times, in an on-again, off-again kind of relationship.'

'Well, they're wrong.'

'Can you tell us how your promotion and pay rise came about? A few of your colleagues said this raised red flags.'

'Nigel will clear this up. The promotion was his idea.'

'We *have* spoken to Nigel. He and Karen confirmed that you'd raised CILEX a number of times and, frankly, the way Nigel tells it, he felt a little blackmailed.'

'Blackmailed?' Harriet snorted, though her pulse quickened.

'Yes, he suspected that you and Rowan were in a sexual relationship, which made it very hard to say no to Rowan when he told his father that's what you wanted.'

'What I wanted? Why's Nigel lying about this?'

No wonder Nigel told her to go straight home afterwards, she thought. He didn't want her marching into his office, confronting him about his lies.

'Is it true you demanded a room share with Rowan?'

The ignorance of it shocked Harriet. As if a secretary could ever *request* to share a room with a lawyer. Had these rookies ever been inside a law firm before? She searched for a comparable example they might grasp.

'That's the equivalent of a special constable demanding to share an office with a detective inspector,' she said. 'Never going to happen.'

The female detective smiled, perhaps accepting Harriet's logic.

'Nigel told us that he reluctantly accepted your move and promotion on a trial basis,' the female detective said, hugging her arms to her sides. 'If it didn't work out, you'd have to go back to your old desk.'

'No way,' Harriet said, sitting back in her chair.

The emails she'd seen on Rowan's computer could prove Nigel was lying, but she'd have to account for how she'd seen them and, ultimately, they'd then be used against her as motive. What's the point, she thought, in saying anything?

'Harriet?' the detective with the mullet said. 'It's best if you cooperate with us.'

'It really is,' the female detective said, nodding.

'Because we're going to find out the truth anyway.'

'We always do,' his colleague agreed.

Hanging her head, Harriet had no words.

'We've taken Rowan's computer, phone and laptop,' the mullet cop said. 'And we'll have to examine yours too, in light of the things your colleagues have told us today.'

Harriet squeezed her hands together and slid her freezing, balled fists between her knees, as though the officers might, any moment, try and snap cuffs on her.

Chapter 14

Kennedy Jones

Dr Stockton says your temperature will go down, but, though you'd do anything to make that happen, you can't force it. You can't eat or sleep, but strange waking dreams make you believe you've been poisoned. You mention this to Boyd when he sticks his head in. He can't stay, but he's concerned that you're getting worse by the hour.

Dr Stockton is confounded, but he's determined to get to the bottom of it. 'You'll feel better soon, I'm sure,' he says, holding his Afternity iPad. 'Mild infections are par for the course with an injury like yours, I'm afraid. We just have to find exactly the right medication and balance the dosage.'

It feels anything but mild, this nausea and fatigue.

He explains the complexity again, as though you haven't learned it by rote. There's the absent tactile sensation. Compromised thermoregulation that puts you at risk of cold-related illnesses. Diminished bladder and bowel ability. A dependence on spasticity medications, PTSD, anxiety disorder and general stressors inherent to living with a life-changing disability. You're hyperaware of your physical capability and your dependence on caregivers.

Quite the specialist vocabulary.

Recently, your team initiation has haunted you and you were trying to get to the bottom of it with your counsellor, Marni. She says it's buried trauma – from your adoption shock at 16 – but you suspect it's not. You have the same murderous headache, sickness and paranoia now that you had after that day with the boys.

Stockton reads your notes for the third time and throws down his iPad to the side with a sigh of frustration.

Back in the past, your teammates in The City Arms smack down a tenner each. Warner carefully lowers a loaded pint of Carling onto a creased, cardboard Guinness coaster. The contents of the glass slop over. It's full of grotesque non-ice cubes – urinal cakes harvested from the gents' urinals.

Your stomach fizzes with fear.

Drink, you arsehole, you think. Drink before you sodding well think about it. Then it's over, the money's yours and you'll be a fully paid-up member of Cardiff Blues.

Billy Joel's turn-of-the-millennium anthem 'We Didn't Start the Fire' comes on the jukebox.

High pitched, your laugh rings with nerves and bravado.

Taking it steady, you try to ignore the sour stink, real or imaginary; you're not sure so you hold your nose anyway. You're a good three quarters through when your brain registers the musty, chemical mothball bitterness and you remember the yellowing cakes in the yawning mouths of the urinals.

Teammates sing Billy Joel's chorus like a rallying cry.

Not unlike a cat puking up a fur ball, you gag with the hairs on the back of your neck standing on end. You shiver with revulsion.

With their hands hovering over their money like puppet masters, your pals hoot, ready to spring those notes right off the table and back into their pockets if you spew.

You drain the last quarter, stomach rolling, with the yellow cakes – there are six – sliding ominously towards your mouth on a crest of foam.

Now, you see yourself on a raft, swept towards the lip of Niagara Falls.

Putting the empty pint glass down, you clamp your hand to your mouth.

When you vomit soon after, you eject the entire pint over yourself with gusto – a physical embodiment of the word no. The front of your indigo Hugo Boss shirt turns into a black waistcoat as the drink soaks in. You'll have to get home, shower and change.

The notes vanish back into pockets and wallets, hands shaking with the force of delighted laughter.

Queasy for days, stomach sensitive, you play like shit, get abuse off the coaches and don't feel right.

What the fuck is in those urinal cakes anyway?

You made the mistake of looking it up.

Fucking carcinogens, rinsed with urine, obviously.

Your only comfort is that you'll get to jeer at the next rookie initiation, but the subsequent one is tame compared to yours – Iestyn Williams, kicked off the bus naked, a quarter mile from the clubhouse. You'd have taken that in a heartbeat.

Not that you mention it to anyone, but you feel cheated, hoodwinked, poisoned. You suspect they were jealous, wanted to take you down a peg or two.

Maybe you should have known then. Your initiation forewarned and foretold. Those bobbing urinal cakes spelled out something truly ominous.

Now, Stockton has delivered the devastating news from the last scan. For the moment, you nurse the information to yourself, that the game you love has already robbed you of the little you have left. It took a down payment on your future even before the SCI.

Early onset dementia.

Perhaps this accounts for the fact you can't remember a thing of the first HIA in the Wales v Ireland game.

'I need Boyd,' you say: a friend as much as a nurse. This is news you don't know what to do with. Chronic traumatic encephalopathy is the kind of shirt-tackle talk that smashes an already damaged man to the ground.

'He's not capable of administering the kind of care you need.'

'He's like family.'

'Too much so, if you ask me. Watch yourself with these nurses. He knows you've taken a step away from family and friends. He may try to take advantage. Boyd Evans isn't someone we'd have chosen ourselves.'

'You think he's after my rugby fortune? That's preposterous. If I had more money, I'd contribute to my care here. And I've known him for years.'

‘He probably isn’t aware of your real financial situation,’ Dr Stockton says, taking a seat on the Chesterfield. He scratches his temple and screws up his mouth as though he’s come to a decision.

‘Okay. You’ll get him back when he’s proven himself more diligent and trustworthy. And don’t worry about the early onset dementia. We can take preventative measures. In the meantime, I’ve got a surprise for you.’

‘What surprise?’ you say.

‘We’ve got an outing planned this weekend.’ Dr Stockton licks his lips and crosses his legs. ‘It’s about time you met the MP, Nicholas Etheridge.’

‘The campaign you mentioned,’ you say. ‘Where are we going?’

He won’t say. It’s a secret.

The outside world is something you’d compartmentalised, but now it looms large. Who wants to see you looking like this? You need more time. It’ll take too much preparation. People will gawp, maybe take pictures – which will end up on social media or in the press. Mum, dad and Danielle will see them. Trolls will ridicule. It’s an unforgiving, uncompromising world.

No, you’re not ready.

Next time Boyd pops his head in, he smiles, but his eyes are pink rimmed from crying. Dr Stockton must have told him your latest diagnosis. Ridiculous, Stockton’s suspicion that Boyd is ingratiating himself for money. But then if you insist Boyd *must* come on the outing too, maybe Stockton will park the idea for a month or two.

Chapter 15

Close to overwhelmed, Harriet arrived back at her block of flats and had the key in the front door before she noticed, and vaguely recognised, the woman waiting on the low honey-brick wall by the communal entrance. Next to her was a leopard print wheelie case with a fringed shoulder bag balanced on top.

Harriet unlocked the door to the flats and threw the woman a quick, polite smile before catching hold of the latch. As she was about to pull it closed behind her, the woman stood up.

'Are you Rowan's assistant?' she asked, with an East London accent.

'Do we know each other,' Harriet said and then stepped back, chin down in surprise. 'Wait. I recognise you. Are you Sorelle?'

In her online pictures, Sorelle had the most striking blue eyes but, up close, these were contact lenses. Otherwise, she was as stunning as her LinkedIn photo, with long, layered hair and perfect, oval autumn-red nails that complemented her rust-coloured maxi dress, over which she wore a distressed leather jacket.

'I hope you don't mind me tracking you down like this. I saw you'd looked at my profile. It's just ... I don't know how you found working for Rowan, but ...'

'Does a leopard change its spots?' Harriet said, inspired by Sorelle's animal print luggage. 'But how did you find me?'

'Your parents own a pub, right? I saw it on your socials. I went there first and they gave me your address. I don't know what I'm doing here, but I still can't believe Rowan's missing. It was an impulse, to jump on a train and find you. Would you have time for a chat at some point? I'm around until tomorrow morning.'

'Where are you staying?' Harriet asked.

'I was going to book an Airbnb.'

'Nonsense,' Harriet said, her eyes on the low clouds, threatening imminent rain. 'You can stay with me.'

Immediately the words were out of her mouth, she realised her mistake. Yes, her 'Let's Kill All the Lawyers' merchandise was taped up in unlabelled boxes, but still. She wanted to trust the other woman, but Sorelle was a stranger nonetheless.

Too late now, Harriet thought. She could hardly rescind the offer when Sorelle looked so relieved and had already picked up her case. And the pair had a lot to talk about, an evening's worth of conversation at least. She didn't want half of it wasted while Sorelle searched for overnight accommodation.

The decent living space in Harriet's one-bed flat, plenty big enough to allow the sofa to open out into a double bed, came at the expense of Harriet's bedroom, which was barely big enough for a canvas wardrobe crushed against the queen-size bed. The bedroom window had a penchant for streaming condensation from October to May.

Keen to hear about Rowan's behaviour pre-Eiriol, Harriet settled Sorelle in with a cup of tea. She dragged the spare bedding from the airing cupboard and arranged it in a pile next to the sofa. As a pretext for making room for the fold-out bed, Harriet moved the boxes of illicit, anti-lawyer T-shirts and notebooks into her already cramped bedroom.

'Can I help with those?' Sorelle asked.

'No, thanks. I've got it. They're not heavy,' Harriet said, making a snap decision to forgo an explanation.

Next, they collected take-out from a South Asian restaurant on City Road, which they ate quickly.

Worried that Sorelle now had to sleep in a room that smelled of Keralan chicken curry and pilau rice, Harriet put the windows on the night latch and put the food waste caddy on the outside landing. Her neighbours wouldn't object this once.

They sat facing each other on the two-seater sofa, conspiratorial.

'I signed a non-disclosure agreement, so I'm not supposed to talk about it with anyone,' Sorelle said, adjusting the fluffy cushion behind her. ‘But it’s getting me down. I figured, if you were in the same boat, you could do with someone to confide in too.’

‘Tell me everything,’ Harriet said.

‘About six months after he arrived, Rowan had me promoted to his assistant. Rowan told the firm’s partners I needed specific legal training and started booking out a meeting room for an hour after the usual L’Escargot lunch. Except I didn’t learn anything I could use with clients.’

‘Disgusting pig,’ Harriet said. ‘How long did that go on for?’

‘Not long. Right up until the day he got his dick out and ordered me to give him a blow job or he’d fire me.’

‘But you tried to take him to a tribunal,’ Harriet said, scratching at her scalp with her nails, trying to rid herself of the shivers. ‘That takes guts.’

‘I’d managed to get good evidence.’

‘Like what?’

Sorelle grimaced and looked away. She reached down into her brown leather bucket bag beside her, pulling out her phone.

‘I recorded him,’ Sorelle said, waving the phone.

‘No!’ Harriet said, laughing with the shock and surprise of it. Arbitrary recordings of colleagues in private conversations were frowned on but, on a one-off occasion to expose wrongdoing might be accepted. Therein lay the problem: knowing in what specific circumstance to deploy.

‘It was easy. Well, it wasn’t really. It was stressful, but the timing was easy. Rowan was predictable. The harassment only happened when he’d been on the T&C. Usually after L’Escargot lunches.’

‘Wait,’ Harriet said, ‘What’s T&C?’

‘Tequila and coke. His signature drug and alcohol cocktail.’

‘Rowan took cocaine?’

‘Yeah. Didn’t you know?’

Harriet felt stupid, thinking back to his twitchiness and unpredictability, and she mentally added drug dealers to the list of suspects.

‘He hid it well,’ Harriet said, screwing up her mouth, trying to recall more signs she'd missed. 'Sorry – I just can't believe you managed to obtain audio evidence.'

'I thought it would be all I needed,' Sorelle said. 'I mean, it's his voice. And, though he's a bit drunk and high, he's clearly coming on to me and I'm saying, "No, no, no, Rowan". This goes on for a while and then it goes quiet for thirty seconds or so – and he gives me the ultimatum, suck his dick or collect my P45.'

Harriet sighed. Nigel's presence *had* probably mitigated his son's abuse towards her to some extent. 'No wonder you went to an employment tribunal. The audio is a smoking gun.'

'Yeah, you'd think,' Sorelle said, her words sharp with cynicism.

Angry on her new friend's behalf, Harriet struggled to understand how such strong evidence couldn't automatically mean anything other than outright victory. She began to question Sorelle's management of the legal situation.

Harriet rose to turn on the table light. A few streets away, at the junction, horns briefly blared. She spent a second at the window, appreciating that time of day when the lights came on in the windows opposite – various size boxes spilling their candlelit glow as the greens of the trees and creams, brick or greys of the city's buildings receded. Always at this time, the wind in the trees seemed more pronounced.

'The employment tribunal never got to see it,' Sorelle said. 'My lawyer felt sorry for Rowan. He thought he just had a drug and alcohol problem, needed some therapy and there was no need to ruin the poor guy's career.'

'You're kidding?' Harriet said, blindsided. That lawyers on opposite sides of the litigation might express solidarity with each other hadn't occurred to her.

'Honestly, Harriet, if it didn't hurt so much, I'd give Rowan props for a genius counter. He said we'd been in a secret relationship, and I'd dumped him. His feelings for me had run deep, and he'd therefore had a hard time adjusting. Hence the drinking and the sexual demands, which he claimed were totally out of character and of the moment. He *begged* my lawyer not to ruin his career. He said he'd moved on and was now in a stable, loving relationship. But it was a lie, from start to finish.'

Putting her head in her hands, Harriet squeezed her eyes shut for a second, fighting a headache that had come from nowhere.

'After hearing Rowan's sob story,' Sorelle continued, 'my lawyer suddenly started screaming down the phone for me to accept a settlement. He threatened to fire me as a client if I didn't cave immediately and sign a non-disclosure agreement.'

'So,' Harriet said massaging her temples where the pain was strongest, 'your own lawyer treated you like the villain?'

'Yes. Rowan has – or had – a great reputation in London,' Sorelle continued, 'so I didn't fancy my chances finding someone else who'd represent me fairly. My lawyer empathised with Rowan: the money he'd paid for his legal practising certificate, the sacrifices he'd made for the training contract and the grind to get promoted. Add in Rowan's success and professional recognition and getting justice for myself was an uphill struggle.'

Unshed tears shone in both their eyes.

This isn't how the law's meant to operate, Harriet thought.

The sound of a car idling below in the car park made them both pause. Harriet checked it out, approaching the window with slow caution, but it was just a resident waiting for her husband before heading out.

Sorelle took the cushion from behind her, fluffed it up and hugged it on her lap.

'How did you end up at Star One?' Harriet asked.

'Ah, finally a career break. I applied for a ton of legal secretarial jobs but each time they'd ask, "Have you ever tried to make a tribunal claim against a former employer?" It was like they knew already.'

'Do you think Rowan made sure the word got out?'

'I don't know. Maybe everyone just asks that question nowadays. So, I started temping for a bit, including Star One. I knew a bit about them because they represented the rugby player, Kennedy Jones. Nicholas Etheridge and Kennedy's agent at Star One set up a meeting with Rowan, but then it went silent for a bit. Kennedy wasn't well and they were waiting for him to get better. So, anyway, I saw an administrative job with Star One and they were impressed. Another few months and they'll let me scout my own clients.'

'Wow,' Harriet said. 'You must've impressed them.'

'It's a dream come true, really, especially after everything that's happened. That's why I don't want to poke the hornet's nest, but that doesn't mean I don't need someone to understand.'

'I get it,' Harriet said. 'I'm so pleased for you. But look, who do you think might have done this to Rowan? What about his clients at Thompson & Hurley? He brought a couple of clients to Eiriol who later lodged complaints.'

'I think I know which clients you're talking about, but I can't see them doing something as crazy as kidnapping and dumping Rowan in the sea. If I'm honest, they're all threats and no substance. What happened sounds like the work of underworld contacts with a lot of money.'

Harriet nodded. She'd formed the same conclusion. Individual judicial review clients were a dead end – unless something new materialised.

'Can you think of anyone else who might be behind this?' Harriet asked.

'All I'll say is it's something bigger than one unhappy client. Rowan always hit the T&C when stressed. Sometimes, he even looked scared.'

'Scared of what?'

'He was in over his head with something and I can tell you, it's nothing to do with Cardiff. He used to hang out with all these politicians. He and Etheridge were inseparable, I honestly thought Rowan was going to give up law and go for a Tory constituency. But then Rowan started to sound paranoid. And that's when he seemed to want me around more.'

Harriet's questions, the ones to be reflected on later, multiplied. Had Rowan *wanted* Harriet around? Was that why she'd been moved into his room? Perhaps there were reasons other than harassment for him keeping her close. Maybe he'd even *wanted* her to know his password every time he updated it, so she could potentially help him if he ever got into trouble.

And what of those sharks, swimming in and out of Rowan's incomprehensible scribbles. Harriet saw them now as Rowan's own demons.

Even 'Wuthering Heights', echoing in her head from time to time, somehow fit better.

Whatever his problems, Rowan's treatment of Sorelle and herself was unforgivable. Fate had metered out justice and she was glad of it. She hoped he'd survived long enough to think about all those he'd hurt.

'I didn't know Rowan was a Tory,' Harriet said, sloughing off her spiralling thoughts.

'He was and so were all his friends. He even got one of our paralegals at Thompson & Hurley a job as a political speechwriter.'

That lost Harriet for a moment. It didn't make sense that Nicholas Etheridge MP would have had anything to do with Rowan's judicial review work. Etheridge would've been against it in principle.

The three judicial reviews Harriet had looked into, *Petty*, *Nicklinson* and *Purdy* had been easy to research because the Conservatives had written so much about them. The assisted dying cases featured among fifty problematic judicial reviews put together by a far right thinktank, Policy Exchange's Judicial Power Project. Interference from judges presiding over judicial reviews was, they said, completely undemocratic.

The JPP alleged the professional classes had lost faith in the working classes to vote intelligently and judicial reviews were an underhand way for liberals and lefties to regain control.

While Harriet didn't trust the Tories, this particular point – the part about the professional classes not trusting the working class – had a possible nugget of truth.

She'd always had the uncomfortable feeling that the regular inclusivity and diversity training at Eiriol Law was viewed by lawyers as more applicable to business services staff and secretaries. They, after all, belonged to the very class of people that had voted for Brexit.

To counter this suspicion of moral inferiority, Harriet brought all her energy to engagement, reminding Eiriol's facilitators she'd always lived in areas with high diversity and was an all-round sensitive and inclusive person who voted Labour.

So, if Etheridge and Rowan Tudor didn't see eye to eye on judicial reviews, what had brought them so closely together, Harriet wondered? Unless it were as simple as a love of rugby. Kennedy Jones, after all, was the common thread between them.

'But that's enough about me,' Sorelle said. 'What's your story?'

For all Harriet's own trauma with Rowan, Sorelle's experience was on another level. While Harriet wanted to share everything, the risk was too great.

'Nobody will understand better than me,' Sorelle encouraged as though Harriet's body language somehow betrayed her desire to close down. 'I mean, Rowan, being the target of a terrible crime, has robbed us of our own victimhood.'

'Did Rowan ever pretend to be a shark?' Harriet asked tempted to confide in her new friend, but she checked herself. If she started sharing, she wouldn't stop until it was all out.

'No, why? What's the shark thing?'

'Nothing. Just something weird,' Harriet said, shaking her head, and waving – a gesture of nothing. 'Maybe I was lucky. His father set up Eiriol Law, so I guess he had to self-censor himself more.'

'You sure you don't want to talk about it?'

Harriet looked at her phone. Somehow it had turned midnight. The surrounding streets had quietened.

'I'll tell you everything another time,' Harriet said, yawning and reaching for Sorelle's sheets and pillows to make up her friend's bed.

Chapter 16

Carwyn's fidgeting, as he waited at the entrance to Wyndham Arcade, caused Harriet to pause a beat and wonder if she'd misread things. He toyed with the buttons on his duffel and adjusted the cuffs of his sleeves in the same nervous way he did before an open mic performance.

When Harriet hugged him, he released her with a tight half-smile and scratched his ear as though nursing a head full of doubts.

When she'd heard from Carwyn, Harriet assumed he was seeking a dramatic, first-hand account of Rowan's kidnap. The alternative was a relationship second chance, but she dared not get her hopes up.

He suggested they get together at 2pm the following day, at their old lunchtime haunt, Waterloo Tea in Wyndham Arcade.

Speciality teas and a veggie menu of smashed avocado, mushrooms or posh beans on sourdough toast made the teahouse a haunt for middle-class creatives.

Not for the first time, Harriet wondered how much better her relationship with Carwyn would have fared if she hadn't encountered Rowan Tudor. The idea that she and Carwyn might get back together in such stressful circumstances was such a comfort. Nobody understood her like Carwyn did, and there was so much he'd missed.

The nicest thing about dating a poet and a writer was that they tended to be intensely interested in the minutiae of psychological experience, even if it was with a view to turning the emotional truth of it into a literary product.

Then there'd been their travels around America, the shared memories which would always connect them.

'I guess you've heard then,' she said, giving him a sad smile and a sigh.

'Yeah. Awful,' he said, studying the cakes on display and ordering two jasmine green teas with a couple of lemon polenta slices.

Harriet mulled over the understatement and produced her debit card, which she tapped against the payment reader.

'I would've picked that up,' he said, though his hands hadn't moved towards his pockets.

This exchange had played out more times than Harriet could count during their relationship. She, without hesitation, picked up the tab and Carwyn attributed slowness, rather than poverty, as the reason he didn't for the benefit of the cashier.

'I popped over to see your dad,' Carwyn said, dragging the oak chair out from under the table with a heavy scraping noise. 'He said you were off for a few days, if I wanted to see you.'

When the waitress brought their chunky orange teapots, Carwyn absently played with his hour-glass timer. They observed their old tradition of waiting for the tea to brew before touching their cake.

'I guess you can't believe it either?' Harriet said, blinking under the scratchy weight of glued-on Eylure eyelashes. She'd worn black, mourning colours, and her dark make-up contrasted nicely with her pale skin and fair hair.

Carwyn glanced at the teapot, then the lemon sponge, then the counter with the moist slabs of cake, and then gazed out at the people passing outside, stepping through rhomboids of winter light from the historic arcade's glass roof.

His silence filled Harriet with apprehension. The longer it took Carwyn to explain, the more her imagination conjured grim alternate scenarios.

'My publisher suggested we meet,' he said.

'You've found a publisher?' Harriet said, trying to sound happy for him, but finding the topic a little narcissistic in the circumstances, and registering that it hadn't been his idea to see her, but someone else's. 'Is this *The Silence of Pauses*?'

Carwyn's last collection had had a few near misses.

'No, this is something new,' Carwyn said. 'It's a big deal. A *really* big deal. I'm so lucky. Brenin Books have only taken on a couple of collections this year, and they chose mine.'

'Fantastic,' Harriet said, mirroring a notable juxtaposition between his enthusiastic words and muted tone. She'd assumed that he'd heard about Rowan's death, but was she wrong? Where had he been? Off grid, writing poems in a forest?

'It's a *really* big deal.'

'Okay,' she said, thinking her boss's murder was the kind of thing that trumped everything else. Her heart rate increased. What was he holding back?

Carwyn's eyes burned into her, as though it were obvious.

'What's up? Why don't you look that happy?' she said, but then things fell into place. Certainty jagged her system. Carwyn had written poems about their relationship, he'd found a publisher and wanted to tell her the news before she found out from someone else.

'There are a few about you,' he said, pulling a slim volume from the seat pocket of his trousers.

'It's already on the shelves?' Harriet said, extending a hand to halt conversational traffic, palm exposed. 'I don't want to read it if I'm in there.'

'It's called *Swimming with Sharks*,' he said.

'Jesus,' she said. 'So, it's all about me.'

He *had* heard. The timing was so awful as to be deliberate.

The shark games had seen her at her lowest point. Time and distance had failed to shed any light on what happened, psychologically speaking. No insights. Nothing. And it certainly wasn't the kind of thing she wanted memorialised in a Welsh poetry pamphlet.

Then there was Eiriol Law and the police. Their speculation, if they read it, would depend on whether the subject matter was obscure or explicit enough for a critical reader to guess the inspiration.

More concerning and hurtful was that Carwyn had been yet another apathetic bystander. Rather than offer a shoulder to cry on, he'd been creatively inspired and shoplifted her trauma.

'It's just a pamphlet, really,' Carwyn said. 'Nobody's going to read it. No-one's probably even going to buy it.'

'It's fine,' she told him, her iciness letting him know the word *fine* wasn't manifesting in its usual form. If he thought she was going to massage his ego about book sales, he had another thing coming. 'As long as the poems aren't obvious.'

'The publisher says the collection is ground-breaking in its examination of toxic masculinity,' Carwyn said, leaning forward and lowering his voice. 'It's not just about your harassment, but my own misogynistic reaction. Coming to terms with the rage and resentment I felt about that arsehole putting his hands on my girlfriend wasn't easy. I fantasised about beating the crap out of him and you know me, I'm not an aggressive person.'

Harriet opened her mouth to interject, but Carwyn nodded with a kind of anticipatory impatience as though he were two steps ahead in their back-and-forth.

'And, yes,' he continued, 'I know it's wrong to have treated *you* as though you were *my* property. The gall I felt was irrational and misguided, but those feeling were so overwhelming. And your diplomatic attempts to resolve the situation infuriated me. I admit it. I wanted you to knee him in the balls and walk out. *Swimming with Sharks* is my way of processing and coming to terms with such repressed feelings and, in a way, it's also an apology. That's why I've dedicated the book to you.'

Harriet's lips moved, but no sound came out. *My property*? She didn't doubt his anger, but his candid explanation came as such a surprise, she wasn't sure whether to believe it. Had he bottled everything up at the time? What else had he concealed? And had Carwyn really overlooked the biggest danger in choosing to express such negative feelings now? Harriet squinted at him.

'You do know ...' Harriet swallowed, 'Rowan's probably dead. You have seen that on the news, right?'

'Yes, but that's got nothing to do with us. You must read this,' Carwyn said. 'This copy's for you.'

'What are the police going to think?' Harriet said, fear making her reckless as she waved a hand at the book and the matching bookmark contained within its opening pages. 'They're going to think you had a hand in it.'

'Nonsense. I'm trying to admit my faults and take responsibility here,' Carwyn said, placing the poetry volume in front of her. 'I'm trying to make things right by admitting I've been a dickhead to you at times. It'll help us move on.'

'There's absolutely no need for you to feel bad,' Harriet said, breathlessly, with her hand pressed to her collarbone. 'I just need you to stop this from coming out for a bit.'

'Stop it? It's already out. There's going to be an article about in *The Western Mail* – a big interview in the weekend supplement – and *Nation Cymru* are doing a piece in the next few days.'

'How abstract are the poems? Could the police or Eiriol Law work out who and what it's about?'

'You can find out yourself if you read it.'

'I'm never going to do that,' Harriet said. 'Never ever. End of. Conversation closed.'

'Please?' he said. 'For me. For old time's sake. For what we had.'

'This is going to make you a suspect too, Carwyn. And if you are, I am. This is probably going to lead them to what I did and these are lawyers – they won't find it funny. Is your fifteen minutes of fame going to be worth that?' Harriet said, on the verge of grief filled tears, losing him again – even though the whole reconciliation thing had amounted to wishful thinking. She slumped down in her chair, hoping those around them wouldn't notice her defeated posture.

'I couldn't kill anyone,' Carwyn said, with an incredulous laugh.

'And yet, you've – for the first time ever – decided to articulate your toxic masculinity and feelings of violence towards Rowan. Not with a counsellor. No, that would be too low-key. You've put it into print and sent out press releases to the Welsh media.'

'They'll know just by looking at me I'm not a criminal.'

'Yeah, the Baby Faced Assassin. That's exactly how the criminal justice system works. I'm surprised you didn't go into law yourself,' Harriet said, her voice tripping with sarcasm.

A pause encircled them like a predator. Carwyn, she knew, was considering which new angle to come in at. He took a great bite out of his cake. Then another.

'At no point do I blame you,' he said, licking his fingers of the sticky citric drizzle. 'You got caught up. Maybe it'll help you – to see it from a different angle. It might be therapeutic to resolve your feelings, considering the guy isn't coming back.'

He still doesn't get it, Harriet thought, harpooning her own cake with a fork in anger at his gratuitous act of pardoning her for being a victim of harassment. 'Thanks for the psychological understanding. Your poetry's going to heal me, is it?' she said. 'Carwyn plays Jesus of Nazareth. They'll be coming for you. Don't come crying to me when they do.'

"Harriet, you need to stop catastrophising. And I don't understand why you're so hostile. I did this for you.'

Carwyn's voice had finally lost the flat, yoga-studio tone he liked to read poems in.

When Harriet said nothing, Carwyn stood, donned his coat and shoved the last of his cake into his mouth, scattering crumbs. He breathed in and choked, coughing dryly into his hand and taking a sip of the small amount of cold tea left in his cup to wash the cake down.

Then he left.

Harriet remained still, her gaze distant and inward, trying to focus on the colour of her feelings about his departure.

No, she didn't want it to end like that.

Harriet hurriedly wrapped the rest of her cake in a serviette – like take home after a bickering-filled kids party – and ran after him. She caught up with him on The Hayes.

'Hey. Wait. Don't leave like this,' she said. The minute the words were out of her mouth, she regretted their ring of desperation.

'You'll feel better if you read them,' Carwyn said. 'Okay, maybe it's not going to be that cathartic for you, but you'll be reassured that I haven't named anyone.'

Carwyn's distress had him on the verge of tears also.

Harriet thought of her own CILEX dreams. For so long Carwyn had dreamed about his own poetry collection. How stoic and generous he'd been in the face of mounting rejections when friend after poet friend of his was taken up by *Broken Sleep* or *Verve*. She could give him a chance, at least. If the poems were obscure, what was the harm?

'Okay,' she said, nodding as she brushed yellow cake crumbs from his duffel coat.

'You'll read them?'

'I guess so.'

Before she could change her mind, he handed her the proof copy with a Chinese ink shark on the cover. Opening the poetry pamphlet gave her the sense she'd dropped into an underwater diver's cage.

Harriet sat down on the damp marble bench and felt the chill of the seat seep through the fabric. Carwyn joined her, grateful now, supportive and reassuring.

Under the statue of John Batchelor, a saxophonist finished the last bars of 'Danny Boy'. He wore a green camo coat and a woolly hat. At his feet there was a burgundy bucket hat for coins.

Behind him, on a shoulder-height ledge of the statue's plinth, the busker had placed a tartan flask next to his cycling helmet. Watching them, the busker stopped playing, poured coffee into the lid and drank.

Her hurt demeanour, Harriet knew, had drawn his attention.

'They're only short,' Carwyn said. 'You could honestly read them now and get it over and done with right away.'

'In public? Right now? Why are you doing this to me?' she asked, wiping away the tears before getting herself under control.

'Isn't it better to do it while I'm here? If there's anything you really don't like ...' Carwyn mimed ripping out a page and throwing it aside, '... it's gone.'

Harriet would have found his promise more credible if he'd come to her before the slim book had been printed, bound and distributed to book shops. From her bench, she could see the black frontage of Waterstones on the corner. She imagined a great pile of *Swimming with Sharks* on a promotional table at the front of the store.

The busker was busily screwing the lid back on his flask, but they'd also come to the attention of two Jehovah's Witnesses, standing behind him with their leaflet trolley.

Harriet wanted to shout over to them that they couldn't talk. A few weeks earlier she'd seen a Jehovah's Witness sobbing uncontrollably on Queen Street. An older woman had been comforting her. No doubt, Harriet thought, it was over some idiot guy, telling her that she was over-obsessing about a *Watchtower* workplace bully.

While Harriet skimmed Carwyn's poems, she didn't take them in. No magical healing enveloped her. All that happened was she hurtled through the dark fathoms of the past, not stopping until she was back in Rowan's room on the Friday afternoon before his disappearance.

Chapter 17

After entertaining a client from New York on the Eiriol Law roof terrace, Rowan had returned to his desk with sweat patches under his arms and his forehead pink and glistening, though it was hardly warm.

In a well-practised but unconscious habit, Rowan slipped two fingers inside his shirt, three buttons down and absently stroked his chest. Harriet, as usual, grossed out and intrigued, speculated. Was it a scar? A particularly interesting mole? A wiry hair? A third nipple? He often worked the surrounding buttons undone. Sometimes, she helpfully pointed this out when he rushed off to internal meetings. More often, she didn't.

When her phone trilled and the receptionist, Petra, informed her a parcel had arrived for Rowan, she was pleased to escape the tension.

As she waited for Petra to finish a call, Harriet listened to the plasticky rattle of cheap black keyboards around the room, printed white QWERTY letters under fast fingers. A paralegal in the corner leafed through a stapled document and applied a breathy rub of neon highlighter to a section of text.

'Sorry,' Petra said, as she scribbled a note to herself. 'Right, here it is.'

Harriet took the parcel in its neat brown paper wrapping and held it in both hands. Gifts often arrived from satisfied clients; she guessed at a magnum of champagne in a box and ripped the paper off. The two women studied the parcel's contents.

'What's that?' Petra asked.

The white box had a pattern of finely detailed cartoons in gold ink and housed what looked like a bottle-sized white pepper grinder or chess piece. Blue laurel leaves snaked around the vessel. There was no label.

'Clase azul re ... pos ... ado,' Petra said, reading off the box.

'Look it up,' Harriet said, nodding at her screen, leaning on Petra's desk with both hands.

'Tequila.'

'Tequila,' Harriet echoed morosely, as the receptionist's search threw up a variety of images and information.

'The bottle's handmade,' the receptionist said. 'Costs hundreds.'

'Hand-painted,' Harriet added, without enthusiasm.

'Who's it from?'

'Not a clue.'

The intricate cartoons on the presentation box, including a Mexican skull, now made sense. Harriet wished she could hide it from Rowan, but Petra had signed for it. It was traceable.

Even the delicate doodles were appropriate and reminiscent of Rowan's shark drawings, how they swam in and out of the numbers and notes on his desk blotter.

Rowan was briefly dumbstruck, then a satisfied smile exposed his red wine-stained teeth.

'It's tequila that's been rested,' he said, admiring the box. 'I don't feel rested, do you? But maybe I will do after I've got through this.'

Harriet watched Rowan over the rim of her mug. The filtered afternoon light emphasised his uneven shave, creased shirt and the bags under his eyes.

'There's no card,' Harriet said.

'Oh, I know who it's from,' he gloated, tearing off the seal and opening the bottle. He slopped his black coffee into the fake fern and poured a double measure of tequila into his mug, which he swirled as though holding a hiball tumbler.

Harriet rehearsed various objections. All of which sounded horribly prim.

'You're not supposed to ...' she ventured.

'So, sue me. What are you going to do? Run and tell daddy?'

Rowan pronounced daddy in the split, sing-song Welsh way, 'da-dee'

'Want some?' he asked, raising his mug before drinking. He coughed, screwed up his face and refilled. 'Go on,' he said in an accent which was a poor parody of Father Ted. 'Go on, go on, go on, go on, go on, go on.'

'No thanks.'

'Bring your mug over. I insist. Let's part-ay.'

'You're all right. I'll stick with the coffee.'

Harriet grieved for her future. She pictured her parents, masking their hurt over a wasted golden opportunity. They'd offer her barmaid work at The Poet's, even though they couldn't really afford it. Then she imagined Debbie, a secretary who'd made it quite clear she thought Harriet had been unfairly promoted just because she was pretty and blonde, coming in with her husband and ordering two pints of Carling.

'You can have the empty bottle once I'm done, if you like,' Rowan said.

Harriet narrowed her eyes and watched him. From time to time, she glanced at the door – praying that Nigel would choose *this* moment to pay his maverick son a visit.

'Do you know what this means?' he asked, picking up the bottle, pouring another good measure and holding out his mug towards her.

'No,' Harriet said. The word flew out of her mouth like a small white ball thrown in a game of beer pong.

She had an envious flash of her secretarial colleagues on the desk-pod, oblivious to the escalating situation, slowly winding down. In forty minutes or so, there'd be the zip of handbags, the snap of reading-glass cases.

'It's a peace offering,' Rowan explained, the articulation of his words slippery with drink. 'I need to make a call. Acknowledge safe receipt and all that. You may as well head off if you're not going to be civilised and join me.'

Harriet smiled at the unexpected reprieve. Much of the anxiety she'd collected suddenly detached and floated free of her. 'Thanks,' she said, gathering her things while her machine shut down, aware that he could, at any moment, change his mind. She was owed an early finish for the unclaimed overtime she'd put into the Kennedy Jones work, but had anticipated having to wait until the following week. She shrugged into her coat and grabbed her bag. 'See you tomorrow.'

'Wait,' Rowan said tapping his screen, as she was almost through the door. 'Before you go. Is this the right draft document?'

A set up, she knew. She'd only emailed Rowan one linked document. A pretence at confusion meant mischief. The ghost in the room pressed its cold hands on the back of her neck.

Harriet glanced around and swallowed. In a clumsy manner, she tried to see Rowan's screen from the other side of his desk, avoiding getting too close.

'Yes, that's it,' she said, unable to really view anything on his monitor, but knowing the game. Her fake breeziness telegraphed her caution. Harriet could see it in his eyes now, that dead-eyed shark look.

'I can't believe you haven't got a boyfriend,' he said, pouting, theatrically sad.

'Plenty more fish in the sea,' Harriet quipped, turning to leave.

Rowan grabbed the strap of her bag as she passed the corner of his desk. From there, he gripped her wrist, tugging her towards him while holding the blue and white bottle on his lap like a great white pottery dildo.

Shaking with embarrassment and outrage, Harriet yanked herself free.

'What are you doing?' she asked, her face on fire and her whole system buzzing with affronted panic.

'It was a joke,' he whined, putting the bottle back on his desk. 'Come on. We're having fun. Don't spoil it. Come back here, right now.'

In a flash, he darted around the desk and reached the door before her. Resting one hand flat, keeping it closed, he cornered her. The fine hairs on the back of her neck stood on end. *You're in trouble. You're in trouble again*, the voice inside her head chimed.

Harriet twisted away, only to find herself more firmly hemmed in by Rowan. With her head at his chest level, she felt small and helpless.

'What am I?' he asked.

‘Leave me alone,’ Harriet said, looking past him, searching for an escape.

‘Tell me what I am, and you can go.’

Harriet remained mute.

‘Say it. I’m the killer shark. I’m the predator,’ he whispered in her ear, moving a lock of her hair aside. ‘The more you struggle and thrash in the water to get away, the more turned on I am.’

‘I’ll scream,’ she said, trembling, her face aflame. ‘Get away from me or I’ll scream.’

This time, Rowan stepped back laughing as though it were all a joke to scare her. Nothing more. He held out an arm to indicate she was free to go.

‘What would your dad say?’ she asked shakily.

She hoped invoking his father would protect her from any comeback on her CILEX chances. Next time a gift of tequila arrived, she’d enlist someone else to leave it on his desk after she’d gone.

‘I’m the only one looking out for you, remember?’ Rowan said, hurriedly. ‘You need me. You’ve no friends here. They all talk about you. I hear them. It’s funny.’

‘You need to think of me as Thomas the Tank Engine,’ Rowan called after her, stumbling to the door so she could still hear him. ‘Thomas is doing the hard work up front – dragging the moaning, whinging carriages along behind him!’

Harriet stopped in the street outside, assessing with shock that, after his promise to behave, he, once again, followed up harassment and rejection with savage bitterness.

You’re a liar, she thought. *You’re* the one with no friends. *You’re* the one they talk about. He wouldn’t change, she knew that now.

‘Are you okay?’ Carwyn asked, when Harriet had finished skimming his stanzas, all of which, in outline, took a different shark shape. Clever, she thought, without feeling.

There was nothing to else say. She felt chewed up, dead inside.

‘I’m really …’ he said.

The word ‘sorry’ hung in the air.

He stood up, wanting to leave and continue with his day.

'Are you okay in there, Harriet?' he said, touching her shoulder with one hand as he pressed the book back into her hand. She'd been about to drop it.

Harriet continued staring at the busker's tartan flask.

'I have to go,' Carwyn said. 'Look, if you want to talk about anything I've written, email me this weekend. Otherwise, I'll assume we're fine, okay?'

Harriet blinked, which Carwyn seemed to take as affirmative, like a waking coma patient who signals once for 'yes'.

The busker, Harriet suspected deliberately, started up the saxophone instrumental of Elton John's 'Sorry Seems to be the Hardest Word'.

An elderly lady in a beige wool coat, sitting at the other end of the marble bench, began to hum the tune as her husband searched his pockets for loose change. He limped over to the busker and dropped coins into the burgundy hat.

The busker nodded in thanks.

Carwyn walked backwards away from Harriet towards the Old Library, keeping an eye on her until, at last, he turned the corner.

'If they read it, they'll think you killed him for me,' she whispered at last.

Chapter 18

Harriet remained on the bench for another ten minutes. She ignored another two missed calls from the employment agency she'd visited immediately after her and Rowan's last dreadful encounter.

After a cathartic cry in the toilet at work, sobbing in silence and mouthing the one-word question, 'Really?' over and over, Harriet had dried her eyes and phoned ESR. If she left, Nigel and Rowan would surely realise they were to blame.

The agency had invited her straight over.

After tearing around there, she realised she'd made yet another mistake. Six young and hip recruitment consultants hooted with laughter at the far end of the echoey, open plan room. They weren't much younger than her and Harriet had a flash of how Eiriol, awful though it was at times, had instilled in her a level of professionalism and decorum around visiting clients.

A girl with tightly braided bleached hair and mousy roots gave Harriet a thumbs up to indicate she was Sasha, mimed acknowledgement of their recent telephone call and raised one finger to signal she'd be with her in a minute.

A fidgeting, emaciated lad in an ill-fitting black school blazer, white shirt and no tie, was filling out forms next to a laptop and keyboard. He had a recent growth-spurt look about him. Patchy break outs of strawberry blond stubble and painful looking cuts told of someone getting to grips with the art of shaving. Sasha sat Harriet next to him and slapped down a new client form and a cheap branded pen.

Harriet wished she could have gone to Phoebe. Phoebe ran a top-rated recruitment agency for legal staff. Going to her was a risk. Harriet didn't want rumours of a job hunt getting back to Eiriol Law.

She studied the questionnaires in front of her, which seemed to demand she replicated everything in her CV. Preoccupied with marketing herself – from her new legal assistant title to her 85 words per minute typing speed – she'd rushed over here assuming the paperwork could be emailed the following day. She was in no mood for form filling. With the raucous noise, plus the toxic drama she'd just left, Harriet could barely remember her own name, let alone her National Insurance Number.

It seemed she wasn't the only one. Next to her, the boy thumped the table in frustration. 'I've filled my form out wrong,' he said, presumably hoping someone would overhear. 'This is wrong,' he repeated, swivelling in his chair to face the office. The overhead lights caught his oily, T-zone, sebum shine.

Harriet told the boy that, in lieu of help arriving in the meantime, once she'd finished her own paperwork, she'd slide over and see if she could help. Such prioritisation was modelled on emergency flight instruction videos: you had to secure your own oxygen mask before helping others. A wise protocol, she considered, for many life situations.

Sasha, breaking away from the group, returned with such heavy footing on the laminate floor that it spoke more of bossy determination than actual physical weight.

'Let's swap you two around, huh?' she said.

Harriet and the boy exchanged surprised looks. Both had expected Sasha to focus on the paperwork error. Harriet gave the lad a nod of encouragement. *Go ahead. Speak up.*

'I've made a mistake on my form,' he said, holding up his sheaf of papers at an angle that suggested an elbowed double-jointer.

'She's got to do a typing test and we're closing in ten,' Sasha said, jerking a thumb at Harriet. 'So she'll have to sit there.'

They switched seats and Sasha logged Harriet into the test screen with hot pink talons so long she had to bow her fingers to depress the correct keys.

She couldn't touch type 85 words per minute with those things, Harriet thought.

Her own nails were clipped short and the most colour she ever applied was a French manicure pink. Yet, when Sasha scratched her tight-braided plaits with those long nails, Harriet imagined it felt good.

They were nails to scratch an itch with – or to cause real damage.

Nex time Rowan trapped her in the corner, how wonderful it would feel to savage his face with those almond-shaped acrylics.

She struggled to concentrate on the typing test with the boy drumming his pen on the table in an attention seeking, nervous way. Why couldn't men just ask for help, Harriet thought, even as a small voice within reminded her that she didn't always know the right way to ask for support either.

Harriet knew the story without being told. His mum was waiting somewhere in town, probably in a local coffee shop, waiting to hear all about the opportunities for her kid in the world of business administration.

Abandoning the test, Harriet helped him with his form. She knew what it was like to be out of your comfort zone, hopeful but scared.

His plight took her right back to being the nervous new starter at Eiriol Law where she'd been desperate for guidance and people were too busy, or too careless at first, to assist.

Maybe it was the fallacy of sunken costs, but she still badly wanted to complete the CILEX training. And she'd enjoyed the judicial review research for Kennedy Jones, even if she wasn't sure what she thought of JRs in general. They didn't have the greatest success rate.

'I can't tell you how I wish the law to be,' Rowan would say to his disappointed clients. 'I can only tell you how the law is.'

In the left-hand corner of her screen, a green numeral displayed Harriet's overall unfinished test speed as a lowly 41wpm. Sasha came over, whistled at her results and drummed her sharp, acrylic nails on the desk. She called for one of her colleagues to collect the boy's paperwork.

'Executive Support Recruitment can't take you on, for the kind of work you're looking for, with a typing speed of less than a basic 65 words per minute,' Sasha said. 'All I can suggest is that you go away and practise until you've improved.'

Harriet, silenced by an oncoming storm in her head, gathered her things. The stress of the day triggered a flickering migraine aura in her left eye. It appeared in a side-on V shape, shimmering along the converging lines, as if viewing the world through a sheet of dissolving pearlescent gelatine.

I would have clocked 85wpm if I hadn't been doing your job for you, Harriet thought.

Sasha had no further words of comfort or encouragement.

When Harriet emerged into the street, feeling as dazed and anaemic as if she'd just donated blood at the NHS mobile unit, she breathed in a lungful of air to steady herself.

The streetlights were searingly bright, and she pressed a cool palm to her pounding head. She'd barely taken two steps when she walked straight into Debbie, clattering along in her too-big court shoes, carrying three large sale bags from Marks & Spencer.

There was a chilly little hello before Debbie took in the Executive Support Recruitment sign. She hitched her loaded shopping bags to get a better purchase on the plastic handles that were cutting into her hands.

'Hmm,' she said, arching an eyebrow. 'What gives?'

'Nothing. I, um ... I've a friend who works there,' Harriet said, a little too hesitantly.

'I believe you,' Debbie said, with a provocative smile, engaging her usual catchphrase. 'Thousands wouldn't.'

'See you tomorrow,' they chirruped, at the same time.

Harriet watched Debbie clop away in her wide footwear, noticing how the weathered dandelion seed head motif around the hem of her colleague's dark grey coat looked a lot like she'd sat in, or brushed against, bird droppings.

The rumour that she was scoping other jobs might well get back to Nigel who, with any luck, would sit Rowan down and tell him to behave once he returned from London on the Tuesday. She pictured a contrite Rowan telling his father his misconduct amounted to no more than banter, but that it would never happen again.

No point wasting time dreaming of how you wished life to be. Harriet needed to deal with the daily, grinding challenge of how life was, until her CILEX opportunity paid off.

Chapter 19

When a text arrived from Nigel Tudor, asking if Harriet could pop into the office for 11am, she sank back on the sofa and closed her eyes in a moment of relief and gratitude.

With no idea what was going on at work or in the search for Rowan, her concentration couldn't fix long on anything. Unable to read a book or watch anything other than the news, she longed for a distraction, anything to put her out of her misery.

The lack of predictability when contacted by other Eiriol Law colleagues shocked and surprised Harriet. Former detractors sounded empathetic and supportive: 'I'm so sorry this has happened. I hope you're okay.' People she'd thought of as work friends only lusted for gossip: 'Karen said it was awful. What did you see? Who do you think did it?'

With her confidence in second-guessing dented, choosing an appropriate outfit for Nigel's meeting proved equally difficult. In the end, Harriet pulled on her jet-black Levi's which, though casual, could pass for work trousers when combined with Chelsea boots and a grey and black quilted jacket.

The choice of what to wear *under* the jacket triggered hot-headed, wild frustration because, as usual, the hangers in Harriet's jam-packed closet seemed to wilfully thwart and frustrate her in moments of stress or difficulty.

As Harriet extracted the very sleeveless white chiffon blouse with the Peter Pan collar she wanted, the cheap, plastic hanger it was on snapped in two, half of it falling through the garment to the floor as though in a deliberate act of wilful self-destruction.

Such domestic anthropomorphism, she knew, was nothing more than a manifestation of stress, but Harriet had still needed to list ten things to be grateful for before she calmed down. Underlying her fears was the bleakest outcome – Nigel making her redundant.

Surely not. It was more likely Nigel intended to extend her compassionate leave for another week. If so, Harriet figured she'd trade the time off and ask for some counselling instead.

On Richmond Road, Harriet realised the prettiness of autumn was almost over. Winter was on its way.

There was a bite in the wind and, in the gutters, double yellow lines found themselves submerged in shallow ponds and covered over by a thin, dirty layer of disintegrated leaves, which turned into farmyard-style mud at the bottom of every driveway.

The wet road glinted with cold sunlight, making her squint, but a spur of optimism hit Harriet. Christmas was around the corner. In the New Year, life should return to normal.

Waiting in Eiriol's reception area proved disorientating, as though she were a visitor, not an employee.

While Petra tried to make conversation between calls, Harriet concentrated on the antique-gold and slate-coloured world map that took up the entire back wall – as though Eiriol's global domination were imminent.

'Harriet,' Nigel said, appearing in the doorway and waiting for her to rise and follow. 'Thanks for coming in.'

When they'd settled in the small meeting room, his expression became grave.

'What's happened to Rowan is a terrible, terrible loss – not just for me and my family but for all of us,' Nigel said. 'However, we need to be practical. You've had a massive emotional blow which probably means you won't be in a fit state to return to work any time soon. And there's no job for you now.'

Harriet's worst fear was materialising.

'Is this because of Cardiff Bay?' Harriet said, her voice thin and high. The cold air con was blowing down her neck and she was suddenly glad of her jacket.

'No, no,' Nigel said. 'I'm very grateful for your level-headed thinking and the courage it took to see it through. If it had been another secretary in the same circumstances, we might have had hysterics and nothing else.'

'Then how about we let the dust settle?' Harriet said, giving him a hopeful smile. 'You never know what might come up.'

Harriet pictured herself collecting her things in a cardboard box. The idea brought red spots to her cheeks. People might even think she was a suspect in Rowan's kidnapping and murder.

'With the timing, my colleagues will read more into it and that's not fair,' she continued.

'You can't take notice of public gossip. In any case, there were constant problems between you and Rowan.'

'But it wasn't my fault,' she said, looking at him. Surprised at the brazen way he returned her gaze, she tested him. 'What if I say no?'

'To being a good leaver?' Nigel asked, incredulous. He winced on her behalf, as though the suggestion were downright dangerous.

'Yes,' she said. 'What if I don't want to leave?'

In that instant, Harriet was surprised at the extent to which she meant it. She didn't want to leave Eiriol Law. Even if she had the savings to get by until she found another job, which she didn't, she preferred to leave on her own terms, to be mentally prepared for going. CILEX was unlikely to happen anywhere else. She'd never get that chance again. And the second part of the plan, driving lessons and eventually her own car, would also evaporate without the legal training.

'You can say no,' Nigel said. 'But, if we find anything in breach of your employment contract, you'll be let go for gross misconduct.'

Harriet fidgeted with her hands, a horrible suspicion growing clearer by the second.

Nigel's stillness and direct intensity reminded her of Carwyn's manner at Waterloo Tea when he'd wanted her to understand without him having to spell things out.

'But why?' she said. 'I don't understand.'

Nigel sucked his teeth as though considering whether to impart more.

'You know Gethin Price?'

'Gethin? Yes. He's your investigator.'

'The minute my son went missing,' Nigel said, 'He got to work. Asking questions. Doing some digging.'

'Into me?'

'Into everyone close to my son. He came to me with this outlandish theory about you. No evidence, yet. But he's convinced.'

'What theory?' Harriet asked, feeling suddenly sick and shifting in her seat to displace the nausea.

'Almost too shocking to believe of you,' Nigel said. 'Shocking and disappointing. An endeavour rather offensive to lawyers in general. Proof of a worrying animosity which speaks to motive in my son's abduction and murder. But I suspect, given the colour you've gone, you'd rather we change the subject.'

Harriet, too stunned to deny anything, knew her low-key reaction had already confirmed her ownership of 'Let's Kill All the Lawyers' eBay products. If innocent, she'd have ranted and raved about the unfairness of it. Now, Nigel would return to Gethin and instruct him to keep going until he had concrete proof. If he'd rumbled her, Carwyn would only be a matter of time.

A gnawing fear had been growing in Harriet since she'd read Carwyn's *Swimming with Sharks*. His pamphlet, while not naming names, laid bare his raw anger at Rowan, but two lines in the poem 'Hammerhead' particularly troubled her.

She was sure she'd kept the worst of the details from Carwyn. Either Carwyn was particularly prescient – not entirely out of the question – or he'd somehow found out exactly what went on between her and Rowan in his office. And such information could only have been extracted from her boss under duress.

The fact that Carwyn's father loved fishing and that this recollection had occurred to her at the very time of the money drop had also grown in significance. Carwyn's father didn't have a boat, but he'd certainly have friends who did.

To the police and Eiriol, her ex-boyfriend killing Rowan would be tantamount to *her* having done it.

What she couldn't do was ask Carwyn if he had an alibi. Not without enraging him. Then, they'd never speak again.

'You'll have to sign an NDA,' Nigel said, taking an envelope from the inside of his jacket. 'We'll keep things in-house, because this will have to be bespoke.'

How would she ever pay the rent, she wondered? What would she tell her parents? From nowhere, Harriet came up with a short-term plan that addressed both her finances and any potential isolation.

Nanali, known as Nana, The Poet's long-standing Georgian barmaid, had recently been discharged from the University Hospital of Wales after a bout of pneumonia.

It seemed so obvious. Harriet could cover Nana's pub shifts while she recovered. She'd pretend to everyone that she was still on compassionate leave. The arrangement meant Harriet could move back into the pub for a few nights and would give her some breathing space while she decided what to do next.

'I'm sorry to have to do this,' Nigel said, without a trace of regret, 'but it can't go any further. We've already suffered so much. What you've done – well, I – the business might not survive another scandal.'

Gethin would follow the trail and there'd be no coming back. Nobody in the legal world would trust her again. The only way out was to find Rowan's killer before everything else unravelled.

Chapter 20

Phoebe Meredith of Legal Recruitment Cymru had always been praised by the secretaries at Eiriol. She ran the go-to agency in South Wales for legal employment across the profession.

Though unsure if she was ready for another law firm, Harriet had no choice. Every hour, it seemed, another Barclays notification appeared showing direct debit payments taken. Text messages pinged from Klarna, ClearPay and PayPal informing her of another instalment for pay-in-three purchases. Covering Nana's shifts was one thing, but without a full-time job, she'd struggle to keep up with her financial commitments.

The promise of CILEX and an eventual legal qualification had provided her with long-term security. With her student loans deferred and the offer of free education, Harriet hadn't worried about incurring a little extra debt. Now, with interest being added, a little threatened to roll into a lot, in no time at all.

As Harriet climbed the stairs to the agency, she wondered at its unassuming frontage on High Street, at the top end of St Mary Street. The office's centrality no doubt provided a regular footfall of disgruntled legal staff sneaking in a lunchtime visit. But the way the old stairs creaked and the heavy doors on each landing put up a resistance, it was as though the city's law firms had tightened the spring mechanisms of the hinges to sabotage staff wanting to jump ship.

Harriet put her shoulder to the last landing door, relieved at the lack of further obstructions. Easy access to Legal Recruitment Cymru itself, once you found the right landing, was guaranteed by the cast iron sheep wedged against the open door.

The doorstop triggered a memory of her and Carwyn, early in their romance, walking past the Welsh tourist shop, where, on impulse, he'd bought her a walnut love-spoon keyring. She put her hand in her pocket, feeling for it, for reassurance.

The receptionist explained that Pheobe had popped out, but was expected back soon. A moment later, the woman herself breezed in, panting from the stairs, clutching two sturdy paper bags from The White Company Tissue paper mummified whatever was inside. Business had to be good, judging from Phoebe's caramel highlights and designer jacket. She put her shopping down beside a waiting room chair and greeted Harriet like an old friend.

'I haven't seen you before, have I? Are you looking for a change? Come, lovely, let's talk.'

Phoebe ushered Harriet into her white office where an 'I Loves the 'Diff' underground poster rubbed up against photographs of local landmarks.

'I worked, until recently, at Eiriol Law,' Harriet said. 'I'm not sure if you've heard ...'

It was impossible Phoebe hadn't. After Rowan's return to Cardiff, he, his father and Phoebe had had photographs taken together at some glitzy event for *Cardiff Life*'s business magazine.

'Dreadful,' Phoebe said sitting down with an unbelieving shake of her head. 'That poor family. Absolutely dreadful. Can I get you anything, my love? Coffee? Water?'

Harriet declined with thanks.

'Are the police any closer to finding those responsible?'

'I haven't heard a thing,' Harriet said.

'There are some monstrous people in this world,' Phoebe said, sucking in her cheeks like she had toothache. 'And how are you doing?'

'You're probably wondering why I'm here.'

'Tell me.'

Harriet had intended to bluff her way through the visit, but she didn't have the energy. She'd been staring at a graphic print of the Norwegian Church in Cardiff Bay. The image was simple, honest and authentic.

'It wasn't my choice to leave. I was Rowan's legal assistant. They said there was no job role for me now.'

'Jesus Christ!' Phoebe said, leaning forward. 'I'm sorry. Eiriol isn't renowned for its kid gloves. And I heard he could be difficult. Did they make you sign an NDA?'

Not supposed to refer to it at all, Harriet couldn't shake the fear that this was a test instigated by Eiriol, to see if she'd honour the NDA when asked about it by third parties.

'Okay,' Phoebe said, with a knowing look, nodding in recognition of Harriet's silence. 'Do you know how I got the start-up funds for this business?'

'No,' Harriet replied. She'd heard vague information once about a compensation award, but it had come from the perma-unreliable Debbie and Ffion.

'This is also confidential. I was an office manager for a law firm now mercifully gone. It had about 40 staff. Great reputation. Only, what clients and most of the staff didn't know was that the firm's youngest partner had a history of exposing himself.'

'You're kidding?' Harriet said.

'With the first victim, they negotiated a settlement agreement with her and the whole thing was hushed up. Two Christmases later, the same guy pulls me into a side-room saying he needs to speak to me and whips out his bits. I left the party immediately and reported it the next day.'

The story left Harriet with many questions. Like was the guy still working in law?

'They didn't want me to leave,' Phoebe said, 'and until then, I hadn't once thought about moving firms. The salary was good. I'd made friends there. Apart from the incident, I loved my job. But I just couldn't stomach being around him. They offered me a straight settlement agreement – six figures. They bought my silence. I guess they'd done the same for the paralegal. You see, his wife worked high up in BBC Wales. And HR didn't want it getting out, embarrassing the firm, embarrassing his wife. They were, from the outside, such a well-known, high-flying couple. I signed the agreement, feeling pretty shit for the next unsuspecting woman likely to be on the receiving end, but the firm folded two months later. I have no idea what sort of financial position they were in to hand out six-figure settlements. Maybe there were more. Who knows? But I chose recruitment so I could keep an eye on all the dirty little secrets and protect people where I could.'

'I don't know what to say,' Harriet said, mourning the unnecessary months she'd stuck it out at Eiriol. Phoebe's experience would have made her an ally rather than an enemy.

'Trust me,' Phoebe said. 'I'm on your side. The only reason I'm telling you all this is because something toxic is going on at Eiriol and, at some point, it'll catch up with them.'

'You think?'

'I will tell you this,' Phoebe said. 'Nothing is forever in this game. Two months and Eiriol will have forgotten all about you. So, we'll fix you up with some temp work for a few months. Then we'll get you a decent permanent position, close to home. How does that sound for a plan? Just to warn you, it's a quiet time, but I'll see what we've got.'

'I can't do a typing test at the moment,' Harriet said, 'or any kind of stressful assessment – because I'll go to pieces.'

'Why would you need to?' Phoebe asked, raising her hands as far as they would go while keeping her forearms on the desk, half surrendering. 'You've been doing the job long enough. Be a bit bloody weird if we only just realised you couldn't type.'

Chapter 21

Kennedy Jones

At fourteen years old, a man called Rhino led you into a dojo that smelled of Tiger Balm and sweat. Two pairs of dirty flip-flops outside the door suggested people were already in there, using it.

Two boys, years older than you, maybe uni students, leaned against the wall-mounted punch bag engaged in fight chit-chat. Shoeless, they wore loose-fitting yoga-style vests and shorts. Their shin bones were prominent, covered with old scars from conditioning. One of them scratched absently at crusting grazes on his right elbow.

As we passed, they gave Rhino a nod of acknowledgement and left.

A heavy bag dangled at the far end of the room, half obscuring a whiteboard covered with abbreviations in green marker pen. At the end nearest you, shelving cubbies held martial arts boxing gloves and kick pads next to a pile of unwieldy body shields.

'Trainers off,' Rhino barked.

As long as that's all I'm taking off, you thought. His name made you cringe, is the truth of it. It made him sound like a male stripper.

How long would this take, you wondered? Dad waited in the car outside.

You stood on one leg at a time, bringing your other foot up and yanking off each shoe in turn.

'You better not use what I show you on the street,' Rhino said for the second time.

'It's to build confidence on the rugby pitch,' you assured him, still not sure if you'd last that long in the game.

Rhino took time to demo his first takedown tackle. He told you to stand normally, then changed his mind, suggesting one foot forward, a more stable stance, he said.

'I want you to push back, hold your ground.'

He swung his solid arm across your collarbone, clothes-line style, gripping your opposite shoulder so your hips touched. The closeness of him alone in a room with you was uncomfortably intimate, but his business-like manner reassured you, as did the no-nonsense soap-powder smell coming from his clothes.

His right hand gripped the back of your neck, his arms forming a brace. Then he tucked in behind and planted his left leg between your feet. A small rotation felled you, like an earthquake.

Your fall started slow, but your body found no purchase or means to right itself. You hit the padded mat flat on your back with a slap so hard you had an instant headache. On concrete, it would have knocked you clean out. Helpless and dazed, you lay there like a beetle on its back, but inspired by the idea you might wield this on others.

'Easy. Now you try,' he said. 'It's just gravity and momentum. Size doesn't factor as much as you'd think.'

It took three goes before you cracked it. You forgot, the first few tries, that he'd flicked his left leg back, like a tango gancho.

'But does it really work on someone bigger?' you asked, thinking of Morgan and Rhys, giants on the Glantaf high school team.

'The bigger they are, the harder they fall. That's why you're here. That's the lesson. Give you some confidence, kid. So let's try it out,' he said.

Rhino left the room. You threw a few punches at the bag.

'Don't hit that without gloves,' Rhino growled, ducking back through the door. In his own mind, you guessed, he was a lot taller.

Behind him towered a guy, six-four, with an impressively thick Viking-style platted beard, wearing army boots. Who wears army boots to the gym, you wondered? Thor remained in the doorway and you realised he didn't want the bother of undoing his laces. Rhino told him he could keep his boots on. It would only take a moment. The floor would survive.

You weren't sure if you could reach Army Boots' shoulders. You'd have to throw an arm around his biceps and hope for the best. When you grabbed the back of his thick neck, what you were about to try didn't seem feasible. You stepped in behind him, ruthlessly hugging him to you, twisting your body and pushing hard. Hopelessly off balance, he smacked down harder than you had. The worn soles of his big black boots showed themselves before he straightened his legs and his heels hit the floor. His arms dropped to each side and when he stared up through his eyebrows at Rhino, he reminded you of a Viking Jesus on the cross, asking his father why he'd forsaken him.

The rush of empowerment was like nothing you'd ever known.

Army Boots gave you another takedown, below waist, technique that you could use on the field and he demoed on Rhino, reminding you of a lion, taking down a giraffe.

'It's lethal,' he grunted.

'One more thing', Rhino said, as Army Boots stomped off, back to whatever he'd been doing. 'Your PE teachers say you're a bit gun-shy.'

You curled your lip and shrugged, trying to communicate ignorance, as though it were the first you'd heard of it without having to outright lie.

'Ever boxed?'

'No.'

'You've never once been punched in the face, lad?' he said, going to the cube shelves and tossing you a pair of bright green RDX gloves. The fact that you dropped one of them and had to run after it didn't say much for your hand-to-eye coordination.

'No.'

Your heart pounded like a speedbag drilled by a boxer.

'Then there's your problem right there. Every man should get punched in the face once, just so you know.'

You tried to process his sadistic philosophy, resisting the urge to back away. He wiggled his fingers into a black pair of gloves and punched the palm of his other hand with his padded knuckles.

You ripped away the stiff Velcro cuff. The green gloves were too big, like you had your hands in two sand buckets.

'You learn a lot from boxing,' he said. 'You find out how you handle conflict. You learn to respect others and not get into situations you can't handle. Do you want to find out who you are, Kennedy Jones?'

'I don't know if I'm the right fit for rugby or contact sports,' you said, even though you wouldn't have turned up if you didn't think it was in you somewhere.

'Don't ask what your sport can do for you, Kennedy Jones,' he replied, thinking he was funny. 'Ask what you can do for your sport.'

'Yeah,' you said, without feeling.

He touched your gloves. Gave them a tap of respect.

'Hands up,' he said.

He threw out some feints and then smacked you in the face with a straight right that you didn't see coming until it swallowed you like a black hole. Shooting stars sparked from your head out into the dojo. Warp speed. How you stayed on your feet at all was something to be proud of. It didn't hurt as such, but the right side of your face burned and throbbed. What it was, more than anything, was wretchedly humiliating.

You remembered a hard-guy threat doing the rounds in school.

There's gonna be three hits:

me hitting you;

you hitting the floor;

and the ambulance hitting sixty.

You gritted your teeth and grabbed him. Animal instinct.

It wasn't easy to articulate afterwards, but something inevitable happened. You were going to teach that guy a lesson if it was the last thing you did. And then you found yourself standing over Rhino, apologising and offering to help him up.

You walked out of the gym wanting to shake everyone's hand and, at the same time, take everybody down and slam them into the floor, from the Thai boxers outside the toilets to Prince Charming on his swivel chair at reception.

More than instilling confidence, domination felt good. Really good.

As Rhino had promised, you'd gained in self-knowledge. You weren't in it for the team spirit. Glantaf had plenty of teamsters, slapping each other on the backs and insisting on rugby socials every five seconds. You were in it for the controlled aggression. Your mission: to neutralise at all costs, to pound the opposition and leave them fighting tears of frustration in the communal post-game shower. Your super-power was selfishness. You wanted to win, for you.

Of course, the downside was that everything Rhino taught you was illegal on the field. A couple of spots in the sin bin taught you that lesson. But coaches taught you to hinge and come in low, bend your knees and wrap your arms, breaking core. You disconnected the strength of your opponent's upper body from their lower. You mastered the short grab.

The reticence that initially put you off had come from a place of fear of allowing yourself this. Something told you, even then, a high price for indulging such appetites might have to be paid.

You were always going to control the situation. Doing so gives you power. Find a way to get control over the nightmare you're in, a quiet voice insists.

Chapter 22

Harriet had pitched the idea of working anywhere apart from Cardiff to Phoebe, but starting work at Redlands Law in Penarth hit her like an enforced exile. Not that three-and-a-half miles south was exactly Siberia, but leaving the capital city to work made her feel the pariah.

It wasn't just the sense of loss Harriet felt over her legal assistant job, but the fear of having such a dreadful story attached to her name that she might never shake off. Her first-hand account of what happened would have to be rehearsed and practised, specifically to avoid provoking suspicion. She feared raised eyebrows everywhere she went.

Even if Rowan's killer were to be found, the conspiracy theories might endure. She thought of true-crime cold cases dug into again and again via podcasts and streaming services. Rowan's high-profile status granted his case a higher level of interest.

She understood why Kennedy Jones wanted to escape his new-life narrative, when he'd been so deftly forging his own impressive path. Now, he represented the cautionary tale in which everyone pretended sympathy, but in truth found fascinating.

The reception at Redlands, in a converted house, was papered with a prim lavender wallpaper, more appropriate to a girl's bedroom. Harriet guessed they had little money and the decorating had been done on a budget.

Beyond the plexi-glass and wood counter, old buff client files, dusty with age, hid skirting boards and teetered upwards, like drystone walls.

Harriet took a deep breath and was led upstairs to a chaotic room and a messy desk.

A peek in the top drawer yielded packets of painkillers, used tissues and a sachet of Lemsip, with only half a teaspoon of powder inside. There was no stapler – the item she'd been looking for.

The second drawer contained only envelopes, compliment slips and a mini hot water bottle, with a blue, knitted cover that portrayed a deer leaping in front of a moon.

At least she knew why she was covering. In leaving Eiriol, Harriet had missed the opportunity for a free flu jab. She rooted around in her handbag for an ancient, travel-size bottle of anti-bacterial gel.

The staff at Redlands were helpful, if not outright friendly. Harriet shared a room with Leanne in the conveyancing department, who couldn't have given off stronger 'do not disturb' vibes if she'd hung a sign above her desk. Her new colleague wasn't ill natured, however Leanne focused on her work to the exclusion of everything else. Every time Harriet asked a question, Leanne had to emerge from somewhere deep within herself before she could answer.

Compared to litigious work, conveyancing was boring and finicky, but Harriet had accepted the job precisely because, by working in a different legal specialism, it was less likely the lawyers would know Rowan or Nigel Tudor.

Her boss, Andrew, was tall fellow with a neat beard. Harriet had half-expected him to flinch with recognition at her name, but when she introduced herself, like Leanne, he'd barely glanced from his screen.

Reassured, she determined to show him he had an experienced secretary on his hands. She'd make no errors in his transcriptions.

Harriet worked through lunch, too anxious to eat. She was so paranoid that any laughter from reception made her think they were laughing at her.

First day anxiety also left Harriet over-sensitive to noise. There was the constant clacking of Leanne's keyboard and, downstairs, the insistent tone of the unanswered phone in reception, which reminded her of her GP surgery.

At 4pm Harriet knocked on Andrew's door and wordlessly left eight letters on his desk, along with the appropriate size envelope paperclipped to each document.

Harriet wondered how long it would take him to sign them and bring them back to her. She didn't expect any amendments, but the post had to be with reception at 5pm. Any changes therefore had to be made immediately.

'You can expect some tweaks,' Leanne said, grimacing. 'He likes to mess about. Can't dictate a sentence without rewriting it ten times. Jane will tell you what he's like when she comes back.'

The idea that Jane, consumer of Lemsips, would chat to Harriet on her return was a conceit. There would be no overlap of their employment. That wasn't how temping worked.

Andrew entered the room and handed Harriet the letters.

'It's not you,' he said, before leaving the room, 'it's me. Once you've amended them, bring them back in and I'll sign them.'

Leanne's eyebrows managed to communicate 'I told you so' on their own. Harriet almost laughed. Her colleague wasn't so bad.

The first letter, written to a conveyancing firm in Cardiff, set out what documents were needed from the seller's solicitors in a numbered list that took up a page and a half. Andrew had annotated further points for inclusion, in what amounted to a complex map that included arrows, stars to sections over the page, PTOs and abbreviations Harriet hadn't seen before.

The seven other letters were the same. Harriet sighed. Leanne stopped what she was doing and came around the desk. Side by side, they deciphered Andrew's handwriting, decoding and incorporating his changes. Harriet must have thanked Leanne at least ten times.

With the amended, reprinted correspondence in her hand, including the reattached envelopes, Harriet hoped there would be no further problems.

Andrew asked her to wait, assuming he'd be able to skim the letters and sign them there and then. As he read, his left hand explored the desk for his pen.

Gesturing Harriet to come closer, he tapped the top of his located fountain pen on the desk to indicate she could take a seat.

'Our receptionist tells me you're from Eiriol law,' Andrew said.

She'd been right, Harriet thought. The receptionist had probably been laughing about her – having viewed her CV when the agency had sent it over.

'That's right,' Harriet said.

'So, you know all about that lawyer that's gone missing.'

Harriet rubbed both index fingers with her thumbs as she wondered how best to reply.

'As long as no-one goes missing here and starts turning up in bits, in the post, you'll be fine,' Andrew said, with a hearty laugh.

Just like that, Harriet saw herself back at Eiriol, snipping through the brown parcel tape on the Jiffy and giving it a shake to dislodge the contents.

'Sorry, I can't do this,' she said, in a whisper, before she rose and left the room. 'It's too soon.'

Andrew, perhaps seeing how the colour had drained from her face, instantly stood up and apologised for the joke.

With her balance somehow affected by the memory of the day it all started, Harriet stumbled back to her desk for her things. All she wanted was to get out, out into the street – away from anything office related.

'What's wrong?' Leanne said, jumping to her feet, in a panic herself about what might have taken place. 'What on earth did he say? What's happened?'

'Is everything alright?' Andrew said, appearing in the doorway. 'I was just trying to make light of things. It wasn't meant seriously.'

'Nothing, nothing. It's fine,' Harriet said, gathering her things. 'I'm sorry. It's me. I'm sorry. I have to go.'

It didn't matter how much air she breathed in, the results were inconsequential.

'Please, sit down,' Andrew said, holding her letters in his hands. 'Let's calm down and talk about it, rationally.'

He thought she was being irrational, which only made the situation more intolerable because she knew she was and there was nothing she could do about it.

'I can't. I have to go,' Harriet said, gazing into the middle distance, holding a hand to her cheek, before walking out of Redlands Law. It was as though all her determination to stay at Eiriol Law had left her with no resilience at all.

She couldn't find the words to explain.

It was only when she stood shivering on the platform, waiting for the train back to Cardiff, that she realised four letters might suffice: PTSD.

Chapter 23

Nana's homemade card stall, draped in black fabric, stood across from eight packed rows of chairs in a cavernous arts building in Grangetown.

Desperate for money, having only picked up a couple more days temping work, Harriet had agreed to help Nana, still weak from pneumonia, on what promised to be a lucrative weekend.

Nana's side hustle of cat cards and headbands complemented the other offerings at the event. There were cat-themed bottled cocktails, care and grooming speaker panels, and local cat cafés and rescue centres. At 3pm, an award-winning animal photographer would demonstrate how to take fabulous photos of your feline fur-baby.

To Harriet's left was the PDSA stall. Its neighbour to the right sold cat litter. Opposite were more craft and jewellery stalls, stocking cat-related products: make-your-own pet collars and colourful scratch posts.

Outside, in the courtyard, two street food trucks took care of lunch and a coffee van sold americanos and cappuccinos.

Nana's lucky waving Chinese cat reflected the gloomy black and midnight-blue decor in its yellow-gold shell.

An hour before arriving, Harriet and Nana had dunked dark Oreo cookies into mugs of tea and noted that day's schedule from the Carnival for Cats website: a weekend pop-up 'paws-itively crazy about cats'. Customers were asked not to bring their own cats, an instruction mitigated by the promise of a free cat toy.

Harriet was morbidly aware of the various claw marks on the soft arms and hands, sometimes even the noses, of adoring cat owners. These sharp, sometimes inflamed, gashes made her wince.

'My cat thinks I'm its toy,' one woman told Harriet, beaming with maternal happiness while Nana talked to other stallholders.

The batteries of the lucky Chinese cat were running out, although Harriet had discovered that if she prodded it with a Biro, it found sufficient energy for a single reluctant wave.

'I wish I look like those lady cats,' Nana said, nodding at three svelte dancers dressed as cats in fur figure-hugging onesies. They popped their hips, swung their tails and batted the air with their paws.

'Me too,' Harriet said, only half-listening as she drew closer to the mirror shine of the exhausted cat. She had spotted someone she didn't expect to see here in its golden reflection, his presence cutting like a cat claw.

'You're already skinny,' Nana chided.

'I'll be back now,' Harriet said, leaving with such haste that she knocked a handful of Nana's cards to the floor.

'Look what you're doing,' Nana said, bending down to pick them up.

'Gethin,' Harriet said, following him out into the courtyard. Quite why he thought he could get away with spying on her for Eiriol at a cat carnival, she had no idea. It was utterly juvenile of him. Pathetic, really. Then it dawned on Harriet that this was the point. Rather than anonymously tracking her, his presence served to intimidate.

Harriet's own claws were out.

'Gethin Price,' she said louder, catching him up and putting a hand on his shoulder, the way she imagined he'd have apprehended someone himself when he was with South Wales Police. 'I had no idea you were such a fan of cats.'

'Oh yes,' Gethin said, turning with a smile, casting a look around before fixing on Harriet. 'Started when I was a kid, with reruns of *Bagpuss*.'

'Yeah – really,' Harriet said.

'No, I mean it', Gethin said, crossing his arms. 'By the way, love that headband. It suits you.'

She'd quite forgotten how well they'd got on when he visited the office and how, despite her best efforts, this cordiality threatened to extend beyond Eiriol Law.

'Cut the bull,' Harriet said, ripping the leopard-print accessory from her hair and pointing it at her stalker. 'This is getting out of hand. You can't treat me like a criminal. Tell Eiriol to back off.'

'Meow,' Gethin said, in a faux wounded voice. 'I'm not here for Eiriol. We need to talk.'

'You need to leave me alone,' Harriet said, as an intense pressure built up in her chest, leaving her breathless and tearful. She put her hand over her heart. 'I'm working.'

'I didn't mean to scare you.'

'I'm not *scared*,' Harriet said, but the heaviness in her chest affected her voice. Turning away from Gethin, she supported herself against on the wall.

'Okay. Deep breaths,' he said, soothing. 'It's just a panic attack. I'm not here to make your life more difficult. We can talk later. When are you free?'

Grateful for the way Gethin had stepped in front of her to afford her a little privacy in the face of her mounting distress, Harriet gave him a shrug of defeat. Her breathing was returning to normal.

'Take your time,' he said, taking advantage of a lull in the coffee queue to buy Harriet a bottle of water. He cracked the cap and handed it to her.

'I'll be at my parents' pub at 8pm,' she said, after a few thirsty glugs from the bottle. 'You can find me there.'

Gethin nodded and vanished into the stream of people leaving the event. Still dazed, Harriet stared in wonder at the people storming past, bristling with silent outrage. Weaving through the thinning crowd, Harriet caught up with Nana inside.

'What's happened?' Harriet asked.

'A man shaved a cat – onstage,' Nana said, pointing to the front of the auditorium. A small heap of ginger fluff served as corroborating evidence.

Whether this resulted from an act of gratuitous cruelty or amateur grooming, neither Harriet nor Nana could tell.

In protest, most of the audience had risen from their seats and left. The rest followed just minutes later.

By mid-afternoon, with the anger on social media growing, the stallholders, dancers, guest speakers and street food vendors had a meeting.

Harriet helped pack up Nana's cards and headbands into two plastic storage boxes and wondered if she were cursed when it came to employment. Sliding the lucky cat into its pocket of bubble wrap, she thought of how Gethin, sitting alone in the back row, had been reflected in its 9-carat lustre.

After the initial confrontation, he had left Harriet feeling strangely safe. Her predicament seemed to amuse and fascinate him. She feared the inappropriateness of finding someone behind enemy lines reassuring.

Getting out her phone, Harriet was keen to know what Gethin had done to warrant imprisonment. The nature of it might give her a clue as to his moral compass.

Scrolling 'South Wales Police Officer jailed', Harriet's heart sank at the litany of cases across the South Wales Police Force appearing on her phone.

She amended her search to 'Gethin Price, South Wales Police' and was rewarded with a series of posts from 2011, relating to the Occupy demonstrations.

Gethin Price, a rookie officer and his sergeant, Marc Munday, had been charged and jailed for assaulting a demonstrator who'd camped at Occupy Cardiff Castle. On appeal, Gethin, who'd only been in the job three months, found his sentence overturned.

In the last paragraph, Nigel Tudor was quoted as saying that, while he agreed with the IOPC that South Wales Police should have sacked Sergeant Marc Munday long before he broke a protestor's jaw at the Occupy demo, the evidence against Gethin had fallen apart under the lightest of scrutiny.

'To send an innocent and idealistic young police officer to prison for a crime he didn't commit,' Nigel said, 'smacks of gross negligence on the part of South Wales Police as well as Mr Price's own legal team at the time.'

Harriet rubbed the tender imprints left by the cat ears headband.

The article, while portraying Gethin as an unfortunate victim, raised more questions than it answered. Nothing in the legal system was ever that black and white. Nigel had, no doubt, exploited the scarcity of evidence against Gethin to further frustrate South Wales Police.

No wonder they hated Nigel, Harriet mused. Even when they took swift action against their own officers, Nigel found embarrassing ways to undermine such efforts and denounce the outcomes as further miscarriages of justice.

As the meeting of the cat carnival contributors broke up, Harriet considered she and Gethin might be heading towards being tentative allies.

Chapter 24

'Eiriol are wasting their money if they're paying you to spy on me,' Harriet said, as Gethin joined her in The Poet's lounge with two pints of the new IPA.

'If you don't want the time,' he said, 'don't do the crime.'

'Thanks for the catchy slogan. PS: I haven't committed any crime.'

'Do the words 'Shakespeare' plus 'tote-bag' mean anything to you?'

Harriet's breath caught in her throat.

'Not,' she said, immediately embarrassed at the squeaky way it came out, 'that it's anything to do with me, but it probably wasn't meant maliciously – just a subversive joke. Hardly criminal. If you think that's bad, wait until you stumble across the dark web.'

'They're not laughing.'

'I know that.'

'You knew it was a matter of time.'

'What was?'

'They're not messing around, Harriet. You have to destroy it all.'

'I don't know what you mean.'

'We haven't got time to play games.'

'I thought I'd covered my tracks,' Harriet said, giving up with a sigh.

'My last check was an hour ago,' Gethin said, holding up his phone. 'Here's a T-shirt and mug in my checkout basket.'

'I asked an IT person to help,' Harriet said, her hands curling into fists in frustration. 'It looks like he hasn't.'

'If you want me to help, I can.'

'I need to get rid of all the stock in my flat as well.'

'I'll take care of it.'

'Why? Aren't you the one who tipped Nigel off in the first place?'

'Yes. I was too quick doing that. I'll get rid of the evidence – all of it –napalm option. There won't be a trace left.'

Grief caught in Harriet's throat. She had to trust someone. Her eyes shone as she looked away.

'Eiriol won't know a thing about it,' Gethin went on. 'It'll be our secret.'

'Why?'

'Nigel's researching the UK's best libel lawyers right now.'

'Shit. Carwyn's book.'

'That's right.'

'Why help us? If Nigel finds out, he'll be furious.'

'I know what it's like to be wrongly accused and lose everything.'

The pair sat in silence for a moment.

'D'you ever wonder what your career would have been like if things hadn't have gone wrong?' Harriet asked.

Instead of answering, Gethin took his phone from his breast pocket and showed her what looked like a movie still.

A figure in a black boiler suit strode through a curtain of fire, head lowered. His downturned face was obscured by a baseball cap, bearing the words 'Police' in white. Flames curled around his legs. It took Harriet a second to realise that this was Gethin, presumably in training.

'Your crotch is on fire,' she said, pointing at the picture.

'Yep. Cool photo, huh?'

The camera had caught an Elvis-like twist of Gethin's hips as he strode through walls of flame.

'Crotch on fire,' Gethin repeated with pride.

Harriet wondered whether he saw the photo as a metaphor – a career up in flames too.

'There's a computer upstairs,' Harriet volunteered.

In The Poet's home office, Gethin studied the icons on the desktop.

'Where do I start?' he asked, pulling a pair of over-the-counter reading glasses from his coat.

Leaning over him, Harriet typed in the web address and the

password, Berlin1972 – which had been Rowan's own and seemed as good as any when she'd set everything up.

Wriggling back on the single bed until her shoulders were supported by the wall, Harriet watched Gethin work. A small voice warned that her vulnerability in the situation might be clouding her judgement. She'd look even more stupid if she trusted him only to find herself betrayed to Nigel. Her ego couldn't take much more.

'I can't believe Rowan treated you like that,' Gethin said, turning back to her, having taken only minutes destroy every business link she'd worked for and invested in. 'If Carwyn's book is anything to go by.'

'It wasn't all the time,' Harriet said. 'Otherwise, I'd have left. I honestly thought it would get better.'

'Hmm,' Gethin said. 'The optimistic yet hopeless mantra of abused women everywhere. But it's not over. Not by any means. They're looking for a scapegoat. Any sort of motive and they'll pin his murder on you too.'

'But I'm in no position to have someone kidnapped, mutilated and thrown in the sea.'

'There's an unsolved murder connected to this pub.'

'Now, wait a minute!' Harriet clambered off the bed and pointed to the door.

'Hang on. Calm down. I'm on your side, remember? I'm just telling you how they could pitch it.'

'This is so unfair,' Harriet said.

'But you're not alone.'

Gethin looked at her with his kind, world-weary brown eyes behind black frames, a man who understood. She resisted an urge to move closer and touch his arm. No, she told herself. It's just vulnerability. It's not real.

'Hang on a minute,' she said, drawing her chin in. 'What Carwyn and I have done looks like motive, but you also know I didn't kill Rowan. Is that because you have someone more likely in mind?'

'My guess is, he got involved in some dirty politics. My money's on Etheridge, but the trail's gone cold. I have a witness who saw a major fall out between them in a London bar. I'm sure Nigel sensed Rowan was in trouble and that's why he wanted him at Eiriol, where he could keep an eye on him.'

Harriet covered her hand with her mouth, wondering what it meant.

'Let me know if you find anything more,' she said.

'I will,' Gethin said, looking at his watch. 'Time to go.'

'If you're going to move my contraband, won't you need me to let you in or loan you a key?'

'What do you think?' he said, with a smile.

'I'm glad you're on my side now,' she said.

Though he wasn't that much older, Gethin leaned down and gave her a fatherly peck on the cheek. Harriet gave him a sad smile.

'That's kind of a Judas move,' she said.

Chapter 25

Kennedy Jones

Getting washed and dressed takes two and a half hours of methodical preparation, but this is nothing compared to the mental groundwork – a week and a half of Marni breaking down your agoraphobic fears and social anxiety.

You're as accepting as you'll ever be, but if a chance comes up to duck out, you'll seize it.

That said, it's odd that you're not drained of energy today. So perhaps, as Dr Stockton and Augusta say, it's a mental rather than physical barrier preventing any improvement.

Your white, wasted legs dangling from the hoist trigger a detached empathy towards them. You recall them tanned from days on the field, pumped from leg pushes and deadlifts in the gym, their first-class muscle definition photographed beautifully in action, more so when blown up on stadium billboards.

'Sorry legs,' you whisper, and look down so Boyd doesn't see you. He'll start crying himself.

Though there were far better distance kickers than you, there was a time when your short-kick accuracy was a thing of entertainment and wonder.

During pre-match warm-ups, you could launch that rugby ball from the side of the pitch and knock the pint from an unsuspecting fan's hands as, distracted, they edged along their row of seats, looking for their friends. Fellow players took to suggesting a target picked from their own family or friends.

That legacy ended only when, on an off day, the ball sailed past your friend's dad, loaded with four beers dangling from a cardboard carrier and ricocheted off a baby cradled in its mother's arms. No harm done, fortunately. St John's Ambulance rushed to check and the mother had shielded the child with her arm.

You had some great times and great games, legs, is the truth of it.

Once you're in the borrowed wheelchair and your head is in a comfortable position, Boyd races you up and down the corridor a couple of times to check you're safe and secure. When you get one, it'll be custom-made.

'Faster! Faster!' you laugh.

By the time Dr Stockton, Augusta and a suited gentleman appear at the end of the hall, Boyd is sweating and exhausted. Panting, he wheels you back into your room.

They wordlessly chide Boyd for the horseplay and step aside so you can get a good look at their sombre guest. Everything about him is contrast monochrome. His suit is black, his shirt is white. His tie is pewter, patterned with clusters of white scratches. Apart from the five o'clock shadow, his skin is pale. His irises are charcoal, his lashes and eyebrows are black, the whites of his eyes glisten.

Very smart, you think, especially compared to your Afternity trackie-bottoms, Cardiff Rugby hoodie and Puma trainers. You envy the luxury of putting on something so complicated and formal.

'I'm so terribly sorry to hear of your struggles with recovery,' the suited guy says, crouching down, frowning and then looking at Boyd with inclusive gratitude, 'but I've known Dr Stockton and Augusta for a long, long time and you couldn't be in better hands.'

'This,' Dr Stockton says, 'is Nicholas Etheridge. The MP I told you about.'

You nod, wondering how much of your confidential patient care they've shared with him. Quite a bit, you suspect. Funny, you think, that he didn't introduce himself, but waited for someone else. Without being told, you know what party he represents. Not a party you'd vote for.

'So where are we going?' you ask, just to say something.

'We need your help with something important,' the MP said.

That gave you a start, is the truth of it. How could you, in your current position, help anyone?

Nicholas Etheridge leans against the end of your bed and folds his hands.

'I'm facilitating an undercover investigation into a local care centre in South Croydon, called Orchid Rise. The police are aware. We just need more evidence. The families of dementia patients there have contacted me. Complaints have been made and the Care Quality Commission is investigating, but the management of the care home isn't taking them seriously.'

'Right,' you said. Not what you'd expected at all. You'd imagined a boat trip along the Thames, maybe. A picnic in the country or visit to the seaside, Brighton or Hove. And then it hits home. Dr Stockton has told Nicholas Etheridge of your recent diagnosis.

'You told him ... about me ... the latest results?'

'Of course not,' Dr Stockton says.

Etheridge squats in front of you again. This time, he keeps a thin, pale hand on your wheelchair.

'Orchid Rise isn't a care facility specifically known for dementia, Kennedy. It's really nothing to do with that. This is how we're hoping you'll help. We're going to take in undercover cameras and pretend you're thinking of paying for care there. Afterwards, we'll have lunch at my house and maybe even check out a film.'

Etheridge's appeal is interrupted so Boyd can administer your usual pills. You expect to spend the next hour keeling with exhaustion, but an instant miracle occurs. The last of the fog lifts, sunshine breaks through.

Pain free, mentally alert, you feel like it's the first day of spring. You're wild with ambition. You perform the dream equivalent of handsprings and cartwheels along Afternity's corridors.

Helping with an undercover job suddenly sounds liberating.

'Count me in,' you say, loud and a little drunk sounding.

Other jobs could follow, you think. Employment goals flickered to life again from a state of dormancy: coaching, managing, designing functional sportswear for disabled athletes.

Hallelujah, you say to yourself. They've found the right dosage.

It's disorientating to see Augusta and Dr Phil Stockton outside

Afternity without their lab coats. It's like seeing coaches or school teachers out socially.

When Stockton pulls his Barbour on over his red cashmere jumper, the only thing missing is a couple of chocolate Labradors on leashes. Augusta comes out wearing hot pink trousers, white heels and a white blouse, shoulder-robing a purple and pink trench coat. By their wardrobe choices alone, it's clear they have nothing in common outside work.

Boyd is wearing a sunny, yellow jumper and claps his hands in excitement, which Augusta misreads as attention seeking.

Orchid Rise care facility isn't Afternity. There are no suite rooms with bowls of roses, wall-mounted TVs, personal menus, tropical fish tanks, fire bars and posh sofas, but the place looks clean and bright.

There are retro radios in the boxy, magnolia rooms, and a communal games and TV area. From the kitchen comes the appetising smell of spicy tomato pasta and melting cheese. The nurses chat and fuss over residents. Granted, there's something universally glum about the patients, but neither you nor Boyd see any red flags. Can it really be as bad as they're making out?

The manager fawns over Augusta, and you understand why she and Boyd wore such bright colours. Like presenters on children's TV, their enthusiasm, compassion and attention light up the faces of the residents. Augusta, particularly, is charismatic and generous. For a split second, they remind you of Princess Diana and her butler, Paul Burrell.

Chapter 26

Harriet waited for Carwyn, who'd asked her to meet on the upstairs balcony of Cardiff Market at a pizza kiosk where the smoke of a real wood oven aggravated the scratchy strep throat Harriet had woken with.

It's a universal truth, she thought, that as soon as a potential new love interest crosses the path of a single girl, previous boyfriends become desperate to retain contact.

From the balcony, Cardiff Market had always reminded Harriet of a railway station, with its Victorian glass roof. Customers milled around the narrow stalls on the ground floor as though waiting for train carriage doors to open. A part of her wished she could hop on board one and rattle off to a less stressful life.

The artisan eateries had moved in and now the old hardware shop, selling everything from telephone leads to sink plugs, rubbed shoulders with a cheese pantry and a boutique Thai noodle stall.

Though about to ambush Carwyn, Harriet justified it by apportioning him some blame for the Redlands Law overreaction. Had it not been for him insisting on a trip down memory lane, she probably would've still been in her temp job.

That said, her entire, albeit brief, experience of temping had been horribly stressful. The bleating Redlands reception phone trilled in her head for hours after she left, like a burglar alarm.

At the counter, a relentless *Grange Hill* ringtone made Harriet's nerves bristle again.

'Aye, I'm on the run, innit,' a woman said to her friend. 'If they can't get me on the phone, they don't know where I am.'

The pair laughed and the laughter grated.

Right now, even smiling again would require huge effort.

Carwyn appeared on time at the top of the stairs on the other side of the balcony, where a life-size model of Elvis advertising Kelly's Records twisted mid-croon at a microphone-less stand. Such punctuality from her ex was unusual. Harriet watched his gaze run along the stalls, waiting for him to clock he'd ascended the wrong steps.

After pressing the red voice-record button, Harriet slid her phone into her jute tote bag. Hooked on the back of the chair, it dangled between her and the seat she'd saved for Carwyn. The phone recording served as insurance. She didn't expect him to confess to murder, but what if Carwyn disclosed his involvement during their conversation?

Evidence once lost was lost forever. Proof uncaptured never existed.

Harriet, shifting in her chair, gave Carwyn a weak smile as he approached.

A customer at the far end of the seating area glanced her way, checked his phone and began to eat.

'Everything okay?' Carwyn asked, giving her a loose hug and scanning the people nearby.

'Yeah,' Harriet said, touching the strap of the jute bag.

'You look worried. I thought maybe you'd seen someone from Eiriol.'

'No, thank God.'

Harriet placed their orders, paid and handed Carwyn one of two cans of San Pellegrino lemonade. They made small talk until the server brought over their Quattro Stagioni pizzas.

'Thanks for meeting me,' Harriet said.

Carwyn started to eat, then put down his knife and fork. 'I'm sorry,' he said, with feeling.

'You mean for the book? I wondered if we could talk about that.'

'I didn't expect you to be so caught off guard,' Carwyn said, popping the tab on his can. 'I started to second guess myself. I mean, the collection is doing well, but still. Who d'you think killed him?'

'Rowan had a lot of things going on,' Harriet said. 'Maybe it's politics or he harassed the wrong woman. But I think his father knows something and is going to cover it up.'

'Huh?' Carwyn said, taking a sip from his can.

'I'm serious,' she said, lowering her voice, hoping Carwyn would do the same. She wanted their conversation recorded, but had to be careful of eavesdroppers.

Harriet forked a mouthful of pizza.

'Okay,' she said. 'I'm in real trouble and I've got to ask you for a huge favour.'

'What is it?'

'Can you not do any more promotion for a while? Calm down on social media about the poetry publication?'

'I knew it was too good to be true,' Carwyn fumed. 'That's what the unsettled feeling was.'

'Something's changed.'

Carwyn shook his head in utter disbelief. 'What now?'

'Gethin Price came to see me.'

'Who's he?'

'A private investigator. He's working for Eiriol, but he helped me shut everything down – because Eiriol are coming after me.'

'You mean about the ... ?'

'Yes, but it's just the start. Rowan was mixed up in something and, whatever it is, they don't want it coming out. Gethin says they're trying to make me a scapegoat. Frame me or something. Make out I had him killed.'

'Wait. You've never mentioned any of this before.'

'I've only just found out myself. They haven't got anything on me – but they suspect. And if they read your collection, they'll happily drag you into it. Two plus two equals Bonnie and Clyde.'

'This is ridiculous,' Carwyn said. 'They won't pin a murder on us just for that. They're a well-respected law firm.'

'You sound just like my parents,' Harriet said, reddening as she recalled once trying to talk to them about the harassment. 'It's a veneer of respectability. Eiriol are ruthless. And I lost a temping job because of a panic attack. Your poems contributed to that. I shouldn't have read them. And now Redlands Law in Penarth also think I'm weird and unemployable. They'll feed that back to the agency. And you're one poetry review away from coming under the suspect spotlight yourself. I mean, even I wondered.'

'Wondered what?'

'Whether you actually had something to do with it. I mean, your 'Hammerhead' poem? How did you know what happened?'

'What happened when?' Carwyn asked.

'The Friday before he disappeared.'

'Huh?'

'The Friday before?'

'I have no idea what you're talking about.'

'What's it about then?'

'You once told me about him cornering you and trying to bite you.'

Harriet took a sharp breath in. 'Ah,' she said.

'So,' Carwyn asked, 'what happened the afternoon before Rowan disappeared?'

'Nothing.'

'Not nothing. Something obviously.'

'I don't want to talk about it.'

'What happened?'

'He got drunk and was a bit of an arse again,' Harriet said, lifting the handle of the jute bag, folding it over on itself and putting it next to her handbag near the leg of the chair, 'but I promise you, he was alive and well when I left.'

Carwyn, having barely taken two bites of his pizza, twisted the Pellegrino can clockwise on the counter as he considered.

'You have to take this seriously,' Harriet continued, tearing at her food with her knife and fork, pulling it apart rather than cutting it. She stuffed a couple of large forkfuls in her mouth and, for the second time, regretted not taking it slower. 'Neither of us wants to be out on bail while South Wales Police scrutinises every inch of our lives.'

'But this collection is my *future*, Harriet. My publisher's going to enter *Swimming with Sharks* for Welsh Book of the Year. It's very hard to imagine Eiriol Law doing anything so underhand.'

'You don't know them like I do. They'll want to know where the original idea came from. Worst case scenario, you might have to give evidence in court.'

Carwyn's eyes narrowed. He pointed his fork at her. Melted cheese clung to the tines.

'You should have told Rowan where to stick it and walked. I told you that a million times. Keep me out of it.'

'Wait a minute. I thought the whole point of this book was an apology for that exact mindset?'

'If I'm dragged into this, I'll never forgive you.'

'But you got a collection out of it first, didn't you?'

'What utter nonsense,' Carwyn said. 'Why don't you just sit down with them? Straighten it out.'

'Sit down with them?' Harriet scoffed, before growing quiet with suspicion.

'Yes. That's all they want.'

Harriet studied Carwyn's face.

'Brenin Books are on the brink,' he continued. 'They've closed their submissions window and the accountants are in. There might not be a Brenin Books much longer.'

'What do you mean, that's *all* they want?'

'Huh?'

'Has Eiriol contacted you?' Harriet asked.

'Yes. No. I mean, yes, someone did, but I told them they'd have to talk to you.'

'Who? Who did? What did they say?'

'It was just a text message, saying you were in trouble and they wanted to help.'

'And you said what, exactly?'

'That they'd have to talk to you.'

'I can't believe this. Didn't I tell you? They're coming after me.'

'Their concern seemed genuine,' Carwyn said.

'I bet it bloody did. They'll have read your collection.'

Carwyn glanced over his shoulder at the diner sitting on his own. The man, having finished his food, thumbed his phone. Crescent shaped crusts littered his plate.

'What's wrong?' Harriet asked.

'Nothing. You're making me paranoid.'

Carwyn checked the time on the central market clock.

'It's a couple of minutes slow,' Harriet said.

Carwyn fired off a quick message on his phone. It pinged and his expression darkened. He looked behind him again and stood up, gathering up his coat from the back of the chair.

'I'm sorry, Harriet,' he said. 'Thanks for the pizza. Time to go. Great haste.'

'What?' she asked. 'What's going on? What've you done?'

'I thought I was helping. Sorry.'

From the direction of the Tikka Tuk street food stall a man was walking towards them with a terrifying sense of purpose. His eye contact, his gait, his leather messenger bag, even his neat, short hair and indigo blue peacoat spoke of ex-military. The click of his heels, thanks to Harriet's oversensitivity to noise, pierced the market's bubbling hum and chatter. Her eyes widened. Frozen, she found it impossible to look away. She stood up straight, unblinking and braced for impact.

Chapter 27

'Don't leave me,' Harriet whispered, grabbing Carwyn's arm.

The approaching man slid his hand into his bag, before drawing out a white A4 envelope.

Harriet leaned back and shrank behind Carwyn.

'Harriet Erskine?' the man asked.

A donkey-kick of fear made Harriet want to double over. Her hands shook with adrenaline. She didn't answer, but her lack of denial seemed enough confirmation for him. With the envelope pressed into her stiff fingers, fear balled to a knot in her stomach.

'Carwyn Hughes?' the man said, withdrawing a second envelope and handing it over.

Without further explanation, the man turned on his heels and walked off.

'Shit. I'm sorry,' Carwyn said, stunned, turning the envelope over in his hands.

'Oh my God,' Harriet said, holding up the white envelope in front of her with disgust. 'What is this? You told them we were meeting?'

'They said they needed to get some papers to you. They didn't say anything about a letter for me and I didn't think it'd be so fucking scary. I didn't think they'd send the Terminator.'

'You idiot' Harriet said, sitting back down, dazed. 'You absolute idiot.'

Harriet had previously thought of UK law as humdrum legal Heinz beans, but this handing over of an envelope had brought with it unexpected terror.

To end the torture of uncertainty and, no doubt, usher in a new nightmare of specificity, they opened the envelopes immediately.

Harriet wiped the table's surface clean of crumbs with a serviette and tore at the gummed end of the letter. Carwyn did the same.

Harriet wondered if the staff behind the pizza counter could see the stress aura hazing off them.

The letters weren't from Eiriol, but from Figgis LLP, a London firm of libel lawyers. Lawyers representing lawyers now, Harriet thought. *Expensive*.

Hers was a three-page cease and desist letter, warning her to remove anything to do with marketing or selling 'Let's Kill All the Lawyers' products.

'What does yours say?' she asked Carwyn.

Rubbing his temples, Carwyn's mouth puckered as he tried to speak and, when he did, his voice sounded strangled.

'They want *Swimming with Sharks* withdrawn from sale and pulped. They say it's libellous. They're going to sue Brenin Books. How could you do this to me?' he asked, showing her the bottom line, under the signature, which informed him an identical letter had also gone to his publisher.

'This isn't any of my doing. This is all textbook Eiriol. Why do you think I was so careful to keep everything anonymous?'

'Brenin don't have any money. They won't have lawyers. They only published my book because they received a grant.'

Harriet swallowed, imagining hundreds of copies of *Swimming with Sharks* juddering along a squeaking, upwardly inclined conveyor, before the crafted tomes tumbled into a churning vat of paper-coloured mush.

'You wouldn't listen to me,' she said. 'You're the one who led them here.'

'I honestly thought I was helping fix your mess.'

Carwyn's phone rang.

'Shit. It's my editor,' he said.

Walking away for privacy, Carwyn listened more than he talked. When he returned, his mouth trembled with fresh emotion.

'They received their letter before me,' he said. 'They've already called Figgis to discuss it. *Swimming with Sharks* will be off the shelves and in the bin by the weekend. My editor is fucking terrified. You need to make this right.'

'What?'

'Do something.'

'There's nothing I can do.'

'There must be something. You went to law school for a few months. Please don't let them take this away from me. Can you speak to Figgis? Speak to Eiriol? Make a deal?'

'What sort of deal?'

'Tell them you were behind everything. You're the one – and I had nothing to do with it.'

'What?' Harriet said, aware that the voice recording needed to be deleted from her phone so that Carwyn's accusation didn't go any further.

'Tell them you're sorry,' he implored, hands outstretched, 'and I wasn't involved in any way.'

'That's not what you just said. You literally asked me to confess to a murder I didn't commit,' Harriet said, raising her voice for the purposes of audio.

'Harriet, you need this put right.'

'Even if it means me going to prison?'

'I didn't mean that. Can't you stop them?'

'I can't do anything,' Harriet said. 'You wrote a collection about how you wanted to kill Rowan and you didn't come to me about it until it was on the shelves.'

'For you. I wrote it for *you*. Please don't let them destroy me.'

'Look, I know this is terrible, but you're the one who told them they could find us here.'

'This is unforgiveable. There must be something you can do. You know the law.'

'Find yourself a good lawyer,' Harriet whispered, wanting him to leave, unable to handle the guilt. She too felt as though she were drowning in a cold vat of post-poetry mulch, as copies of *Swimming with Sharks* rained from above. She could almost smell the wet, pulverised paper.

'I can't afford a lawyer,' Carwyn said.

'Then try Citizen's Advice.'

'Fuck you,' he said, his voice thick. 'You did this. I bet you're secretly delighted.'

As Carwyn strode away, hurt and offended, he looked back over his shoulder as though she might have a last-minute idea to protect them both. Harriet slid her letter back inside its envelope.

She'd toyed occasionally with the idea that Eiriol might one day find out about the merch. Now they had, she knew she'd seriously misjudged it.

Since Rowan's death, everyone was at pains to paint themselves as his closest confident – or as an ally of Nigel.

Not once had she ever considered that Carwyn might write about it too – and that, cumulatively, it would be viewed as a creative pincer attack on a law firm coping with trauma and grief.

Harriet winced at the idea that a board meeting had probably been convened, at the very moment she was laying her cheap flowers, to discuss what she and Carwyn had done, brainstorming damage limitation and countermeasures.

When it came to Rowan, the fact that the dead couldn't be libelled counted for little. He'd been alive at the time the poetry collection was published. These were lawyers who would find a clever, technical way to show Carwyn had libelled him and his father and, by that token, she'd probably killed him when Rowan found out and confronted her about it – or got her unemployed boyfriend to kill him.

If only Carwyn hadn't been so stupid. Yes, he'd wanted to have his own voice, but he should have respected the fact that, when it came to her employer – or employers in general for that matter – he had zero experience. His understanding of law firms and offices came from TV shows or the few writer friends who temped for a few weeks when they were skint.

Circling back around to solutions, Harriet's first hurdle was how to convince them her product line was eradicated. She appreciated it made her look sneaky and subversive – exactly the kind of person who might have killed Rowan.

Chapter 28

Kennedy Jones

The minibus drops you next at Nicholas Etheridge's palatial address. They wheel you down a level garden path, past a small orchard of apple trees, to the back of the property, where a ramp with intricate metalwork leads up to a pretty patio and into Etheridge's kitchen.

'I had all the modifications done for my wife,' he says, running his fingers along the polished marble of the kitchen island.

'Is she here?' you ask.

Nicholas Etheridge smiles with one corner of his mouth. The expression speaks of fortitude in loss.

'I'm sorry,' you nod.

'MND,' he says. 'But let me show you everything I did for her.'

He demonstrates the swing-clear hinges and how the main door of the fridge opens above wheelchair lap height. Light switches were lowered. A modified wheel-in shower was customised with an additional fold-down bench. Natural stone flooring was chosen for its warmth.

His attention to detail impresses you. Boyd claps and oohs and aahs like he's on a game show.

'We also saved a little money,' Etheridge continues, 'by installing bathroom height cabinets rather than kitchen. That's a three-inch difference. Much cheaper than bespoke and every bit as good. Note the cut-outs under the kidney-shaped sinks, work surfaces and hob for rolling leg room.'

His having been married explained the contrast between Etheridge's person – so sombre in his style and dress – and his property, decorated in earthy, feminine colours. And now you know why Etheridge is interested in care homes and your own story.

After lunch, they show you into a plush six-seater home cinema.

'Is there popcorn?' Boyd asks, but further snack questions are shut down with a frosty glare from Augusta.

'This is where things get a bit serious,' Etheridge says to you. 'You've been to Orchid, right? Nothing looks out of place, but some of the relatives had cameras installed. I mentioned a documentary, right? Documentary-cum-undercover exposé.'

Your thoughts go to the patients. The indignity of secret recordings capturing not just abuse, but the victim's health problems and vulnerability.

'As it happens,' Etheridge says, nodding towards the blank, black screen in front of you, 'I've just had the first cut back from the editors. Will you watch it with us?'

You know when you're being played and this is one of those times. Augusta is unusually quiet, engaged in phone texting, multitasking work. Aware, perhaps, of your eyes on her, she blinks and looks up.

'I think you should watch this, Kennedy, for so many reasons,' she says, sounding distracted. 'Nicolas, Dr Stockton and I are on the same page. We're passionate about ending the dreadful legacy of underfunded care combined with pious belief that suffering brings us closer to God.'

A presenter explains that, despite numerous complaints, nothing is changing.

How you hate those managers, having seen an old lady you recognised from the care home crying piteously, on screen, to be assisted to the toilet in the dark. Lights, the presenter explains, go out at 10pm. Staff are deaf to her mewling and calls. And, when she soils herself, they slap her and yank her off the bed.

'Dehumanisation,' the presenter explains. 'It's institutional abuse.'

'This isn't *your* future,' Augusta says, as Boyd begins to wheel you back to Etheridge's kitchen, where coffee, water and biscuits have been arranged by some unseen hand. 'But it is for so many others.'

'What do you want me to do?'

'Boyd, would you leave us please?' Dr Stockton asks.

Boyd's jaw falls open and he jerks his right ear towards them as though he needs to hear the instruction a second time to believe it.

'You can take your coffee and biscuits out there,' Nicholas Etheridge says, pointing to the patio.

With Boyd on his way out, the remaining three crowd in.

'You're the great Kennedy Jones,' Nicholas Etheridge says. 'Nobody's going to abuse you in a care home. That's never going to be *your* story. But what about regular folk? If you'd only seen what a terminal illness did to my beautiful wife. Before that, I was firmly against assisted dying and voted against it. Then I saw it rob my wife of her personality, her wonderful sense of humour and her happiness. Pain made a haggard skeleton of her.' The MP speaks with increasing passion. 'She was unrecognisable at the end. Didn't know who she was or where she was. And do you see anyone, other than us, trying to address or improve the situation? All we get is talk about how much it costs to keep things degrading at the rate they are.'

'You've seen how we do things at Afternity,' Augusta says. 'And you'll have also seen, when you arrived, the plaque in reception, dedicated to Richard Holmes, my great, great, great-grandfather and one of the four founding fathers of John Hopkins Hospital.'

You nod. You've seen it. She herself pointed it out.

'At Harvard,' Augusta says, 'I set out to disrupt public sector medicine in the UK. I came up with a plan to introduce an assisted dying model to Britain, similar to that in Canada. We want you to help us.'

Fantasyland, you think, eyes on Boyd for a moment. The sunlight puts fire in his hair as he paces on the patio, pulling at the railings like a sulking child.

'The time's right,' Nicholas Etheridge says, 'to end the unnecessary and protracted suffering of our weakest and most vulnerable members of society. We need to have managed practices, with monitored systems. It's better than things happening behind closed doors. More and more, we're hearing about a husband trying to kill a wife or a wife trying to kill a husband – people who've never harmed a living creature in their lives – out of love. Nobody should have to endure that or face that unenviable burden alone.'

'That's a complicated area,' you say, though you are reminded of a similar news item about an elderly couple from Birmingham. 'I'm just a sports guy.'

'The early onset dementia is going to make things difficult. That's why we need to talk now. Because it's going to rob you of your dignity. And because you're famous, there won't be as much privacy as you deserve, even with the high-end, specialist care we can offer.'

It's surreal to talk about your own death, but the bravery of it thrills you a little.

'It's like writing a will or funeral planning,' Augusta says. 'Only there's another layer of choice we're adding in, which is taking control of when and where.'

'I'm not going to lie,' you say, 'there've been plenty of times when I wanted a way out since the spinal injury but, on days like today, when I feel better and the sun is shining, I know that I'll get back to my family and friends. There are better days to be lived and enjoyed.'

'That's the spirit,' Dr Stockton says. 'We're just opening the discussion. We can park it for as long as you like. But, if you do decide to help us – whenever you decide – we're inviting you to play a pivotal role.'

Augusta opens the kitchen door, a signal to Boyd that he's allowed back in.

'A pivotal role, how?' you ask, but the conversation has come to an end.

Chapter 29

As Harriet was printing off the first draft of her cease-and-desist reply letter to Figgis, her phone rang. She didn't recognise the number but, with a Cardiff code, she assumed it was safe: someone local, calling on a landline. Answering, a voice she vaguely recognised said her name.

'Yes?'

'It's Mike.'

'Mike?'

'Yes, your dad gave me your number.'

'Ok-ay?' Harriet said, clenching her jaw, her anxiety building. Mike must have given her dad a compelling reason for needing her number. She noted too, his lack of a conventional apology for calling out of the blue.

'We need to talk. It's urgent. Can we meet somewhere?'

'I've got a lot on,' Harriet lied. 'Can't we discuss whatever it is over the phone?'

'It's not a good idea. Can you be at Roath Rec, say, in half an hour?'

Outside, the chill in the air made Harriet's nose red and numbed her fingers, even with her oversized fleece and coat. When it started to spit with rain, she searched her bag for her compact umbrella. It unfurled with an aggressive flourish that Harriet rather liked.

Mike met her by Penylan Library, dressed in his customary vegan leathers and tried to rub warmth into his hands after blowing his nose in a tissue.

On the recreation ground, five kids kicked about a white and orange football on the muddy field. They'd left their bags in a pile on the sidelines. Harriet watched the cold manifest in their vapour breath.

‘Thanks for coming,’ Mike said, stuffing the tissue into his jacket pocket. ‘We can’t talk openly on the phone. You never know who’s listening.’

The cloak and dagger stuff grated on Harriet. She had no intention of letting Mike get carried away.

‘What’s going on?’ she said, in a light tone.

‘Why don’t I buy you coffee at Terra Nova?’

Oh God, Harriet thought. Terra Nova café was at on Lake Road West, overlooking Roath Park Lake, a fifteen-to-twenty-minute walk away.

‘Can we stick to the Rec?’ Harriet asked. ‘I’ve got to keep an eye on the time.’

For a moment, Mike rounded his shoulders and let his arms hang like a disappointed child, but he trailed after Harriet towards the narrow footpath that edged the field.

‘Your merch has completely disappeared,’ Mike said.

‘I know,’ Harriet said.

‘What’s happened to it? I was worried about you.’

They stopped on the path, allowing a dirty, white poodle to cut in between them, its leash trailing behind, followed a second later by its owner.

‘Why?’ Harriet said, walking on, refusing to dawdle at Mike’s drawn-out pace.

‘Who took it all down?’ Mike asked.

‘Does it matter?’

‘It does to me. I thought I was your IT guy. You should have come to me first.’

‘I did speak to you, but you didn’t listen. Maybe if you’d sorted it out when I asked you, Eiriol wouldn’t have sent me a letter before action about it.’

‘I never thought they’d cotton on. So, who shut it down?’

‘His name’s Gethin. He’s Eiriol’s private investigator but, even then, we weren’t quick enough.’

‘And you just trusted this random guy? I’m here to help you. There are lots of people on the internet who can help.’

'In what way?' Harriet said, tipping her umbrella back so she could confront Mike. 'I don't understand.'

'People are making headway with who's killed Rowan,' Mike said. 'They have a suspect.'

Harriet shivered and pulled her coat around her.

'Please tell me you don't mean YouTube detectives?'

'Yes. This is why I couldn't talk on the phone. There's this ex-police officer with a big grudge against Nigel Tudor and Eiriol Law. He's got the motive and the contacts from doing time in Parc Prison. I mean, you can imagine, can't you? He's estranged from his son. An eye for an eye and all that. We're pretty sure it's him.'

'What else have they got, because I've found stuff like that too: previous clients whose cases ended badly, plus other instances of him sexually harassing women in the workplace. Is there anything concrete against this guy in particular?'

'It's solid. I'll send you links to everything they've found. Why don't you send me your list of suspects?'

'Mike,' Harriet said. 'We're not playing a detective duo here. I'm in enough trouble with Eiriol. Don't you understand? I've been running around trying to find whoever killed Rowan precisely so the police don't think I'm involved. These internet nerds are going to get me arrested way before some ex-police officer nobody's ever heard of.'

They reached the end of the field in silence. The rain fell on the wide, stony stream, the kind of watercourse that dwindled to a trickle in summer. A crisp, brown leaf glided downstream. Harriet watched it float along like a little brown bird, its five leaf-tips curled back like feathers.

Mike, sulking, pulled at the tall weeds.

'You tell them – these true-crime nerds – that this isn't a game,' Harriet said.

'That's going to be hard,' Mike said. 'The more you tell them not to do something, the more they'll wonder what you're hiding.'

'What I'm hiding? What *I'm* hiding? Call off the murder vultures or I'll never speak to you again,' Harriet said, hurrying away.

By the time Harriet got back home to her flat, a peculiar bronze storm light had overtaken her, forcing motorists in her street to switch on their headlights.

Chapter 30

During a second catch up with Gethin at The Poet's, a couple Harriet had never seen before sat down at the next table. The guy threw a faded black denim jacket over the spare chair opposite him.

Harriet overheard the woman mention money, that things would be okay. Empathetic to this kind of conversation Harriet glanced their way.

An attractive middle-aged couple, they both had the lean, tanned, super-fit outdoorsy appearance of endurance runners or cyclists. The man's bronzed face had the faintest, pale band at eye-level that spoke of a summer spent in wraparound mirrored shades.

Gethin and Harriet leaned in towards each other.

'So, what happened with this Mike guy you mentioned?' he asked her.

She had the difficulty concentrating around the nerdy Mensa Monday group in the corner, but at least Mike hadn't arrived yet. She hoped he'd sent the group his apologies.

There'd never been a woman member, other than her mother or a girlfriend-guest of one of the guys. As a child, Harriet hadn't questioned this, thinking the sticky carpets and torn upholstery of The Poet's Arms had probably put the cleverer ladies off.

By the time she was a teenager, Harriet viewed the group for what it was – an ego boost for working men oversold their potential in school, an abstract promise they'd failed to grow into.

The real bind of the group was the idea that a high IQ entitled them to something and mild resentment because they weren't quite sure what. If they thought it led to automatic respect, they were disappointed.

Competing openly in quizzes was the only way they could assert their genius, which meant decent conversation didn't always happen.

More often, one of them, with a gaze fixed on his beer or a pattern in the carpet, would recite the periodic table or the books of The New Testament, in chronological order.

Harriet filled Gethin in on Carwyn's betrayal, the Terminator's visit to Cardiff Market and Mike's rogue investigations.

'I'm really sorry,' he said. 'That all stinks. At least Carwyn will have learned his lesson about staying out of things. Sounds like Mike is at risk of the same thing.'

'I know.'

'I'm also sorry you-know-who was such a blue-ribbon arsehole.'

'It's okay. At least, while I was working at Eiriol Law, I got to do a bit of interesting research on a JR.'

Harriet mentioned the judicial review in a last-ditch attempt to come across like a variously experienced legal person whose talents were better employed in a solicitor's office than on the shop floor in Tesco. Though why she was trying to impress Gethin, she didn't know.

'Sounds interesting.'

Gethin, she remembered, had his own debenture seat in the Principality Stadium.

'It was,' Harriet said. 'Famous rugby player.'

'Ah, even more interesting.'

'I'm not sure what'll happen to those JR files now,' she said.

'Look,' Gethin said, checking the time, 'I'd better head off. But let me know of any further developments.'

Five minutes after Gethin had left, Harriet finished her drink and stood up. At the same time, the sporty guy on the next table put his hands on the sides of his chair and remained there for a moment, poised to rise. He straightened up slowly and followed his female friend into the small entrance hall.

When Harriet used the same door a moment later to go upstairs, the couple were waiting in ambush.

'I heard you in there talking about Kennedy Jones,' the man said, donning a pair of black wraparounds. He was taller than he'd looked when at the table and Harriet took a step back.

The woman, to her left, blocked her escape and acted as lookout.

'Who are you?' Harriet said, steadying herself and hoping someone would interrupt and call her dad. The pounding between her collar bones returned. Breach of confidentiality was serious.

'Kennedy Jones – the international rugby player. You said – in there – you enjoyed working on his judicial review.'

'No, no, no,' Harriet said, shaking her head and shooting the guy a warning look that he'd got things wrong. 'I'm not stupid. I didn't say anything of the sort.'

She couldn't think fast enough to recall *exactly* what she'd said, but she definitely hadn't named names.

'And that guy ... that investigator guy with you ... he called you Harriet. So, if I were to check around the local law firms, they'd have no idea who you are? There's no link between you and Kennedy Jones or his judicial review?'

'What's this about?' she asked, thinking of three scenarios, each worse than the last. 'Did Eiriol Law send you to blackmail me, or is this just straight spying?'

It had to be Eiriol. How else could the guy know she'd worked on Kennedy Jones' case? Perhaps they suspected Gethin was getting too friendly with her. She'd have to warn him.

From the bar, beyond the adjoining wall, she heard the nerdy guffaws of the Mensa group.

'You've committed a serious breach of confidentiality. The rules exist even when the client is dead.'

How much of the couple's conversation about money worries was true, Harriet wondered? It had sounded so authentic. Is that why they've taken on a shit job, she thought, following me around, listening to my conversations?

'Wait. What?' Harriet said, puzzled. 'You mean when the *lawyer* is dead.' Rowan Tudor was dead, but his client, Kennedy Jones, was very much alive.

'You know what I fucking mean,' he said, grabbing her by the arm. 'It's in play whether the fucking lawyer, the fucking client and/or their useless fucking secretary is dead.'

'Don't you dare threaten me,' Harriet said, raising her chin. She became her father's daughter, uncomfortably at home with working-class confrontation. In her scathing eye contact was an admission that, beyond the legal secretarial veneer, she came from a tougher place. And yet her heart drummed so loud in her chest, it undermined her bravado.

If Eiriol had hired more people to follow her and prove her an untrustworthy, blabbermouth liar, she had to protect herself and lie her way out.

'I couldn't have disclosed anything,' she said, wrenching out of the guy's grip in an exasperated way, as though he'd merely tried her patience, 'because I never worked on anything. Rowan did all the work. All I ever did was type attendance notes. I was just trying to impress Gethin. So you can stick this ridiculous charade right up your ...'

'Keep your fucking mouth shut,' the guy said sticking his finger an inch from the bridge of her nose, but nodding to his girlfriend that they were done.

Chapter 31

Kennedy Jones

You'll never see her again. You know that now.

How the mighty have fallen. A late developer, once you'd done a bit of training at Sophia Gardens, you'd bulked out – and how the women came running.

Some of the guys in the team started training at Llandaff Boat Shed and raved about CrossFit. As expected, you loathed it. You visited only once, undergoing the kind of physical training where you mourned the hours you'd never get back. By then, you'd all the flexibility of a scaffolding plank. Supporting your entire bodyweight with your hands and fingers: pull ups, ropes, ring-pulls and rock-climbers, were brutally unforgiving for a rugby player who served as a walking advert for muscle weight gain. Too much of a unit. Too much of a World War II tank.

Pissed off and about to make your excuses, a girl you'd spotted banging out chin-ups like a Silicon Valley AI robot sauntered over with a look of amusement on her face. She clapped you on the back like an old college buddy and asked your name. How you liked her confidence, not to mention her green Gym Shark two-piece.

She had traps, biceps, no boobs, a wasp-waist, a six pack so taut her skin formed soft creases when she twisted and the kind of hard, defined ass that you'd only ever seen on Action Man figurines. Her thighs were disproportionately rounded out and solid. Her buttery, tanned skin was dusted in places with chalk dust. Her palms were also white with it, like a baker's, and a number of fingers were taped due to callouses.

Individually, her features weren't so attractive. Her horsey teeth glowed synthetically white. Her dyed blonde hair showed the roots, scraped into a pony further controlled with a second elastic hair band sitting only an inch from her hairline. But, taken together, you couldn't stop looking at her. The creases on each side of her mouth suggested she smiled a lot.

She did.

You wanted to pick her up in both senses. You wanted to see how much she weighed and take her out. Something told you, she wouldn't mind either.

'Can I lift you?' you said.

'Sorry?' she said, with a mischievous twinkle.

'I want to see how heavy you are.'

'Sure,' she said, amused, happy to go along.

You'd expected her to leap into your arms sideways, but she demurely turned her back and crossed her arms over her chest as though you were going to bear hug, cracking the knots out of her back. You wrapped your arms under hers, held her tight, lifted her up and leaned back so her feet left the floor.

Her hair smelled of shea butter.

You put her back down and nodded, impressed, ready to carry her out of the place like Richard Gere in *An Officer and a Gentleman*. A girl like Danielle looks like a nine stoner and feels more like a ten and a half. Worth more than her weight in gold.

Obviously, she wasn't going to hang around after your accident. You'd only been together a year and two months. You'd sent her packing for her own good.

Tough love.

Boyd says he's single but he's lying to you. The way he constantly checks his phone and then pops out of the room. You hear him talking in the hall and have definitely overheard, 'Love you, speak later,' before he ended a call. You're jealous, even of his secrecy. It must be new. He doesn't want to jinx it by talking about it. He's gay, of course.

'I know it's frustrating,' Stockton says, 'but I've never known such treatment complications. Have you ever taken anything in the past that might inhibit the drugs and treatment we're administering?'

'What do you mean?' you ask. 'Like performance enhancing?'

'Yes.'

'Go fuck yourself,' you croak, mouth dry, head blasting.

You ignore Rhino and Army Boots standing in the corner. There's Ellis, touching his mouth. Not real, you tell yourself.

You hear your old Cardiff Blues Academy coach, Dean: *Don't worry about what's going on out there. Stop them in here. And play, play. Squeeze. Squeeze. Squeeze, boys. Who's got the man at the back? Are you guessing, Jones? Or do you know?*

'I'm not trying to insult you here. I appreciate you're in a world of pain. It's like your system is fighting us.'

Army Boots does a chopping motion with his hand at his neck. Enough is enough, he means.

He's right.

'I've had it,' you say. 'I want out. Enough with this shit. I've thought it through. I want to help you guys get the message out. People shouldn't have to live like this.'

'Really?'

'Yes,' you say and retch emptily. Then groan.

'Okay, Kennedy. I'm sorry that it's come to this, but we understand. I'll call Rowan Tudor. He's a lawyer who can help us get a judicial review underway. I'll tell Nicholas Etheridge you're on board. Once Rowan's sorted his end, we can organise a press conference.'

Chapter 32

Harriet, working a quiet three-hour shift in her parents' pub, leaned on the bar and recalled Rowan's stories about the game he used to play to liven up his train journey to London.

It was guaranteed that travelling in the same first-class carriage to Paddington were one or two other lawyers from the bigger Cardiff law firms, on their way to their respective central London HQs.

After identifying his peers, Rowan would make sure to go down the aisle as they worked on their laptops. Whenever possible, he'd eavesdrop on their phone conversations. Any near reveal of private client information – an open file, a laptop without a privacy screen or a legal case mentioned, however obliquely, during a call – and he'd rap his knuckles on the individual's table or on the hard plastic edge of their seat. Then he'd remind them, in a bellowing voice for the other passengers' benefit, about client confidentiality and the danger of conducting legal work on trains.

The victim of his train game was inevitably indignant, embarrassed and angry.

Rowan would then return to his seat, pull open his laptop and, thoroughly entertained, continue with his own work.

No wonder Leighton had described his brother as 'too much of himself' Harriet thought.

Though Harriet hadn't mentioned anyone by name in the pub, the accusation of a client confidentiality breach spelled real trouble for her.

When she'd asked, Gethin told her he had no idea who the scary couple were, though he promised to find out if they'd been hired by Eiriol.

With breaking news flashing up on her phone, Harriet stopped drying pint glasses, found the TV remote and switched on the pub's flatscreen.

'Yes, yes, yes,' she said to herself. 'They've got someone.'

The red rolling info news banner said no more than the police were talking to a person of interest, but a sense of glorious freedom tingled through her. She wondered if DI Lennon would tell her anything about the guilty party, given Harriet's proximity to the crime, but it didn't matter. All that mattered was that she was off the hook.

Harriet was about to run upstairs and tell her parents, who were having a night off, when DI Lennon walked in, accompanied by a uniformed officer.

'I've just seen it on the news,' Harriet said, with a giddy smile. 'You've arrested someone.'

'Not quite. The news reports state we have a suspect, which we do. Harriet Erskine,' DI Lennon said. 'I'm arresting you for the murder of Rowan Tudor.'

The news sucker-punched Harriet low in the stomach. 'No, no, no, no.' she said. Her mouth gluey, she put her hands on the back of her head, hunched over and brought her elbows together, trying to protect her ears and her brain all at the same time.

Producing handcuffs, DI Lennon raised an arm – an instruction to turn around – and, before Harriet knew what had happened, had snapped them on her wrists. As she moved, the cuffs tightened with a series of tiny clicks.

The shock of it all and the tourniquet feeling of the cold cuffs set Harriet's head spinning.

When a line of officers trooped up the stairs, Harriet was unable to warn her parents.

'What the hell?' Louie roared, no doubt thinking they were being burgled as he flung open the living room door brandishing his second-best baseball bat with Lottie cowering behind him.

'Back up. Back up,' an officer shouted, with one hand on his yellow taser.

'Oh my God,' her mum whimpered, grabbing her dad and pulling him back as the bat tumbled to the floor. The officer kicked the bat out of her dad's reach.

'Dad!' Harriet shouted, but her parents had retreated out of sight.

She wanted to tell them she was sorry, but with the racket the police were making and the *Newsnight* theme blaring in the upstairs living room TV, they wouldn't have heard. Besides, there was the risk DI Lennon might interpret it as an apology for Rowan's murder.

'Where's your mobile phone?' DI Lennon asked, as an officer handed her a plastic zip-lock evidence bag.

Harriet pulled her Samsung from her pocket and handed it over.

'Do you have a lawyer, Harriet? We can provide you one for free if you'd prefer.'

Harriet asked for a duty sol – the greener in terms of experience the better – hoping to keep her predicament a secret a little longer from the wider legal community.

By the time they got Harriet to the station, she felt in need of a personal Richter Scale. Random thoughts fizzed up through the quake fissures, like how much energy and how many calories did shaking use up? People can't shake for hours, she thought, not without their bodies taking the toll.

The police explained the procedures, and offered Harriet water and a cup of tea. Kind little jokes were put out there as they encouraged her to calm down.

'Do you know what we're holding you for?' DI Lennon said.

'You think I murdered my boss,' Harriet said, welling up, her heartbeat pulsing in her ears, 'but I didn't.'

Harriet's run of misfortune continued with the arrival of her legal rep, Kerri, a young, social butterfly criminal solicitor wearing an updated 80s look of a beige blazer suit with shoulder pads and ruched three-quarter sleeves.

When Harriet asked whether she knew a lot of people in Cardiff's legal fraternity, Kerri confirmed Harriet's fears. She'd attended all the law awards, charity legal walks, Beaujolais days and networking events that she could cram into her already packed diary.

More worrying still, Kerri appeared a little tipsy. She sharpened up as she listened, breaking a soluble paracetamol in two and dropping each half into the neck of her water bottle.

'Sounds like he was an arsehole,' Kerri said, looking at the notes she'd made after Harriet had no choice but to confide in her. 'I believe you when you say you didn't have any involvement in his abduction and murder. I've seen their evidence. They know about the 'Let's Kill All the Lawyers' product line and they've seen email exchanges between you and Rowan where he's apologising for being a complete dick. Other than that, they've got nothing concrete, so just answer as you see fit. Anything that makes you uncomfortable, just say "no comment".'

Despite the reassurances, at the start of her formal interview, Harriet's legs still trembled under the table.

DI Cerys Lennon introduced her colleague Detective Fitch. Unlike DI Lennon, who looked like a lithe club runner, Fitch, judging by the bags under his eyes, appeared to have been on the job for three straight days and nights.

'You mustn't believe everything you've seen on the TV,' DI Lennon said, reading Harriet's nerves. 'If we behaved like the cops on *Line of Duty*, we'd all be on suspension. Isn't that right, Detective Fitch?'

Ironic, thought Harriet, given the dramatic storming of her parents' pub wasn't far off a scene from the hit show.

'Now,' DI Lennon said. 'Do you need a glass of water or anything before we start?'

'I'm fine, thanks.'

'Okay. Good. Now, Harriet, why don't you start by telling us about your time working with Rowan? Tell us how you went from being his secretary, working in the open plan area, to working alongside him as a legal assistant?'

DI Lennon and her sergeant threw Harriet off balance when they both assumed an air of patience, ready to listen for as long as it took. An alarm bell sounded that this was a clever technique. It probably even had a name, like active listening or building rapport or something. They'd get her to open up as though they were all friends and then, later, pounce on everything she said like a Temple Street barrister at the Old Bailey.

'I'd done a couple of semesters at law school,' Harriet said, 'so my skills were in listening and polishing as I typed. Not that the lawyers noticed, but that's the point. They never remember waffling in the middle of the third paragraph or getting the client's name wrong twice. Sly editing is the opposite of gaslighting, I guess.'

'You wanted to be a lawyer, then?'

'Once upon a time.'

'So, Rowan was giving you another opportunity to study law?'

'Well, it didn't happen like that. Rowan could be a menace when drunk,' Harriet said, with a what-can-you-do shrug. 'You know – handsy. When I got up the courage to complain to Nigel, he said he'd talk to Rowan.'

'And did he?'

'Yes, and that's when they said, given my interest in law, they'd pay for my Chartered Executive training if I worked as a personal assistant to Rowan. He promised to behave himself.'

'So, you complained about him, and they promoted you and moved you into his room?' DI Lennon asked, giving her sergeant a look of surprise mixed with scepticism.

'Yes.'

'And did Rowan keep his promise?'

'No. Anytime he got drunk, it still happened. He always apologised the next day. Promised it wouldn't happen again.'

'This must have made you angry and frustrated?'

'Of course,' Harriet said, swallowing.

'Then my next question is, if his son was sexually harassing and assaulting you at work, why didn't you complain to Nigel again?'

Carwyn had asked the same, asked it repeatedly and didn't like her lack of answers. She'd had plenty of time to reflect on that question since. It all came back to the fear nobody would believe her and that Nigel had started visiting her parents from time to time, and they'd never been prouder.

'I was drafting a grievance,' Harriet said. 'It was saved on my work computer, which you already have.'

'Were you sharing what you were going through with anyone else?'

'Just Carwyn,' she said.

'Just Carwyn,' DI Lennon repeated. 'Okay. It's getting late. Let's pick this up again in the morning.'

Harriet looked at Kerri for help because she was facing a night in the cells.

It was the cell in the custody suite that caused Harriet to unravel.

Laceless pairs of trainers to the left of the metal doors told Harriet that she had three neighbours, all of whom were quiet. This came as a surprise. She'd expected banging and hollering. Harriet averted her gaze from the CCTV monitors above each cell as they'd led her to hers, not wanting to witness a foreshadowing of her own incarcerated predicament as she took off her boots and placed them side by side outside.

How unjust it was, to be locked in a grubby box with a squat, metal toilet for the safety of wider society. She wasn't a danger to anyone, least of all Rowan Tudor.

The hours of overnight confinement under dimmed lighting, when time slowed to a standstill, made Harriet rue the day she ever started working at Eiriol.

But for her creative outlet and Carwyn's collection, the police would've had nothing apart from office gossip and some apologetic emails from Rowan that she might easily have explained away with a few easy lies.

Could've, would've, should've.

Her parents must be in turmoil, waiting for news.

Defensive, Harriet curled up in a ball, covered her eyes and wept in silence.

Chapter 33

'What? No!' Harriet said, failing to keep the lump from her throat, strangling her words. 'You know I didn't kill him.'

The quiet certainty with which DI Lennon spoke set the room spinning.

'Harriet,' DI Lennon said kindly, 'the difficulty is, given what you've told us, you've an even more compelling motive for killing Rowan than when we started.'

Her solicitor, with the smallest lift of her eyebrows, disagreed.

'If you *can* prove what you're saying,' the DI continued, 'not only did Rowan sexually harass, belittle and demean you when he was under the influence, but when you reached out to your boyfriend, he didn't understand either. How painful. And you went through a subsequent break up, I understand.'

'I didn't kill Rowan,' Harriet promised.

DI Lennon covered her mouth with steepled hands. When she took them away, her eyes were full of sad sincerity.

'But his being out of the picture is very convenient, right? Not only does the harassment stop but you've given your ex's literary career a boost. Maybe you were hoping you'd reconcile.'

'You don't understand ...' Harriet said, tailing off and looking at 80s-modern-fusion Kerri, thinking it was about time she stopped notetaking and spoke up.

'You have to be careful here,' Kerri said to DI Lennon, pointing a perfect caramel-painted nail at her interviewers in turn. 'My client is a victim. A victim in and of a legal world that knows exactly how to protect its own at the top level. She's cooperated, answered all your questions and you've shown us nothing but circumstantial evidence.'

DI Lennon, unmoved, wasn't done.

'It's a little strange,' DI Lennon said, turning a page in her file, 'that your client asked to share Rowan's office. Were you monitoring his movements in order to orchestrate his downfall, Harriet, from the very start?'

'The room share was his idea,' Harriet said. 'It was part of the deal – the package Rowan had asked for.'

'We'll check with Eiriol again.'

Again?

Nigel's blatant attempt to frame Harriet could only mean the cover-up she feared was underway. It was, she thought, the law of parsimony, Occam's razor. In problem solving, the simplest explanation was usually correct.

'The question you should be asking is why is Nigel setting me up.'

'He's setting you up?' DI Lennon echoed, in such a casual tone that it could only be read as lethargic dismissal.

It was galling how people implicitly trusted lawyers in expensive suits, Harriet thought.

'But why would I kill Rowan?'

'You tell me. Maybe you had a crush on him. Perhaps you gave him the come-on and then realised he was a sleaze.'

Rowan's features were already growing vague in Harriet's mind. She remembered his flaky complexion, in need of a flannel exfoliation and moisturiser, caused by too many high-temperature gym showers at lunchtime.

'Trust me, I didn't. That's such a cliché.'

DI Lennon didn't reply and, in the vacuum, Harriet's mind raced, wondering how many people at Eiriol were in on the cover-up. A couple of sequence steps at a time, she filled in the blanks. Unable to mention Sorelle without admitting she'd been in Rowan's private email folders, Harriet hoped hints would suffice.

'And their reaction means it won't just be me. There'll be more. You need to find out how and why Rowan left all his former employers. There won't be any trace of obvious complaints from victims of harassment. They'll all have been paid off. Trust me. And you certainly won't get anything from the HR departments. Lawyers don't mess about. It's a world of confidentiality. And they're the ones most benefitting from NDAs. You'll be lucky to get former support staff to talk about things they have merely witnessed.'

Harriet's words tumbled out as though her unconscious had been working on a rough draft for a while, just like that grievance.

'Can you tell me why you went for that particular strapline for these, what is it ... tote bags and coffee mugs?'

'It was just a joke.'

'You wanted to kill *all* the lawyers, or just Rowan?' DI Lennon said. 'I understand he was drunk sometimes, but it's an odd phrase – more a call to action. Did you plan to be the author of his downfall, in the same way as Carwyn authored *Swimming with Sharks*?'

'No. Of course not. And it's just a quote from Shakespeare. Worst-case scenario, I would've taken Rowan to an employment tribunal.

DI Lennon, having absorbed everything without betraying her thoughts, suspended the interview by asking Harriet and her lawyer if they wanted a cup of tea or a comfort break. She left the room, saying she'd be back in a moment.

Kerri encouraged Harriet, telling her she was doing okay.

Harriet half expected DI Lennon to say it was all over when she returned. But when she did, her tangent caught Harriet off guard.

'Did Rowan attack you? If you killed him in self-defence, we *could* help.'

'No, that's not what happened,' Harriet said.

'He never touched you?'

'He grabbed my wrist. I pulled away. That was it. I left at around 4.30pm and, on impulse, went straight to ESR – a recruitment agency on Working Street. But they were closing at five thirty, and it all felt too rushed.'

'We've spoken to them already. They described you as stressed and behaving strangely. Didn't even finish the typing test, they said. Nigel Tudor says you're one of the fastest, most accurate typists they have at Eiriol. But you couldn't finish a standard typing test that evening? You can see why it looks odd. We also have a witness who spotted you in the street immediately after.'

Debbie.

'She says you looked like you'd been crying. Now's the time to tell us the truth. Did he assault you before you left? You fought him off and, in the process, accidently killed him?'

'No,' Harriet said. 'I wasn't crying. I had a migraine coming on. Rowan was alive when I left. And how can I possibly have been in Cardiff Bay handing over the money as well as on a boat throwing him overboard? Or are you suggesting I have a whole team of colluders?'

'He honestly didn't lay a hand on you?' DI Lennon said, ignoring Harriet's question in return.

'No. He grabbed me. I shook him off.'

'Not in all the time you worked together?'

'Not really. Sometimes he brushed up against me or pinned me close to him and then later said it was a joke. Another time, he grabbed me and tried to kiss me. I knew he'd deny it. Nobody would believe me. And the fact it only happened now and again, and he backed off when I objected, probably meant I worked for him longer than I should.'

'Come, now, DI Lennon,' Kerri interjected. 'My client can't weigh more than nine stone. Do you really think she killed Rowan, carried him out – in front of a whole floor of lawyers and their secretaries – who didn't notice a thing. Then manhandled him into the lift, dragged his unconscious body past reception, drove him somewhere – though my client doesn't drive – and then chopped off his little finger to lay a false trail and extort a million in cash, which she then doesn't deliver?'

'This is where our inquiry is really going,' DI Lennon said. 'Did your then boyfriend offer to get rid of him for you? Or this IT guy who helped you set everything up. Mike, is it?'

'What?' Harriet said, covering her mouth as she began to laugh. When she waved a hand to apologise, DI Lennon's astonished face made Harriet laugh all the harder. She succumbed to nervous near-hysteria because, though utterly preposterous, Netflix, Harriet knew, was chock full of similarly bonkers, larger-than-life true-crime stories.

Chapter 34

Kennedy Jones

Without the blather of the TV to distract, the winter sun throws you a long-time-ago light.

Dr Stockton comes in with an armful of papers and says you need to talk.

Wordlessly, he spreads out the broadsheets and tabloids.

The morning lurches into one of those surreal moments where some terrible, sick initiation prank is being pulled once again.

Every front page, bar one, carries a picture of your lawyer, Rowan Tudor.

Your word-cloud from the collective headlines gives you: *brutally kidnapped and left to drown.*

'I'm sorry,' Dr Stockton says. 'That's why I left the TV off. Wanted you to have all the information I could get.'

You'd liked Rowan from the off, even if he was a bit strange. You've always liked quirky characters. They're interesting. Weirdos like Dr Stockton and Rowan Tudor give you something to puzzle over.

Rowan was the sort of guy who hid behind the confidence conferred by a hard black briefcase. Physically, he was a game of two halves. Over-developed leg muscles and an under-developed upper body gave him the look of someone planted, but not strong.

Rowan's visit lasted hours. When you thanked him for coming to your bedside, his reply threw you.

'Usually, I don't see clients at all. Make a point of it.'

You looked at him like his answer gave you mild concussion.

'Oh,' you said. 'You mean, you normally do Teams or Zoom or something?'

'No. God no,' he said. 'I have as little as humanly possible to do with my clients.'

You wondered at his point. You were a client. Was he saying your situation was so fucked-up he'd made an exception to the rule?

'You mean your secretary deals with them?'

'No, I can't afford to have my assistant tied up all day listening to meaningless waffle, people bleating "The world is flat. The world is flat", thinking they're contributing to their case. It's insane how many people can't answer a straight question. I bill by the hour, so I'm doing people a favour. If they want a therapist, they can hire the best therapists in the UK for half the money I charge.'

What a strange thing, you think. There was something funny in the way he delivered it too, made you want to laugh. Like a comedian, warming up on a subject.

'Then why come all the way to London for me?' you asked, ready to be offended and kick the guy out if he exhibited pity.

'I have a talent,' he said, 'for finding the weaknesses in law that demand a second look. Normally, the outcome of a judicial review is that a rule of law or legal decision is reviewed. That's it. But with you, there are societal consequences. I'm not sure how successful we'll be, but I needed to meet you first.'

You imagined, though you didn't know why, that you'd become friends during the process.

'And your case is so broad,' he continued. 'The first step is to look for anything to challenge the assisted dying aspect of the Suicide Act of 1961. That's not something you can help me with. I'll need to examine, in painstaking detail, constitutionally entrenched human rights laws, particularly in the areas of choice, liberty, welfare, non-interference, dignity and, given your sporting fame, privacy. I'll have to identify those rights that contradict our laws against assisted suicide and drill down further to see whether there's any sort of challenge.'

If there was a way to change a broken system legally, Rowan would find it.

You think of someone snatching him, applying restraints and the terror he must have gone through. Did he get the chance to fight back? Feeling scared and helpless is the worst feeling in the world, is the truth of it.

'None of this makes sense,' you say to Stockton. He gazes out the window, waiting perhaps, for you to absorb the shock. 'Rowan mentioned an assistant. Maybe her name was Helen or Hazel. I can't think. I'd like to drop her a line or speak to her on the phone. Ask her some questions. At least offer my condolences. Can you get hold of Boyd? He'll give me her number?'

'I'm not sure we want to be bothering them at Eiriol Law.'

'They'll understand. He mentioned her when he came here. Hannah? Or Harriet something? She sent Boyd my paperwork.'

'Boyd's gone,' Stockton said.

Burned out and too tired to talk, this new information powered some reserve energy in the tank.

'What do you mean, *gone*?'

'Family emergency. He's in Wales. He told me to explain, but then,' Stockton pointed to the papers, 'this happened.'

'I'll doubly need to speak to him.'

'He's entitled to a private life,' Stockton said. 'You're getting too reliant on him. He'll return soon enough, but we're going to give you a new nurse in the meantime. Lori. She's good. Maybe you won't want Boyd to come back.'

'I don't want anyone else,' you say, welling up, unable to stop hot tears running down your unshaven cheeks. 'Get Boyd on the phone. Please.'

Stockton turned on the TV news, slid the volume up and left the room. Your tears dry as you wait for the news bulletins showing the search for Rowan's body in progress.

A minute later, Stockton returns with your temporary nurse.

Lori isn't what you expect at all. She reminds you of a nervous bird, her calm watchfulness undermined with all these slight movements, working the skin between her index finger and thumb, pulling at her bottom lip or catching her thumb nail under her fingernails. Some sad energy is always at work. You don't flatter yourself it's for you. She has something else going on in her life.

She already knows about the plan. Stockton must have told her.

Later, you tell her in your own words, about your season coming to an end. How you picture it, peaceful, pain free, drifting away, surrounded by family and friends.

'That can happen,' she says. 'Exactly that way if that's what you really want. But listen, Kennedy ...' She reaches out, then looks over her shoulder at the open door.

Is she afraid?

'What?' you ask.

A moment's silence.

Lori withdraws her hand and raises it to her mouth. You hear the soft click of her nail against her front teeth.

'Nothing,' she says, but a tear slides down her face. She laughs at herself, then sighs.

Chapter 35

Harriet emerged from Cardiff Central Police Station at four o'clock profoundly changed.

The glistening streets around the Civic Centre, speckled with gritty bits of vegetation, informed her she'd missed a rainstorm. A wet dust smell hung in the air, reminding her more of a cold spring than winter. The afternoon sky, scudding grey blue clouds, made it feel like March or April.

The police interview experience had aged her. After her bout of hysterical laughter, which had then morphed into ten minutes of unconsolable tears, a detached acceptance had come upon her.

Some surreal, inner narrator had interrupted Harriet's thought process throughout her questioning with clichés like: 'Is this really happening?' and 'I can't believe this.'

She had a sense she hadn't yet woken from the dream and was now sleepwalking towards home.

Harriet cut through the university buildings in the direction of Lowther Road, pleased her mild state of shock was presenting as quiet, controlled dignity.

On the corner of Park Place stood the prestigious Cardiff University Law School. Harriet stopped and watched as a student couple, arms around each other's waists, exited the building.

They even find love there.

The students, walking or cycling along Park Place loaded with textbooks, reminded her of the other life she'd dreamed of pursuing. How happy they looked, carrying weighty corduroy totes, relating academic exchanges they'd had in class. And how dreadful her legal experience was in comparison.

Stay in university and get your law degrees, kids, she wanted to tell them. There are no shortcuts.

A voice in her head whispered that she should have saved the student loans and deferred until the following year. That's what Roddy would've wanted, for her to get back on the right path.

Not only was the career of a Chartered Executive different enough from a qualified solicitor to make it not the same end-goal, but Eiriol Law had saddled her with something even worse than debt – more trauma, more tragedy and potentially wrongful imprisonment. Carywn would probably never speak to her again. Old colleagues would cross the street to avoid her. What were indefinitely deferred student loans compared to all that?

The next morning, back at her flat, the metal clap of her letterbox and a smack of paper landing on carpet caused Harriet to let out a gasp of apprehension. Collecting the franked letter, marked Figgis LLP, she sat cross-legged on the floor in front of the sofa, wanting to feel hard support beneath. Her chest tightened and her palms grew sticky. Whatever Figgis wanted now, she'd have to deal with it alone.

The single page of correspondence took two read-throughs by Harriet before the contents sank in. The letter, she double-checked, bore her name and address – no mistake. The details in the subject line were indeed correct. Rubbing her temples, Harriet massaged away the unwarranted headache and was flooded with relief, then righteous anger, then exhilaration.

'In the interests of bringing this matter to a conclusion,' it began, 'our client has confirmed that they are prepared to take your assurances at face value.'

Harriet tried to figure out why they'd let her off.

Perhaps Nigel thought the criminal action sufficient punishment and anything else a gratuitous waste of money. Or perhaps he didn't want to be perceived as the antagonist.

Had Gethin successfully appealed to Nigel on her behalf?

Eiriol Law had agreed to drop hands, as the saying went. A technical truce, it felt like outright victory. She wanted to text Carwyn and see if they'd stopped threatening him too, but as his books were already pulped, he'd have mixed feelings even if they had.

It was time for Harriet to turn her full attention into who really killed Rowan.

By the time she got to The Poet's, she'd parked the legal worries and her head burst with an inner debrief. She tried to recall all the questions she'd been asked at the police station, then attempted to analyse the detectives' probable impressions and intentions. Reasonable throughout, they'd also been straight with her about the seriousness of her situation.

The Poet's was empty of clientele. A foreign love duet, clarity distorted by old, built-in laptop speakers, warbled around the lounge. Nana, who was perched behind the bar, one arm propping up her head behind her screen, sang along in a pleasant vibrato.

'You look so much better,' Harriet told her.

Nana's dark hair, glossy with fresh amethyst colour, was tinted to ear level with the same hue as the purple chocolate in a tin of Quality Streets. Harriet suddenly craved something sweet and comforting. A hot chocolate drink would have to do.

'I feel so much better,' Nana said, coming around the bar and embracing Harriet.

'Where are my folks?'

'They went to visit you.'

'At my place?' Harriet asked.

'Yes. A man visit. They rush off to find you.'

'What did he look like?'

'I didn't see him. Just heard his voice.'

Harriet went to check her phone and remembered the police still had it. She ran through the options and figured a police officer had probably stopped by to tell her folks she'd been released. That's why her parents had gone to her flat, not realising she'd go straight to theirs.

'Would you message dad and tell him I'm here?' she said.

A piano and violins took the duetting couple on Nana's laptop to a passionate crescendo at odds with Harriet's sense of unease.

'I'm sorry about your lovesick lawyer,' Nana said, with a shrug. 'So sad.'

'It wasn't like that,' Harriet said, accustomed to her parents and Nana mistaking aggressive advances for love ever since she'd first tried to discuss her problem with Rowan.

She remembered Rowan's supposed girlfriend Natasha. Was it possible a grain of truth lay at the heart of Debbie and Ffion's gossip? Rowan might have met someone in London who'd rejected him. Was that why he'd downloaded his hurt and humiliation Harriet's way each time he returned?

'You all right, love?' Nana asked.

'Yes, just something you said – about being lovesick – made me think.'

But Harriet had no names to go on. There was nothing in the emails, unless she'd missed them because of the lack of time or Nigel – or Rowan himself – had already deleted them.

Wishing she could have another dip into Rowan's computer, she made herself and Nana a hot chocolate from the machine.

There it was again, something nagging and stirring her, just outside her grasp.

'You really do look so much better,' Harriet said, taking the canned cream from the fridge, adding a swirl to the velvety surface of each drink before sprinkling over a handful of pink and white mini marshmallows. Harriet popped a few in her mouth, savouring their powdery, soft, fluffiness.

'I never want to go to Heath Hospital again,' Nana said, having previously shared her experience of spending three nights in a hard chair. 'If I get sick when I'm old, I ask Louie to finish me off.'

Nana concluded her declaration with a karate-chopping swipe.

It came to Harriet in a flash of inspiration. In a sudden rush to see if the pieces fitted together, she grabbed a teaspoon from the caddy, kissed Nana on the cheek and headed upstairs, taking her mug with her.

Spooning off the cream and toppings, Harriet shovelled the sweet mess into her mouth, recalling the day when Rowan had asked her to log onto his computer. Perhaps he'd also wanted to give her a name: Augusta Hertz. 'Not a client' he'd said. Then who the hell *was* she?

Harriet had spoken to the American on the phone, enjoying the novelty of Augusta's confident, New York accent rather than listening to the things she'd said. Rowan had got it wrong, Augusta had insisted, sounding exasperated. There was no problem with him not attending, because she and Rowan weren't due to meet. It had to be some mistake in his diary.

What if he'd been harassing Augusta, Harriet thought, trying to set up meetings with her that she didn't want. After all, he *was* a man who struggled to take no for an answer.

While the interminable wait for the old computer to boot up ran its course, Harriet drummed her nails on the desk. When the computer's internet search flickered to life, she typed in Augusta Hertz. Her instincts triggered goosebumps as she tried to make sense of the articles. Then, she selected the images tab.

'Holy ...' Harriet whispered. There, halfway down the page, was the MP Nicholas Etheridge and Rowan at a glitzy London breakfast event with Augusta Hertz. Was it her imagination, or did Augusta's body language appear ill at ease? The article featuring the image corresponded to a date when he'd returned drunk mid-afternoon and tried to straddle and snog her.

Struggling to connect the dots, Harriet massaged the back of her head before raising a second arm above her head to stretch. Another unpleasant encounter with him corresponded to Rowan meeting someone from New York at the office and schmoozing them on the terrace. It *had* to be Augusta.

But why kill him? Harassment didn't seem a big enough reason. It wasn't like Augusta had the tale-as-old-as-time power dynamic of Rowan being her boss. If anything, the power dynamic existed the other way around. She had power over him, as a wealthy American.

Blackmail?

Another half an hour on the age-discoloured computer and Harriet had a working theory and a flurry of notes so extraordinary, so outlandish she hardly knew what to do with it.

Instinct told her to type it up into a report or a memorandum. Only then could she decide whether her theory might convince others.

An hour and ten minutes later, her research and digging translated to a scant four pages of suppositions. She had no evidence, but the pages had an inevitable ring of truth.

The opening was a little dry but, without it, her piece lacked sufficient context, so she'd put it back in. Being Welsh, she could be forgiven for reminding the reader of a little historical background.

Who, though, could she show it to? The police would consider it fantasy, an attempt to deflect suspicion from herself.

She should go straight to Gethin but baulked at the idea. If he betrayed her, she'd never trust anyone again.

What Harriet still didn't understand was where Kennedy Jones fitted in. Harriet read through her summary again and that's when she saw it – a plan so heinous she brought her hands to her mouth in prayer.

It would take a miracle to stop it, but the nature of the conspiracy made it less likely that Gethin was involved.

Yes, she had no evidence and, yes, there was nobody she could wholeheartedly trust, but they had Kennedy Jones and maybe she could rally Gethin and Kennedy's Welsh nurse, Boyd – if she sold them the idea of a struggle in the name of two Welsh heroes.

It took Harriet a few minutes, in her state of intense concentration, to notice her parents' return. From downstairs came the indistinct mumbling of conversation and questions fired at Nana.

Close to a breakthrough, Harriet was relieved she might soon be able to share the whole story with them.

Her dad called her name, his tone terse, and she heard heavy footsteps on the stairs.

Harriet's first thought was Nana had guessed she was in trouble and passed her concerns on to her parents.

'Harriet?' her dad said, swinging wide the bedroom door. Behind him, Lottie stood with her head lowered, wearing a pained expression.

'Dad?' Harriet said, experiencing a contraction of fear in her chest.

'We've been looking for you all over,' Louie growled. 'Nigel called earlier to see your mother.'

'Nigel?' Harriet said, thinking of the last time she'd seen him.

'He said he'd had to let you go, for gross misconduct,' Lottie volunteered, taking a step closer to her husband and holding his arm for support. 'After everything that's happened to his son?'

'You need to come downstairs, right now, and explain what's going on,' Louie said. 'Are the police really speaking to you about Rowan's abduction and murder?'

Clever Nigel, Harriet thought, biting her lip. She swallowed her anger at her parents. It was unfair. People couldn't read minds.

The unlikely friendship that Nigel had cultivated with her parents now served only to divide and conquer. Harriet blamed herself for not seeing it coming.

'I'll tell you everything, later.'

'What did you say?' Lottie whispered, staring at Harriet like a stranger might.

'You'll speak to us right now, my girl,' Louie demanded.

'I'm in the middle of something urgent,' Harriet said, adding sheets to the printer tray. 'There are things I have to do first.'

'Is this something to do with Carwyn?' Louie said, 'I knew that boy was trouble the minute I laid eyes on him.'

'It's nothing to do with him.'

'Well, it can't be a coincidence that the boy smokes weed and then Nigel turns up, saying he's very worried about your mental health,' Lottie said.

'I'm sure he is,' Harriet said, shaking with anger as she pressed print and the printer whirred into life. Moments later, Harriet grabbed the document, pushed past her parents and ran down the stairs.

She wouldn't do battle for their loyalty. As an only child, her relationship with her parents was strong. Their confusion was situational. Once she'd proven her theory, they'd understand everything.

Yet again, underscoring everything, lurked the fear that, until she had everything in place, she wouldn't be believed – even by them.

Chapter 36

Statement of Case by Harriet Erskine

The obstacles and barriers to treatment that existed *before* the establishment of the National Health Service are hard to imagine, given the catastrophic state it's now in.

Labour's Aneurin Bevan, a former Tredegar miner and Minister of Health for three years from 1945, proved a tenacious pioneer, launching the NHS on 5 July 1948.

To deliver such a socialist concept to British society, he'd needed to persuade a range of interests to go along with his vision, including the British Medical Association and the Royal Colleges.

All were deeply suspicious of a state that wanted to control the doctor-patient relationship.

Bevan made the point that under the existing arrangement, the patient's money, or lack of it, lay at the heart of administering medical assistance. Further, the current system fostered competition rather than cooperation between doctors.

Many denounced his plan as totalitarian and overtly communist, but Bevan wouldn't budge. Parliament would make it work, come what may.

For years, free-market conservatives accepted that there was little money to be made from the state-run NHS, yet it didn't stop some bemoaning the commercial opportunities going to waste.

As the years went by and the increasingly underfunded NHS began to show cracks, corporate interests and politicians saw profits to be gained with the sharp end of a capitalist crowbar.

Private providers without medical qualifications assessed disability claims for the Department for Work and Pensions. Lucrative pandemic contracts were handed to business cronies.

In 2015, a wealthy, 22-year-old Harvard graduate named Augusta Hertz began to monitor the situation from across the Atlantic with the thoughtfulness of a doctor taking a sick patient's pulse.

Augusta was the beneficiary of a sizeable entrepreneurial trust fund from her New York grandfather, who had great plans for his five granddaughters.

Her older sisters, Georgia, Danielle, India and Camilla, all attractive and intelligent, used their respective millions wisely, seeking further major investment from their grandfather's acquaintances to go into real estate and art, and to establish new fashion and beauty lines.

As the youngest, Augusta witnessed her sisters charming their way into exhausting the financial goodwill on offer from family friends. She needed a business plan with a story ambitious and poignant enough to reopen old wallets or find new ones.

Harvard taught her to plunder both the past and the future for ideas.

Prominent in medicine, her great, great, great-grandfather, Richard Holmes, had studied under William Stewart Halstead, one of the four founding fathers of John Hopkins Hospital. Both Halstead and Holmes shared English ancestry, of which they were proud.

Back then, the Holmes family had owned a grand five-storey on Fifth Avenue overlooking Central Park. By the time Augusta was born, they'd downgraded to a penthouse off Madison Avenue.

Augusta was sure there was something in her English ancestry for her. Her grandfather and his cronies loved London. Perhaps she could invent a British business start-up, she mused, and make her mark that way.

Augusta also connected spiritually with her great, great, great-grandfather. At Harvard, she dreamed of ways to further link their lineage through medicine. It would make for a great business-origin story.

Her subsequent business plan, to disrupt public sector medicine in Britain, stamped her out as someone serious and special, a visionary. The more her lecturers encouraged her to explore untapped markets, the more she realised that getting there would take astonishing ambition and bravery.

With Medicare, the US market was cornered. The medical device industry turned over $300 billion a year in profits. Disruptors had already reimagined funerals, but the liminal area between life and death still had untapped potential.

It took $3.5 million to test the American market in assisted dying and she hadn't made a dent. Her four siblings thought her an unconventional maverick. A little Goth style crept into Augusta's wardrobe. She'd blown over half the trust money, but she had faith in her vision. At night, the ghost of Richard Holmes whispered to her to keep going.

A visit to England in the autumn opened her eyes to their potential market and the benefit of being the first to gain a foothold. The NHS was ripe, low-hanging fruit and Augusta could see it. The Conservatives in power at the time viewed it the same way.

She began to test out a fake story on anyone who'd listen about her grandmother dying a lingering, painful death and a revolutionary plan to ease suffering. Augusta considered it impromptu market research. The truth was that the grandmother in question, an entitled woman with an unpredictable temper, had passed peacefully on Boxing Day in an Upper East Side nursing home two years before.

From English taxi drivers to politicians, everyone she shared the tragic grandmother story with seemed to have their own, often more harrowing, story. They all agreed something had to be done.

She returned to the US and set up meetings with investors, seeking out those with long-term disability in the family or who'd lost loved ones in tragic circumstances. Those getting in on the ground floor of a business start-up often invested on instinct and emotion rather than spreadsheets, profit predictions and audits.

Next, Augusta demanded meetings with the family friends who'd helped finance her sisters' businesses.

Colour returned to Augusta's wardrobe. She adopted an English, Kate Middleton style, adding glasses with a smoky tint, as though she'd learnt a lesson in grief and her eyes were delicate to the light. Her accent became more polished and formal.

Augusta rebranded herself as the caring and sensitive youngest sister forging ahead with a dream that combined business with hypocritic virtue.

To her grandfather's friends, it was as though they could see Augusta for the first time. Her business proposal made her sisters' existing endeavours seem trivial and superficial. Augusta was Cordelia in Shakespeare's *King Lear* and they regretted having not mentored her earlier. To this end, they encouraged their wider family and friends to invest in her idea alongside them.

Once she'd secured $100 million, Augusta arranged to meet Nicholas Etheridge in London.

Nine years before, Etheridge had voted against an Assisted Dying Bill, but times had changed. His main objection had been that the original bill was badly drafted, but his wife had been a nurse with strong views on the issue and she'd persuaded him to think again. The BMA was neutral on assisted dying and the RCN largely sympathetic to the idea. Etheridge's personal situation, his wife's illness – on which he maintained privacy – had turned him from sympathiser to activist.

Augusta and Etheridge just needed a high-profile individual case to hit the headlines, to give a national debate momentum and make people think and empathise.

After compiling a team of doctors, lawyers and PR strategists who she might engage in persuasive, behind the scenes work, Augusta visited vacant properties in and around Harley Street.

At the same time, she secretly bankrolled a new UK-based pro-assisted dying grassroots organisation that lobbied on behalf of terminally ill pain patients called Determined Dignity.

Progress was slow and soon Augusta's paranoia that someone would beat her to it as the debates grew.

Sure, she had Etheridge, but who were his political peers were talking to?

With more and more MPs becoming favourably disposed to Etheridge's assisted dying bill, Augusta knew it would just take one beloved celebrity in the public eye.

Their gruesome, botched suicide would act as the ultimate cautionary tale of letting people suffer and tip the balance of approving her as the main provider in that sector. If the celebrity died a short time later – so much the better.

Through Etheridge, Augusta learned of a former international rugby player, seriously injured after a game and clinically depressed, who was Googling Dignitas once a month.

Among Augusta's heroes as a teenager was the late, great John F Kennedy. Coincidence and synchronicity spoke to her. She'd found her man.

But, in all her planning, the one man she hadn't accounted for was Rowan Tudor.

Chapter 37

Nothing placates grief like obsession, Harriet thought, as she waited for Boyd by Bangor's red-brick clock tower.

After the long and slow train journey from Cardiff, when icy air squeezed through the narrow gap in the automatic doors, Harriet's fingers were numb and bloodless to the second joints. She rubbed her hands and longed for indoor warmth.

When Boyd arrived, he embodied Welsh Valleys Male Nurse – a caring and open guy with a penchant for male grooming.

Were Harriet to open his bathroom cabinet, she knew it would be a smorgasbord of cosmetic gels. His pale brows were a marvel of shaped, feathered and set symmetry. Fine comb lines were frozen in place by super-hold styling products. And only whitening trays could have got his slightly overlapping front teeth to such a pristine shade of Alpine white.

He led her to a nearby noodle bar, an eatery with orange crackle-glazed tea-light holders and paper-wrapped plastic chopsticks. A wall-mounted TV ran Japanese anime with the sound off.

Harriet wasted no time.

'I'm so sorry about your grandfather,' she said.

'It's been a tough time,' Boyd said. 'But he's at peace now. When he was home, he wanted to be in hospital. When he was in hospital, he wanted to be home. He'd contributed to the NHS all his life, so he expected them to give him a magic pill that would make him thirty-years-old again. When they couldn't, he sort of gave up.'

'Poor man,' Harriet said.

Fearing that Boyd's loss might cloud his conclusions about Afternity, she changed the subject. 'So why did you become a nurse?'

The waitress delivered the steaming bowls of noodles they'd ordered. Taking the small paper napkin, Harriet weighed up whether to tuck it under her chin or place it on her lap. Boyd ignored his altogether. In the end, she tucked it in the neckline of her brushed cotton, oversized shirt.

Boyd smiled.

'I'm the perfect nurse,' Boyd said, opening his arms, a cheeky invite to agree. 'I care about people – bond really fast. But what is it about our international rugby player that brings you all this way, that you can't discuss by phone?'

Harriet recalled how she'd felt when Mike insisted on an in-person meeting. She hoped Boyd didn't view her with the same scepticism she'd treated Mike that day at Roath Rec. No, this was different.

'How long have you worked for him in London?' Harriet asked.

Boyd tossed his head. His hair didn't move.

'Since the day Kennedy was admitted there. I went with him, you see.'

'You knew him in Cardiff?'

'They – Augusta Hertz and Dr Stockton – wanted to take over Kennedy's care exclusively, but Kennedy wasn't going anywhere without me. That was the deal.'

'He must think a lot of you.'

Boyd paused and gave Harriet a pointed stare. 'I think a lot of him. And he won't allow his family to visit, you know. But he needed someone.'

Harriet's instincts told her to have patience.

'Why no family?'

'It was something they all agreed. He had this idea that he'd make a fifty percent recovery or more and surprise them all. Sadly, it's not working out like that.'

'Things didn't go to plan?'

'You could say that.'

'You're a personable guy, though. I bet you fitted straight in.'

'They loved me!' Boyd said, pretending to slap her hand across the table, as though it were the silliest thing she could have come out with.

But there *had* been problems. Harriet could sense it.

'Is there anything specific you wanted to know about Kennedy's treatment?' Boyd asked.

'I think he's at risk,' she said.

Boyd fell silent. Harriet gave him as much time as he needed.

'You think they're doing something to him at Afternity?' he finally asked.

'Is it plausible?'

'Things have been a bit weird.'

'I think they're gaslighting him.'

'Why? Why would they do that?'

'To promote the Assisted Dying Bill,' Harriet said. She'd wanted to drip-feed her suspicions but, once she'd started, it couldn't be contained. 'You see, Nicholas Etheridge, the MP, won a ballot to introduce legislation and his Assisted Dying Bill is the result. Rowan, when he worked in London – before he even took on Kennedy Jones as a client – must have bribed enough MPs and members of the House of Lords to get it to a third and final reading. His emails were full of meetings with MPs. I'm just reading between the lines here, but he was always the one doing the shmoozing.'

Harriet paused to allow Boyd to interrupt, but he waited for her to continue.

'The government, which has always viewed assisted dying as a controversial issue, changed its stance and gave the bill its wholehearted support. So, my guess is that the legend that is Kennedy Jones, desperate for a way out of his suffering, will attempt suicide. And the mess he creates is the catalyst. The decision on assisted dying has already been made, but they need something to point at for rushing a load of American clinics through – something that will serve as an obvious explanation.'

'They can't do that.'

'They most certainly can. If I'm right, Augusta Hertz also had my boss, Rowan, killed. Maybe he was blackmailing her about it. He was scared, I know that much.'

'This is a lot to take in.'

'You've been looking after Kennedy. Have you seen anything that fits what I've said?'

'It may sound weird,' Boyd said, nodding, 'but I started to suspect they were manufacturing his estrangement from family and friends. I did what I could to counteract it.'

'I know the website says Afternity is a medical centre but I have a feeling that when the bill is 100 per cent finalised, it'll transform itself into a mercy hospital within weeks. Maybe even days.'

Boyd's jaw slackened. 'No,' he said, but Harriet noted the way his eyes darted around the restaurant, putting things together.

'There's more, isn't there?' Harriet said.

'A woman called Lori is Kennedy's nurse now. She's totally trusted. Her brother was already working for Afternity in the medical advertising department. I couldn't understand the reaction Kennedy was having to the drugs they were giving him. They made him depressed and sick, but Stockton insisted they were working, sometimes doubling the dose. Once, I swear, Stockton administered a drug that *causes* temporary muscle paralysis. It was like they were trying to make him worse, not better. I started asking too many questions – if it weren't for Kennedy's insistence, they'd have fired me months ago.'

'You see what I mean?' Harriet said.

'What do we do? Do we call the police?' Boyd said.

'I would've called them already, but it's my word against Augusta's. People are already trying to discredit me. Do you think the police would take you seriously – if we went together?'

'No, they've been trying to get rid of me at Afternity since I got there. I've already had a verbal and written warning.' Boyd fell into a brooding silence. 'Dr Phil Stockton has to be in on it too.'

Now Harriet had an ally, anything was possible, but she'd expected to feel better about being proven right.

'Sometimes Kennedy's hallucinating and delirious,' Boyd continued, his shoulders stiffening. He pushed away his bowl and put his elbows on the table. 'Other times, he's just out of it for no obvious reason. He should've been recovering as much as he could with the

SCI, going off to physio. Stockton told me I should stick to changing bedpans.'

'Will Lori help us, do you think?'

'I don't know. Like I said, they're carefully chosen, but Dr Stockton bullies her. I've seen her crying. And I think she's even had a few conversations with Kennedy when he's more lucid. She cares about him.'

'Have you seen anything that would back up this assisted dying stuff?'

Boyd bit his lip and nodded.

'What?'

'There's a mortuary in the basement,' he said, sounding embarrassed to say it.

'Are you winding me up?'

Everything that day had been permeated with something sinister, Harriet realised. Now, it seemed prescient. On the journey, shifting light and dramatic cloud patterns over fields and ancient woodland gave Harriet the sense of moving through a dark fairy tale, where the lushest dell might be an attractive lure into a waiting ambush. Her mouth went dry with a mixture of elation and dread that her theory might be right.

'Augusta said a few clinics are adding a mortuary space – call it emergency planning – to cater for future pandemics. The whole thing sounded odd when she explained it. The government gave them post-Covid funding. I can't go down there.'

'We need to get evidence of this,' Harriet said.

'I'm not going anywhere near it,' Boyd replied. 'Lori told me someone's down there.'

'What, like a security guard?'

'No, she said there's already a body down there. One of the cleaners told her. I thought she was trying to scare me. She knows I find it creepy.'

'Do you think – if me and a friend, supposedly from Eiriol Law, visited Afternity to see Kennedy Jones on some legal pretext, you could help us out? We'll need a rough blueprint for a start.'

'Done,' Boyd said.

'Maybe we could get Kennedy out of there?' Harriet said, running her hands through her hair.

Boyd shook his head. 'Won't work. We wouldn't be able to move him. They'd be on us in seconds. And remember, he's a big rugger lump.'

'Then we'll have to talk to him and convince him he's in danger. And we'll have to find some other evidence and persuade the police to check it out. You'll back me up, right?'

The flicker of uncertainty in Boyd's eyes made Harriet feel queasy. They studied their untouched noodles.

'Count me in,' Boyd said, a touch of surprise in his voice. 'And I'll go back to work tomorrow rather than wait until my shift starts on Monday. It sounds like the sooner I'm there, keeping an eye on our boy, the better.'

Boyd raised his arm to request the bill.

'It's a shame you don't speak Welsh,' he said, looking rueful on her behalf.

'How do you know I don't?' Harriet asked. She had school-girl Welsh, but that didn't extend far beyond polite greetings, such as good day and thank you.

'I just know. It would have been useful for your visit, if we were able to communicate without them understanding.'

'Gethin, the private investigator coming with me, might,' Harriet said, stung by the idea that her Cardiff comp schooling and lack of linguistic patriotism had her at a disadvantage. She had no idea if Gethin could speak Welsh and she hadn't Boyd's talent of knowing without asking.

'Chwarae teg,' Boyd said.

A phrase Harriet knew, *fair play*. But nothing about any of this, Harriet thought, is fair.

Chapter 38

Harriet stared up at what Landseer would probably have called a Prussian-blue sky. The cold wind stinging her cheeks refreshed her more than the bitter, half-drunk, take-out coffee. Her gaze travelled east along the platform where puddles glinted, so dark they reminded her of the two-way glass used in interview rooms. She watched the railway lines disappearing into the darkness, waiting for the beam of light that would signal the oncoming train.

Every time she heard hurried steps behind her, Harriet turned to see if Gethin had arrived. When he rang, her fear he was going to miss their train made her irritable.

'Harriet, calm down,' he said. 'We don't need to visit Afternity. I know who killed Rowan. It's nothing to do with Augusta. It's Marc Munday.'

'We're going to miss the train,' Harriet said, too tired and confused to process the abrupt, unplanned change to their itinerary. 'Wait. He's your old sergeant, right?'

'He's had a grudge against Nigel for years. I don't know how they got the info they did, but these internet true-crimers got to the bottom of it.'

'But how do you know? A lot of those people are fantasists.'

'Munday runs a large security firm in London, but he lives in Penarth, opposite the marina. A couple of his friends keep boats there and the YouTube detectives can prove he took a boat out the day of the drop. Coincidence? I think not!'

'But what's his problem with Nigel?'

'Nigel got me out of prison and left him there to rot. Munday's also got contacts from his time inside. How much do you want a bet those guys you met in the Bay are his known associates? Anyway, there's only one way to find out. I'm outside his place now.'

The final statement got Harriet's full attention. The electronic sign showed her train was delayed by five minutes, but Gethin would never make it if he was breaking into the home of a man who might have killed her boss.

'Are you trying to get yourself killed? Leave it to the police.'

'It's perfectly safe. There's no car in the drive and the house isn't alarmed. I'm going around the back.'

'He's ex-police,' Harriet said, hurrying to put distance between her and two suited gents with leather man-bags who'd crowded her on the platform. 'He's not going to be stupid enough to leave evidence around, is he? He's not going to have 'Dear Diary, today I killed Rowan' written in a leatherbound journal, now, is he?'

'I need to satisfy my theory.'

By the time Gethin spoke again, he was inside Munday's kitchen. Harriet didn't want to know how he'd got in so fast.

'Here,' Gethin said, panning the phone camera around as he made his way to the front of the property. When Harriet lifted her coffee cup to her mouth, parched with anxiety, her hand shook.

In Gethin's torchlight, Marc's home spoke of discipline and order, from the military and war books, arranged by size, to the state-of-the-art TV and the masculine black bottle reed diffuser on the large, bay windowsill.

Gethin swept the room, allowing Harriet a view of the charcoal tweed sofa opposite a cast-iron mantelpiece.

Marc Munday was making a success of civilian life now, Harriet thought, comparing it to her own rundown rental.

'He must have served in the Army before the police,' Harriet said. 'But how's he making his money now?'

'It was a long time ago, but I remember him mentioning it,' Gethin said, zooming in on a weighty bronze of army boots and beret on a wooden base with an engraved brass plaque: 1st The Queen's Dragoon Guards.

'Gethin, do you think it might have been PTSD? The assault at the Occupy demo. Did anything like that come out at the trial?'

'I think it was mentioned, but they didn't make a big thing of it.

Not as much as of a deal as they'd probably make now.'

Gethin's torch lit up a wicker basket that contained various remote controls. Next to the basket was a sports flask which Gethin unscrewed and sniffed.

'Water,' he said.

Something about the neatness and the sports flask reminded Harriet of the guy who'd menaced her at The Poet's.

'Are there any pictures of him?' Harriet asked, relieved that there was still no moving pinprick of light along the rails.

'When I knew him,' Gethin said, 'he kept himself fit. He's about 5' 10", brown hair.'

Gethin found what Harriet was looking for on the fridge. Even the fridge pictures were neat, clipped into magnetised charcoal frames. Of the three sports-related pictures, two were of Munday and a woman, glowing with health, arms around each other as dawn broke on a mountain – Pen-y-van perhaps. The sun's glorious rays opened out across the sky behind them like the orange-red folds of a great Victorian fan.

'It's him. You're right,' Harriet said, blind to anything but her phone screen. 'He's the guy who threatened me in the hallway of The Poet's. Get out of there and call the police.'

With Gethin's phone capturing a jerky blur as he left via the rear of the Munday property, something caught Harriet's eye.

'Gethin, go back. Go back,' she said.

'What?' Gethin said, obliging by shifting Harriet's view across the kitchen.

'That box on the counter,' Harriet said, looking at the London train pulling in.

A woman in heels tottered to a halt in front of her pulling a small green wheelie case. With a smack, the woman depressed the long handle, grabbed the carry strap and waited for the train to stop.

'This?' Gethin asked, putting his hand on the box.

'Yes,' she said.

There, on the counter, behind other liquor bottles, was a white box, covered with fine gold cartoons.

'Open it?' Harriet said, 'What's inside?'

To free up a hand, Gethin put the phone down. Finally, his face appeared again on screen.

'It's a bottle of tequila,' he said. 'White, with blue, hand-painted leaves.'

Harriet again felt Rowan's iron grip on her wrist as she tried to escape him mimicking masturbation.

She quickly considered the various explanations for the appearance of a second bottle of the expensive Tequila Reposado, while the beeping signal of the train doors about to close underscored her breakthrough.

'Oh God,' Harriet said. 'He's not a rogue agent at all. He's just another person working for Augusta Hertz.'

With the platform guard's whistle blowing, she flew through the door of the carriage and hurried along the narrow aisle looking for her seat. Just as she found it, the train lurched forward and gained speed. 'I'm on the train,' Harriet said, swapping her phone to her other hand as she wrestled out of her coat and threw it on the overhead shelf. She held her phone screen up, but the line had disconnected. When she called back, the call cut off after two rings. When she tried again, Gethin's phone went straight to voicemail.

Chapter 39

The London Underground carriages to Harriet's left and right swung in and out of view in a way that settled her nerves a little. There was no need to panic. The chances were, with Gethin having used his camera so much, his phone had run out of battery and he'd follow her to London on the next train.

Over and over, she replayed the morning's events, lingering on reassuring details. There'd been no car in Munday's drive and, clearly, nobody in when Gethin had gained access.

Gethin would default to Plan B, which they'd run past Boyd the previous night while studying the Afternity website.

On the clinical care menu, the senior life care tab was access-blocked 'for security reasons'. Their assumption was those pages would go live the moment. Afternity, as an end of life provider, was given approval.

After a short walk, Harriet found Afternity located between a women's clinic and a private dentist, on a side road off Harley Street.

Sickened again with anxiety, Harriet managed to mask this. Her emotional temperature was something she'd been monitoring since arriving in London.

Two guys passing, one on a bicycle, whistled at Harriet and she'd flicked her long blonde hair away from her face with what she hoped was haughty metropolitan disdain.

The gleaming freshness of Afternity's white walls set it apart from its brown-brick neighbours.

Swinging open the front door, Harriet experienced the same dread tinged with excitement as when she'd accessed Rowan's computer. The ceiling air con sent an invisible cone of cold draught downward, but she could feel herself beginning to sweat, nonetheless. The scent of aloe vera and rosewater hung in the air.

From behind reception floated the muted strains of Vivaldi. The receptionist was a petite girl with an elfin cut and an air of self-esteem that suggested a successful side-hustle. Harriet imagined sales of organic cosmetics or hand-dipped candles.

'Harriet Erskine from Eiriol Law,' she told the receptionist with a smile. 'I'm here to see Kennedy Jones. I'd also like to see Boyd if he's around – Kennedy Jones' nurse. I grew up in the next village to Boyd. I know his parents.'

The receptionist smiled, nodded and pointed at the waiting room chairs with a Biro. 'Take a seat. I'll let Boyd know you're here.'

'Thank you,' Harriet said.

'One minute,' the receptionist said, calling her back to the desk.

Turning, Harriet prepared to be grilled.

'I forgot to give you these. Please don't remove your pass during your visit. The keys are for the lockers over there, where we ask you to leave your bag and phone. You'll have to go through the scanner on your way in, but wait until Boyd comes.'

'Will you need my passport and boarding pass too?' Harriet said with a dry laugh.

Harriet pinned her laminated visitor card to her lapel with the crocodile clip, slipped her bag into the Bisley locker and set a passcode.

The clinic looked even better in reality than on the website. A grey marble wall plaque with silver lettering dedicated the Afternity Clinic to Richard Holmes. A thickly varnished oil painting of the man himself hung nearby.

Overall, the place had an unused, not-yet-open for business feel. The winter-green Orla Kiely print sofas looked unused.

'Harriet, I can't believe you're here,' Boyd said, extending a hand. 'Let's find a room where we can catch up.'

After a quick exchange with the receptionist, Boyd spun theatrically back towards Harriet with the kind of sharp 360-degree turn normally seen on catwalks. The receptionist rolled her eyes.

Boyd was masterful, every bit the convincing actor. How pleased Harriet was to have found an ally, although, remembering Gethin, she wished she'd waited before placing her phone in the locker.

They took the lift to the third floor and stepped into a corridor lined with closed panelled doors. Each nameplate was blank. Access to the rooms was via keycard – without one, she wouldn't be able to enter.

Halfway along the corridor, Boyd led her into a meeting room.

'How's Kennedy doing?' Harriet asked.

'He's ...' Boyd seemed to struggle for words. 'He's not doing so great. But you were right. Lori has her suspicions too.'

At that moment, the door burst open.

'I'm Dr Stockton,' the newcomer announced, in a brittle tone. 'I understand you're from Eiriol Law? Representing Kennedy Jones?'

"I'd like a few minutes alone with my client,' Harriet said. 'You know, confidentially – client to lawyer, privileged conversation.'

'He's sleeping.'

'I can wait,' Harriet said.

'He sleeps a great deal. It's his body's way of fighting infection.'

The doctor's sanctimonious tone contained an undertone of threat and Harriet had the suspicion that he was acting too. He knew why she was there.

'I wish I'd known,' Harriet said, standing and brushing herself down, to rid her clothes of creases amassed on the long journey. 'Having come all this way.'

'It's hard to say how he'll be. It fluctuates from day to day. Tomorrow, for example, he might rally.'

'Can I at least give Harriet a little tour of the clinic?' Boyd asked. 'I've known her since we were kids.'

Harriet swallowed as she considered quitting. Gethin would understand, she thought.

Dr Stockton looked at his watch. 'There's literally nothing of interest. Kennedy Jones is our *only* patient.'

Decide, decide, Harriet told herself.

'Yes, at the moment,' Boyd said, with astonished enthusiasm, 'but I want to tell her about your grand plans.'

'What plans are those?' Dr Stockton asked, sucking his teeth.

'The amazing facilities for those contemplating paying private – leather Chesterfield sofas, enormous TVs, luxury bathrooms, bespoke online menus prepared by top chefs.' Boyd held his arms aloft and, like a dancer, he began to turn, as though manifesting everything into life. 'I'm sure she'd love to see the showroom.'

'And I need the ladies,' Harriet cut in, seeing Dr Stockton had reached the point where he would have agreed to anything to shut Boyd up.

'What ladies?' Dr Stockton said.

'The ladies' toilets,' Harriet clarified.

'Oh, Boyd will show you. Ten minutes,' he said to Boyd, heading for the door. 'Then please show our guest out and get back to work. I'm sorry you've come all this way for nothing, Miss Erskine.'

After Dr Stockton left, Boyd moved closer.

'Where's Gethin? We need a third man, at least.'

'Change of plan,' Harriet said.

'I'll sneak you in to see Kennedy,' he said. 'Once we're done, head for the basement. There's a fire exit from the mortuary out into the street. If you give me your locker code, I'll put your stuff down there ready. There are cameras all over, so you haven't got long. If you get caught, say you got lost. If they find us in Kennedy's room, I'll say you nagged me into it because you're a Welsh rugby fan.'

Harriet wiped her brow. She'd made it this far, she had to see it through.

Kennedy's suite was dominated by the huge bed.

Seeing the former international player lying there, Harriet recalled some footage she'd seen time and again on YouTube: Kennedy running through the Dragon's Mouth at the Principality Stadium, rugby boots clacking on concrete, breath evaporating in the cold. A great, Welsh sporting-soldier, bounding into battle for Wales, bursting onto the pitch through poppy-red pyro smoke.

How pale he looked now, with grey smudges under his eyes. And how strange that life had brought her here to try and help this giant. He snored with a light, restless rasp that made her wonder if he had a mild chest infection.

Reaching out, she touched his warm dry hand, fingers curled inwards.

'Kennedy,' she whispered. 'Kennedy?'

The snoring remained consistent.

'You won't wake him,' Boyd said, standing back.

Harriet took Kennedy by the shoulders and swore under her breath at herself. Had she honestly thought that she might bundle him into a wheelchair and rush him to safety? Who was she kidding? She'd struggle to lift one arm. In film and television, they made this kind of thing look so easy.

The hoist appeared too complicated to try, given there would be no second chances. Even if they managed to get him into it, they'd probably drop him on the floor.

Boyd stood back, allowing her to form her own conclusions, rather than pointing out the obvious.

Tender compassion for the rugby player flooded through her.

'Kennedy. Please wake up. It's Harriet, from Eiriol Law.'

His eyelids flickered.

'See what I mean?' Boyd said.

'It's Harriet. Rowan's assistant. Please wake up. I've spoken to Danielle, your fiancée. The news stories about her in the press were planted. She's been sending you letters and emails every day. Your family want you home, in Wales. The WRU want you home. These people, they don't care about you. They're using you, Kennedy. It's politics. Can you hear me? We have to get you out of here. We've got to get you safely back to your family in Wales.'

Kennedy opened his blue eyes a millimetre or two, his lids fluttering. Boyd was wrong: his patient was waking up. Then his eyes closed and Kennedy's snoring recommenced.

Harriet was considering what they should do next when they heard the distant ping of a lift.

Boyd quickly ushered her out the door and followed. They shot into the room next door using Boyd's keycard as multiple hurried footsteps echoed in the corridor.

They heard voices and then the sound of people entering Kennedy's adjacent room.

Harriet and Boyd pressed their ears to the wall. Harriet was shocked to recognise Nigel Tudor. What was *he* doing here?

'Let's not panic. When we find her,' Nigel said, 'we'll make use of her.'

'We can still use the angle,' Augusta said in her New York brogue, 'that Kennedy was utterly desperate for a way out and they struck a deal.'

'You'll arrange a transfer?' Dr Stockton said.

Harriet and Boyd exchanged a stricken glance that Kennedy might be moved somewhere they couldn't reach him.

'It's all taken care of,' Nigel said.

'You've got to get out of here,' Boyd hissed.

Chapter 40

Kennedy Jones

The brightness of their laptops and tablet screens were reflected in the journalists' reading glasses. Maybe it's your new drugs, but their lenses transform them into CGI zombies and robots – eyewear glowing blue-white or green with optical VDU filters. This creeps you out, is the truth of it.

'The BBC are team-handed as usual,' Augusta's head of press says, nodding as she points people out. 'You've got the health correspondent, the political correspondence, news correspondent, sports correspondent and the network guy. The woman over there checking her phone works for the BBC online division. This story literally straddles all divisions.'

You wonder about the huddle of journalists across two rows of seats, collectively leaning in when one of them whispers something.

'The nationals,' Augusta explains. 'You watch. They'll get together afterwards to discuss the line they'll all take. And at the back you've got freelancers and local press.'

You study the faces. Two women at the back, in particular, catch your eye. A lady with a shaved head and gold cross studs in her ears has the air of sitting above the conference, like a senior lecturer auditing a colleague's class.

Next to her, a young woman plays with blonde ombre braids, the ends of which perfectly matched her cream polo neck, and sheepskin and corduroy coat. Together, they radiate hostility, which surprises you, until you realise that they probably represent the religious and pro-life press.

Nicholas Etheridge reads out his statement and, as rehearsed, you answer two brief, prepared questions. Then it's over.

For the journalists, it's only beginning.

'How can you possibly justify doctors executing patients?' the woman with cream braids shouts, looking at Augusta. 'And what about unscrupulous doctors when this 'service' isn't going to be free?'

Standing up, the woman with the shaved head tries to wave down the other questions, many about your rugby career. 'You cannot destroy a life without asserting dominion over God,' she yells. 'The church holds that life is the property of God and destroying that property is an attack on His name. What do you say to that?'

Your brain pounds with a chorus of airhorns again.

Other reporters groan. Their questions get louder to drown out the two women.

Eventually, the press accept it's over. Augusta and Lori prepare to move you out of the room and the futility of the exercise begins to affect the various groups. You can see them strategising how else they might get more information. Who, in the room, might give more later. They exchange whispers, reach for their coats, and close their notepads and laptops. The reading glasses are put away and the eyes become human again.

An hour after your press conference, the messages flood in – more messages than you received during the British & Irish Lions' Tour. Social media blows up. Augusta hires extra PR and media support to deal with the interview requests alone.

You'd sent personalised messages to your close family and friends in advance, but now they're clamouring to speak to you too, to find out if you're all right. Augusta and Dr Stockton deal with them personally, saying you need complete rest.

Two days later, Lori shakes letters from the first of three postbags onto the bed. You're surprised, but then it makes sense. The older generation trust pen and paper. You imagine them watching you on television, then struggling up out of their armchairs, crossing to the bureau or the drawer and pulling out their writing sheets and a pen.

All envelopes, most written in juddery Biro, without the full postal address, have been pre-sliced with a letter opener.

Lori slips out the contents and reads, paraphrasing many. The letters are returned afterwards to their original envelopes and are set aside in neat piles. The cards are paraded on your shelves. Afternity staff will reply later, on your behalf.

The letters and cards are all positive, not a single note from angry religious folk or people who take the opposite line. Afternity have obviously screened them.

Just as Augusta promised, you're inundated with people sharing their stories. You had no idea the scale of the problem. It's an audit of suffering. Your eyes are open. You're getting publicity for them, for all of them.

Change *must* come.

Augusta stops by and runs her hands along the lines of cards, picks one up and reads. Lori stops sorting the mail and watches.

'We're going to change the world,' Augusta says, in a soothing voice, putting the card back and picking up another. 'Afternity has the answer for end-of-life uncertainty, the unnecessary pain and suffering. We're going to disrupt and force positive change. It will be a beautiful thing. British society will never go back. Mahatma Gandhi said a civilisation is measured by how it treats its weakest members. We dump the elderly and terminally ill in care homes and hospices, dose them with morphine and let nature take its barbarically slow, impersonal course. History will judge what we're doing here and wonder why it took us so long. We're offering dignified emancipation from suffering.'

As if bestowing a blessing, Augusta crosses the room and places a hand on Lori's shoulder. Then she looks at her watch and leaves.

Lori shrugs and smiles at you.

'Only five more letters and we've finished this sack,' she says, continuing to read.

The letters are short, full of sympathy and solidarity.

There's something else you're listening for. Have they seen you on the news?

Your birth mum, the story goes, abandoned you in Merthyr.

She was Welsh at least.

For years, you hoped your real dad had been a professional rugby player sowing his wild oats in the Valleys towns.

Always, you were looking for a face in the crowd, on the coaching staff, on the bench, or in the history books – a face that looks like yours.

And then this nightmare, something no parent would want and certainly not your loving, adoptive family.

Stockton agrees you're doing the right thing not tracking your biological parents down at this point. There are always loose ends, he says, and it's best to make peace with this.

Maybe one day they'll learn about their son's journey. Maybe you'll still make them proud, the way you made your adoptive parents proud.

Lori shakes another load of mail onto the bed. She gathers it in a pile and opens the first, a creased envelope addressed by an unsteady hand. The contents will be emotional, is the truth of it.

'Ready?' she asks.

Chapter 41

A quilted-canvas liner protected the lift walls from bumps and scratches, with a plastic cut-out giving access to the elevator buttons. The grubbiness of the buff-coloured shielding fabric suggested it served its purpose, preventing dents and scratches, but it felt more to Harriet like a moving padded cell.

Her dry tongue stuck to the roof of her mouth and she found it hard to swallow. She'd made a dreadful mistake and underestimated the situation. Where the hell was Gethin?

The lift, at basement level, opened to a small corridor where a door with a glass porthole showed nothing but darkness beyond. Drawing nearer, a couple of green exit lights cast a ghoulish glow across the room beyond.

The cold hit her the minute she entered, as did the whirr of refrigerator fans.

To her right was an office, also in semi-darkness, with a large window overlooking the sterile mortuary.

Harriet took in the pristine gurneys and the wall of cadaver coolers. Goosebumps tracked across her shoulders, upper arms and back. To get back home, she'd need her things from the Bisley locker. For now, she had no Gethin, no bag or phone, and no Boyd Evans.

Thinking she could wait for Boyd in the street, Harriet rattled the bar of the fire escape door, but it wouldn't budge.

Harriet looked around the mortuary. One of the cadaver drawers hadn't quite closed to the full horizontal position. She recalled what Boyd had said about someone being down there. Curious, she pulled down the drawer and found herself looking at a sheet-covered body.

'Oh my God,' Harriet said, slamming the drawer shut.

It took her a full minute to compose herself sufficiently to take another look and establish the identity of the mortuary's sole resident.

When she did, she gasped. Rowan Tudor lay naked underneath the cloth, eyes closed and looking like a Madam Tussaud's waxwork. With the exception of his missing finger, there wasn't a mark on him.

'Rowan,' she whispered.

Nigel wouldn't have his own son euthanised, she thought.

How long had Rowan remained in hiding before Augusta had really had him killed, Harriet wondered? Had he watched the search? The news reports? Or had Augusta given him a lethal dose the minute he'd agreed to lose a finger to the greater cause.

'Speak to me, Rowan,' Harriet whispered. 'Tell me what happened. Did you fake your own death first?'

Harriet's thoughts went back to the day of the tequila bottle. Rowan's surprise at the gift still struck her as real and authentic. Perhaps it *had* been spiked. Augusta, perhaps, hadn't trusted him to stick to their plan.

She remembered Nigel's plangent insistence on a DNA test – and how controlled and determined he'd appeared.

'He doesn't know, does he?' she whispered. 'He thinks you're out there somewhere. Nigel's still expecting you to make contact.'

When the fluorescent lights flickered into life, Harriet froze, knowing that Boyd wouldn't have announced himself in such a way.

'If you're talking about Nigel, no, he doesn't,' Augusta said, walking into the mortuary. The grey glint in her hand could have been another piece of medical equipment from one of the mortuary's many metal drawers and cabinets, but as Harriet's gaze focused, she could see the other woman was holding a small, pearl-handled gun.

Apart from an air rifle some teenage boy had once brought into the pub to show off, she'd never seen a gun in real life.

Experiencing the same kick of fear she had at Cardiff Market, Harriet desperately tried to piece things together. She'd let her guard down. *Stupid, stupid, stupid.*

"I thought we were being burgled,' Augusta said. She was holding the gun out sideways, her palm flat. 'There's a lot of significant intellectual property in this company that our competitors would *love* to get their hands on. Breaking into our basement is as good a way in as any.'

'Why?' Harriet asked her. 'Why take the trouble of faking Rowan's death only to actually kill him? And why keep his body here?'

Augusta ran a hand through her auburn hair and fastened the clasps of her fur gilet over her silk blouse, shielding against the clinical coldness.

She gave a little laugh. 'Did he try it on with you?'

Harriet didn't respond. Harassment, however unpleasant, featured lower than murder on the criminal scale, but she knew better than to articulate that to an American brandishing a firearm.

'He did, didn't he? Which means a part of you must be pleased he's dead?'

'Sure,' Harriet said, 'I don't miss the guy, but it wasn't all the time. I was dealing with it in my own way.'

'Oh, come on now!' Augusta said. 'You Brits are always so diplomatic.'

'I've already figured out your business model,' Harriet said. 'I just don't understand why Rowan had to die and why Kennedy has to be next.'

'Oh, I think you do,' Augusta said, gesturing towards Rowan's body with a sardonic smile.

'Rowan loved you,' Harriet said, although the idea anyone could admire such a cold, calculating murderer was beyond her. Yes, Augusta was beautiful, but there was a predatory hunger in her ice-blue eyes.

'My goodness, I'm starting to think *you* loved him. What a cliché! Did you harbour thoughts of shagging the boss? Or marrying him?'

Harriet ignored Augusta's provocation. 'I think he did, you know.'

'Whatever *love* is,' Augusta said. 'He told me he'd take on Kennedy Jones as a client if I met him at L'Escargot, on Greek Street. Did he ever take you there?'

'No,' Harriet said, thinking it a strange, irrelevant question.

'Rather than eat in the main restaurant, he'd booked us a private room. It was so over the top. It felt as if we were dining in the Jane

Austen Museum, although not, it has to be said,' Augusta said, pointing at Rowan, 'with Mr Darcy.'

Harriet knew where this was going. Rowan had fallen for a psychopath masquerading as a visionary.

'His goddamned flirting reminded me of plane turbulence – one minute flattering, one minute teasingly insulting, one minute deferring, the next demeaning. And he didn't want the meal to *end*. He showed off with the wine list, ordering Château Batailley. He spilled lobster bisque on his tie, which he tried to clean at the table by dipping his napkin into his waterglass and giving it a spot clean. You can literally see it, can't you?'

Augusta broke into a screeching, overblown laugh that made Harriet think Rowan wasn't the only one with a taste for cocaine.

If Rowan had thought of himself as Hugh Grant, Harriet thought, imagining the scene, he'd been dangerously mistaken.

'So, you killed the guy because of his poor table manners?' Harriet said. 'Watch out humanity!'

'Oh, that was just the start,' Augusta said. 'I escaped and, what do you know, the next thing he's leaving me messages accusing me of *using* him. Begging me for another chance. When I refused, he got angry. What kind of games was I playing? Was I sleeping with that "fucking idiot, Etheridge?". Rowan threatened to ruin everything. He literally threatened to walk straight into the offices of *The Daily Mail*. He should have known I don't respond well to blackmail.'

'So, you came up with your plan,' Harriet said.

'I told Nigel an investigative journalist was onto Rowan and we needed him to fake his death and get out of the country – or we'd all end up in prison. Nigel believed it. Rowan thought we could reunite in New York and run Afternity from there.'

'He wasn't murdered,' Augusta continued, shaking her head. 'The original plan was to make a believable cast of his finger, but it was amateurish. The fake finger literally wouldn't have fooled anyone, so we had to go take more drastic steps. Unfortunately, a medical blunder with the anaesthetic when we took his finger meant he never came round.'

Harriet didn't believe a word.

'But let me explain the wider picture,' Augusta said. 'The UK has an epidemic of suffering. Life doesn't have to be this inhumane – a world of people stoically enduring pain. I'm challenging this country's archaic attitude to assisted suicide. Centuries of Christian claptrap have brought us here: the terminally ill suffering agonies in the name of grace and salvation. It's downright philistine.'

'Sounds really noble,' Harriet said, her eyes fixed on Rowan.

'I'm a figurehead for women in business', Augusta said, lifting the gun. 'I was not about to let a man like that threaten everything I'd built.'

'But why not bury him,' Harriet said. 'It's a little weird, isn't it, keeping him around? Or is it to hurt Nigel? Or blackmail him if he also becomes a problem?'

'You misunderstand. We're doing a beautiful thing here. We're changing the world. If you don't agree with it, you don't have to use us, but don't deny others the right to a beautiful, carefully curated death.'

'I was talking about Rowan,' Harriet said.

'And, in a way, I gave you an answer. He's staying there because I'm too busy dealing with societal change to think about him. The man is literally an afterthought.'

'But Nigel thinks he's alive?'

'What do you care? Why do I sense working-class gratitude towards Nigel Tudor? It's the working class we're setting this up for. The hundreds and thousands of suffering elders, lingering on for decades in poverty. It's their children I feel sorry for. For a paltry £16,000 fee, we can relieve everyone's burden. It's a very moving process. Very clean.'

'Yeah, nothing says clean like killing grandparents,' Harriet said.

Augusta waved the gun as though dispersing Harriet's sarcasm into the air like cigarette smoke. 'It is clean. Everyone says their goodbyes together. It's very beautiful. It's a beautiful moment. Otherwise, any inheritance is squandered on nurses and care homes. The old folks don't want that either. They don't *want* to be a burden.

Everyone says their goodbyes together. And talking of goodbyes ...'

Augusta stepped forward with the barrel of the gun facing Harriet, before bringing the butt down on Harriet's head. She hit her a second time. Harriet fell to her knees with a muffled 'oh'.

She felt little pain at first, just a hot sense of buzzing and swelling at her temple and a wet trickle creeping around her left eye and down her cheek. While Augusta rifled through the metal drawers, Harriet crawled slowly towards the door. Like a bomb on a timer, her head was starting to throb just as she felt a sharp scratch to her upper arm.

Numbness spread throughout her body, with a cold, uncomfortable itching sensation. Brain fog followed. The reflected light, bouncing off the grey polished vinyl flooring, shone brighter and brighter. Then it went dark.

Chapter 42

Someone was repeating her name, insistent and concerned. Feeling groggy, Harriet groaned and tried to sleep.

Harriet. Harriet!

Nigel's voice.

Had she fallen asleep in work? Her neck ached as though she'd slept at her desk. When she moved her head, liquid pain sloshed around. Her brain felt like the inside of Karen's souvenir snow globe, but with shards of glass instead of glitter. There was something important, but she'd have to come back to it later.

Thinking of work set a chain of small thoughts in motion, like a marble rolling through a marble run. Her workplace reminded her of Rowan, which reminded her of Kennedy Jones, which reminded her of Boyd and Gethin and Augusta.

Harriet squinted and blinked at the light until the blob of shadow came into focus. She looked around and wriggled her fingers and toes, checking her limbs were still there.

'Where's Kennedy Jones?' she said, emotion cracking in a parched throat. Even speaking unsettled the delicate snow globe of her skull.

The room was beige and bare. She was lying on a bed without restraints. Nigel sat next to her in a tall-backed chair, like a concerned relative. Across from him was another chair, still plastic wrapped. A roll of new carpet lay against the freshly painted skirting.

'I'm sorry Augusta struck you. She was scared.'

'*She* was scared,' Harriet said. She cleared her throat and Nigel handed her a plastic cup of water. Harriet couldn't imagine Augusta scared of anything. 'What did she give me?'

'Nothing. A regular over-the-counter painkiller. You've had a couple of stitches. There shouldn't be a scar.'

The weirdness of the situation rendered Harriet mute. She'd been given something a lot stronger than paracetamol.

'Let me tell you my story,' Nigel said. 'There was a time when I used to threaten to sack anyone discussing it at work, but context is important. Maybe then, you'll understand. Perhaps once you've heard what I have to say, we can come to an agreement, you and I?'

'What sort of agreement?'

'A truce, of sorts. You wanted to be a legal exec. We could give you enough money to study law at any university you like, debt free. Mentoring too. You could stay at Eiriol Law, which we'd very much like, or you'd be free to work at any other firm. Entirely up to you. Or, if you wanted to work for Afternity in some high-end administrative role, that could be arranged. Are you willing to listen?'

Harriet rubbed her eyes. How long had she been unconscious?

The fact that Nigel hadn't mentioned her or Carwyn's subversive activities worried her. He couldn't trust her to keep Afternity's secret and he knew it.

'Will you give me time to explain?' Nigel said. 'Then we can talk over everything else.'

Harriet, eyes on the door, feared Nigel's company might be a stall for time while they killed Kennedy and framed her for it.

'Go on,' she said, resigned.

Nigel looked towards the window. Grey light and faraway thoughts clouded his eyes.

'When I was a law student at York, in my second year, I lived in a shared house. One of my housemates – an unkempt fellow, studying archaeology – packed his things in the middle of the night and left without paying his share of the rent. The rest of us had to chip in and cover it, so we put ads out for a new housemate. Then, one rainy evening, Siriol knocked at the door. An ancient history student in her first year, from north Wales, she'd heard my housemate had skipped town, was looking for a room and wondered if it was still free. It was love at first sight. We were so wrapped up in each other, we almost flunked our courses.'

When Harriet groaned in response to pain, Nigel paused.

'We married straight after university,' he continued, his

expression hardening, foretelling difficulties ahead. 'Had our two boys. Bought our first house in the Vale of Glamorgan. Siriol and I named it Tŷ Newydd.'

'What happened?' Harriet said, realising that Eiriol Law really was an amalgamation of his wife's name and the old Welsh for advocacy.

'A drunk driver ploughed into her Fiesta on the outskirts of St Nicholas. Someone phoned 999 and said they thought they saw a car at the bottom of an embankment off Duffryn Lane. Not one police officer followed it up. I found her myself the next morning.'

That Harriet had never heard the story proved that Nigel's punitive warnings to his staff had worked.

'I'm sorry,' Harriet said, imagining Siriol hadn't survived.

'It was like a miracle when I found a faint pulse, but my beautiful girl never recovered from the traumatic brain injury. Her personality changed. She needed round-the-clock care. She didn't want to live but went on doing so. She begged me constantly to end her suffering.'

Nigel's eyes filled with tears. His involvement with Afternity, putting his career and reputation at risk, finally made sense.

'And you helped her?'

Nigel dropped his head and blew out a tremulous sigh.

'No, I couldn't, God help me. I just couldn't do it. She called me selfish and I was. I couldn't let her go, wanted her with me, hoping for a miracle. I knew she would find a way somehow and one day she did. She died of an overdose.'

'I'm so sorry.' There was nothing more Harriet could say. He'd explained himself, but it made no difference. Only by stopping things going any further could he redeem himself.

Nigel wiped his tear-filled eyes and composed himself.

'The police questioned me over a fourteen-week period over whether I assisted her suicide. *Fourteen weeks*. You know how much time they spent finding the drunk driver? *Zero*. The lack of CCTV made the task impossible, apparently.'

'And that's why you made a career out of suing the police.'

'The first case I brought against the police was my own. But you and your family saw how nothing had changed when it came to Roddy

Roberts. He was innocently helping you with your homework, right?'

'My A level maths revision.'

'Right. And some thick-necked moron thinks he's showing off. On his way home, Roddy is stabbed. Everyone's life changes. And yet, no arrests are made. What we're doing here is hardly the crime of the century. Politicians are failing us. The NHS is failing us. The police are failing us. So, let's do things differently. Augusta has some wonderful ideas. She's a visionary. She planned all this in her first year at Harvard.'

Oh my God, Harriet thought, filled with disgust. Nigel's eyes had shone with tears talking about his wife, but how they sparkled when he mentioned Augusta. A terrible thought occurred to Harriet. Had Nigel been happy to go along with Augusta's plan to get Rowan out the country because he harboured hopes of embarking on his own relationship with her?

'Oh, I see,' she said, propping herself up and forming a heart with her thumbs and index fingers.

'Don't be so ridiculous. I'll never get over what happened to my wonderful Siriol. My boys, Rowan and Leighton, grew up doing their homework and eating their evening meal in daddy's office. They spent summer holidays being entertained by my secretary, Clare. I never thought they'd go into law, with my bringing them to work before and after school. Even though they hated it, it affected them. That's why I'm passionate and committed about Afternity being a success. So's Rowan.'

'He was passionate and committed, past tense,' Harriet said.

'I agree.'

'He's dead, Nigel.'

'You don't have to tell me. I'm the one who failed to get the ransom delivered.'

'I mean *really*. Not faking it. Not drinking cocktails on a beach somewhere under another name. Dead-dead. He's in the mortuary in the basement. And you might just have a thing for your son's killer.'

Nigel's expression turned dark, brooding.

'Who told you such nonsense?' he demanded. 'You just settled on these absurd facts and came straight here from Cardiff?'

'He's in the mortuary – in the basement. Go and look for yourself. That's where Augusta confronted me.'

'You're a cunning little liar – one unforgivably malicious little bitch,' he said, grinding out the words.

Nigel bunched his hands into fists; he looked like he wanted to punch her. His barrister's wig hair trembled. He took a step forward, breathing noisily through his nose. Though Harriet shrank back, she'd seen such theatrics in The Poet's enough times to know impotent rage when she saw it.

He was, she thought, like the elderly victim of a sophisticated scammer, still caught up in the hustle, denying he'd fallen for a con.

'He's not coming back,' she said. 'He's never coming back, Nigel.'

Nigel left the room without another word. The door swung closed, but the lock failed to engage.

Harriet, sluggish and weighed down with whatever sedative they'd given her, attempted to pull herself off the bed. The medical fog was lifting, but she was cold, hungry and unsteady on her feet.

Gripping the doorframe, she tried to shake herself out of her lethargy. She wasn't leaving without Kennedy Jones.

Chapter 43

Kennedy Jones

Game over, dad waits for you in the place he's always parked during home games or under 18s Cardiff Blues training: in the compound of Cardiff Arms Park. A sharp west wind blows through the hoardings that separate the stadium from the Riverwalk and the Taff. It shakes the tarp, howls through the tunnel and whips the corrugated iron until it groans.

He parks there because it's near the stand he likes best – block 11, north, always quieter. If there are too many kids, he'll move again. It's the evangelical rugby parents he avoids most, the way some of them, with hands raised heavenward, eyes brimming with passion and fury, scream abuse at children and coaches to exorcise them from imperfect play.

Dad will yawn or stretch as you exit the Wendy House, otherwise known as changing rooms three and four, joshing with your friends and juggling your open kit bag and a polystyrene tray of pasta and meatballs, or curry and rice.

The engine is off because he knows you'll have forgotten something. When he runs through the list of things you should have with you, you'll remember what you've left behind. Throwing your bag in the boot of the red Fiesta, you'll leave your food on the front seat and offer him the garlic bread or the poppadom.

So, back you go, often limping as your joints stiffen after all the on-field exertion, to changing room 3, scuffing in your sliders and socks to recover your overlooked gumshield or your water bottle. The coaches depart with netting-sacks of balls, tackle bags and coloured cones.

The changing rooms are empty now save for the Lynx spray and tiger balm hanging in the air and line-out, lifting tape littering the floor. You'll reunite with your lost property and wonder how you missed it in the first place.

At the Taff end, you'll pause at the north-west corner and survey the empty pitch.

Echoes of old training sessions come to you: *Don't start backing off ... Get low ... Make space in here ... Quick as you can so we can fit in more reps ... Yes, turn square ... As soon as we're going, we've all got to go. Yeah? ... And now play, play, play. Let's go.*

The stands are cleared of fans. Only the cleaner remains, bent over his clear plastic bag, pecking the ground with his litter stick. Gulls glide down to the grandstands. A single steward, in a size-large neon orange coat, gathers up the line flags from pitch-side. The astroturf has a faint shimmer until the floodlights are extinguished.

Then, only the lights from the clubhouse and the south lateral tunnel illuminate the players and fans leaving through the courtyard still.

The vanished crowd and the sigh of the wind off the river give you a shiver of pleasure. It's in that moment of reflection that you were never more alive to your adoptive family, life, the sport of rugby, to your fellow humans, the history of the club and your myriad dreams for the future. It's an athletic afterglow, is the truth of it.

Dad parps the horn and you turn and smile. He's always been there for you. You couldn't have asked for better.

You didn't expect this to be the moment, but it all makes sense. Your adoptive dad is here for you, waiting where the dark-green Taff flows past the Arms Park and the clubhouse lights catch the white breast of a gull as it lands on the crossbar of the rugby post and shakes out its wings.

Chapter 44

The door to Kennedy's room stood ajar. When Harriet crept in, it was like intruding on a deathbed confessional. In the dim glow of a standard lamp, offsetting the gathering storm outside where rain ticked at the window, the arrangement of figures had a theatrical lean, as though posed for painting by a modern Caravaggio.

Dr Stockton, set on a course of action, broke the spell by snapping on a pair of blue gloves.

'Ah, good of you to join us, Harriet,' Augusta said.

'Whatever you're doing to him – or about to do – stop it. This isn't happening,' Harriet said, bluffing. 'The emergency services are on their way.'

'Who are you?' Kennedy asked, weary sadness etched on his face. 'What's going on here?'

Harriet hadn't expected to find Kennedy lucid. She crossed the room to join him at his bedside.

'This is Rowan's assistant Harriet,' Augusta said.

Running footsteps in the corridor became louder and Nigel burst in. He took one, deliberate step in and shut the door behind him.

'Nigel,' Augusta said, waving a hand at Harriet. 'I thought you were dealing with the situation?'

'It's okay,' Dr Stockton said, his gaze fixed on the needle point of a syringe. 'She's here now.'

'Explain this,' Nigel roared, crossing the room and thrusting his phone screen at Augusta. 'Is that or is that not a picture of my dead son?'

Augusta pushed Nigel's phone away. Distracted by the drama, Harriet was too late to react as Dr Stockton turned Kennedy's arm upwards and administered an injection into a vein. Harriet, assuming it a lethal cocktail, let out a scream of reproach.

'What have you given him?' she cried, held back from cradling Kennedy's arm by Augusta.

'A mild sedative,' Stockton said, shoving Harriet so hard she almost lost her balance over a chair. 'All this fuss will cause him distress. Did you think I was going to euthanise him? That's still illegal – for now.'

'What's going on?' Kennedy asked, sleepily.

'Kennedy,' Harriet said, fighting everyone off and holding the side rails of his hospital bed, 'before you decide anything, you need to see your family. Augusta lied to you. Lied to your family too.'

The lack of concern or any response at all from Augusta and Stockton undermined her case. Harriet would have preferred to be met with anger and objection. Her desperation made her unconvincing.

'Poor Harriet was in love with her boss,' Augusta said, going to Kennedy's bedside, leaning over him while Dr Stockton took the initiative and held Harriet. 'She hasn't taken his death at all well. It's terribly sad. Really, tragic. She did a little work on your case and has developed an unhealthy fixation on his clients. Nigel can tell you all about it. She doesn't even work at Eiriol Law any longer.'

Then, without warning, Kennedy moved two fingers, just enough to brush against Augusta's arm. She froze, her astonishment clearly evident, before she pulled back.

'How ...?' Augusta whispered.

'Not a miracle,' Kennedy said. 'Let's call it a little medical counter-experiment. You told me, Stockton, that my recovery had *plateaued*.'

'Kennedy, I can't stress how dangerous it is,' Dr Stockton said, turning to Augusta for an explanation. 'If someone's been messing around with your medication. Where's Lori? Someone find that girl.'

'It's a curiosity,' Kennedy said, with sarcasm, though his words were developing a sleepy slur. 'You want to write this down, Stockton. Patient, on certain days, is clear headed, no longer feels sick or depressed, and has recovered a little unexpected movement in his left hand.'

'There can be dangerous false positive results,' Stockton said. 'What might look like partial recovery can last a day or two, only to be replaced with agonising spasticity and debilitating cramps. The Nursing Council will hear about this.'

Kennedy's head tipped back as though he were considering the situation. Tears of exhaustion seeped from the corners of his eyes. He gave out a relaxed nasal sigh as his head hit the pillow and his arm dropped back onto the covers. His wet eyelids fluttered briefly before closing, then gradually his breathing became deep and regular.

'Did you honestly both think I wouldn't find out?' Nigel said, raising his voice again, so Augusta would focus on his plight rather than their drugged patient.

'We had no choice,' Augusta said.

'What was wrong with our original plan?'

'For God's sake, Nigel,' Dr Stockton said. 'Your princeling son was threatening to go the press if Augusta didn't have sex with him. You knew what he was like and you turned a blind eye.'

'You killed my son just because he made a drunken come on? He wouldn't have meant it. He was always making passes at this one.'

'Hang on a minute,' Harriet said.

'No, *you* hang on,' Nigel said turning on her, spit flecking his lips, eyes wild. 'I have a real animus towards people who, from some bottom-rung job, are narcissistic enough to believe that *anyone* is interested in their uneducated, ill-informed and uninvited opinions.'

'Your son's unpredictable behaviour threatened to derail the whole operation,' Augusta said. 'I wanted to find a more palatable way to present it to you, granted. A mugging in America, perhaps. Something like that. It wasn't my intention for you to find out like this.'

'How did he die?'

'He didn't suffer, Nigel. He didn't. He had a bad reaction to the anaesthetic. Can we move on now, or do you need to take a moment?'

Hesitating by the door, uncertain, Nigel looked at Harriet, then Kennedy.

‘We’ve come too far to back out now,’ Augusta warned. ‘If you can’t control yourself, you’d be better off staying out of the way, in my office.’

‘Nigel, please,’ Harriet said, pulling on his arm and gesturing to Stockton, who lifted Kennedy’s eyelids in turn with his thumb to check his state of consciousness. ‘Please stop this. It’s madness. None of you will get away with what you’re doing.’

Nigel shrugged her off and turned away. Harriet sensed he knew what was coming next and had no desire to watch.

Stockton turned Kennedy’s arms so both his pale, blue-veined wrists were exposed. In a cruel, flicking motion, the doctor sliced at each in turn with a scalpel.

Harriet screamed at the horror of what was unfolding in front of her. Nigel tried to grab her, but she bit him. The doctor lifted the knife, about to wound Kennedy for a second time when she rushed forward and seized the blade from his grasp. Dr Stockton allowed her to take it with minimal resistance.

‘Back off,’ she said, brandishing the glinting knife.

‘Thank you, Nigel,’ Augusta said, leaving Kennedy’s bedside and walking over to him. ‘Glad to see you’re back on Team Afternity.’

Harriet tried, ineffectually, to lift Kennedy’s wrists as high as she could while applying pressure using the bedclothes as bandages, but found it impossible to keep tight hold of the knife at the same time. Dr Stockton carefully extracted it from her with his gloved hands.

Too late, she thought of her fingerprints on it.

The blood flow from Kennedy’s wrists wasn’t as severe as she’d feared. She hoped that meant the wounds were superficial.

Though covered in Kennedy’s blood, her amateur first-aid efforts seemed to be working. It took her a second to realise her new predicament.

She couldn’t let go of Kennedy.

‘Here’s where you come in,’ Augusta said to Harriet, sitting on Kennedy’s bed by his feet. ‘Let’s start with the fact that *your* prints are now on the knife and you’re the one stopping Kennedy from bleeding to death. We were going to say that Boyd Evans, paid to kill

Kennedy, botched it, then killed himself in desperation. But Boyd is no longer in the picture.'

'What does that mean?' Harriet said, her forearms beginning to shake and her hands aching with the effort of staunching Kennedy's blood. In the drama, she'd forgotten Boyd entirely.

'So now *you* took money to kill Kennedy Jones. The money's in your account. Boyd heroically died trying to defend his patient from you.'

'You killed Boyd?' Harriet said, thinking of the bright and radiant nurse and all he'd had to offer future patients.

Augusta kneeled to retrieve something from beside Kennedy's bed. When she stood up, she cupped Boyd's gold nurse's watch in the palm of her hand, which she tilted this way and that to catch the light. After wiping it with great care, Augusta put it in her pocket.

Continuing to apply pressure to Kennedy's wrists, Harriet prayed for a miracle.

'Or,' Augusta said, 'there's an alternative – let's call it Plan C. We wipe your prints and stem Kennedy's bleeding. Help him recover. Leave the money in your account. Blame everything on Boyd. You go back to Wales. Afternity gets the green light. We give you a cash top up. Do what you like with it. Go to university.'

'Harriet,' Nigel said. 'Don't be naïve. You don't survive Plan A and B. The only plan you walk away under is C.'

'Don't take too long to decide,' Augusta said, confident. 'Kennedy Jones' life blood is ebbing away.'

Stockton wheeled over a metal table and began to assemble bandages and a surgical kit to sew and dress Kennedy's wounds. He laid them out, then waited for Harriet's decision.

'If I agree,' Harriet said, 'you'll become the UK equivalent of Dignitas? You get to provide end of life care to the terminally ill of Britain?'

'That's right.'

'For £16,000 per patient?'

'That's the starting point. We'll offer different packages: bronze, silver, gold. Once that's achieved, we can look at the wider privatisation of health care.'

'Aneurin Bevan would turn in his grave,' Harriet said, looking at Nigel, who rolled his eyes. 'My answer's no. I'm not having any involvement in your angel of death agenda. The police will never believe I killed anyone.'

'I wasn't expecting that,' Augusta said, looking mildly amused. 'But it's your choice.'

'Harriet,' Nigel said, 'I know you don't think there's enough evidence, but we were also at work, behind the scenes, from the very beginning. The small amount of billing done on the Kennedy Jones assisted dying judicial review file was done by you. Rowan barely touched it. You pushed it on my son and you blackmailed your way into sharing a room with him. And there's the debt you're in, as well as the recent transfer of funds from Kennedy Jones' account into yours. Your fingerprints are all over this. And now you're here, in the clinic. You came voluntarily. I'm sure we can find witnesses who will attest you travelled here of your own free will.'

They'd capitalised on Harriet's blind faith and ambition. The choice they were offering her were the only options left: join them or spend the next few years defending a murder charge. And yet the latter still presented as more palatable than they'd anticipated, because she couldn't leave Kennedy Jones in their care. They'd never let him live, whatever they said. Even if they did, he'd be drugged forever to ensure he was never lucid enough to recall what happened. And she couldn't betray Boyd's name – have him go down in history as the would-be killer nurse who took advantage of Kennedy Jones.

Kennedy's blood began to dry on her arms in sticky streaks of rust-coloured glaze. Harriet had an overwhelming urge to scrub it off with soap and warm water.

I must approach the situation like any legal problem, Harriet thought. She weighed the probability of a murder charge. Best case scenario, someone else might expose the truth about Afternity before her sentencing. Harriet rated the likelihood of that happening as slim. Where were all the investigative journalists and lefty lawyers when you needed them, she wondered?

As Harriet was about to make her position clear, in walked

Rowan, wearing jeans, a crisp cotton shirt, and with a navy, cable cardigan slung over his arm. If the others in the room hadn't reacted with gasps and blanched faces, Harriet would have thought the figure a ghost, a figment of her imagination.

'Dad,' Rowan said, 'What the hell have you got us into?'

'Leighton?' Nigel said, trying to cut his son off at the door. 'What are ... Why?'

'What the hell is going on?'

'Nothing that involves you,' Nigel said. 'You're supposed to be looking after the business.'

Though Leighton looked like his brother, with the same thick brown hair and of a similar height, he was thinner in the face, Harriet observed. And his voice had less London polish.

'I am looking after the business. You're going to ruin everything we've built? For what? For more money? I have to do what's right for the company. We've got clients and employees to think of.'

'Rowan's dead, Leighton,' Harriet volunteered, trying not to cry. 'They've killed a nurse. Now they've hurt Kennedy Jones and they're trying to frame me for it.'

'The police are on their way,' Leighton said, dragging his dad aside, despite the old man's resistance. 'I knew you and Rowan were up to something dodgy, and I didn't want to know. Even when Rowan went missing, I buried myself in my work, but you've been AWOL for days. Clients are complaining. The managing associates can't get hold of you. I needed access to your emails to check what you'd communicated to your clients before vanishing. But, once I was in, I had the shock of my life. I phoned Gethin earlier to find out what he knew.'

'You've called the police?' Nigel said. 'What the hell are you thinking? Do you have any idea how much how much we'll lose?'

'Is that why you're doing this, dad? For money?'

'No, for your mother. For Siriol.'

At the news Leighton had spoken to Gethin, Harriet clutched Kennedy's wrists tighter out of sheer relief that her friend was okay. She'd also stopped the worst of Kennedy's bleeding. With a few positives on her side now, she willed the arrival of the police. A sheen of sweat coated Nigel's face as Leighton squared up to his father. His lips took on a greyish hue and his skin blanched, then he clutched his left arm and sank to the floor.

'Dad?' Leighton shouted. 'Are you alright?'

Sirens, outside, grew louder.

'You're impossible,' Augusta shrieked at Nigel as he writhed, gasping and wincing on the floor. 'You and your family are a bloody menace.'

'I really didn't want to be a part of any of this,' Dr Stockton explained to Leighton, raising his arms and stepping over Nigel, heading for the door.

'It was all Nicholas Etheridge's idea!' Dr Stockton shouted. 'All Nicholas Etheridge – and Augusta Hertz.'

Chapter 45

Kennedy Jones

The streets to the Principality Stadium are arteries to a beating heart on match days. Fans are swept along, towards the great nautical stanchions.

The stadium overwhelms you. You imagine it's the way an old actor feels, returning to a beloved theatre after many years. You feel old and wise, your spirits rekindling.

Applause resounds from the fans you pass on your way to the seat. You'd forgotten how good it feels to be recognised for who you are as a person, not the disability you represent. The emerald grass of the pitch has never smelled so sweet and so earthy, even from this distance. There is a hazy, misty quality from the pyros. The experience is dreamlike.

Danielle panics when your face crumples and tears flood your cheeks, but it's just happiness, gratitude, astonishment.

'Oh, Kennedy,' she says, before wrapping her firm arms around your neck, warming your cold cheek with hers. You both laugh.

Waiting in the corporate box for Harriet and Gethin are bottles of champagne on ice and roses in white, rope-handled gift bags.

Danielle puts her hand in yours and you still can't believe you can feel a flicker of warmth transfer from her hand to yours.

She smiles at you with her big teeth and her kind eyes.

'Come here,' you whisper. 'I want to tell you something.'

She leans in and you plant an awkward kiss on her. She tips her head back and laughs.

Harriet and Gethin arrive.

Tomorrow, you'll be at Cardiff Arms Park for 10am, coaching the visually impaired. In a couple of months, you'll be back at the

Principality Stadium, commentating on the wheelchair rugby competition. Before then, you'll have media and sports commentator training at the BBC.

This summer, you're taking Danielle to the Seychelles, where you'll propose. A photographer will be waiting to capture the moment.

'Come here,' you whisper to her again. 'I want to tell you something.'

Maybe the day will come when you design the end exactly as you want it, but that's a ball kicked far down the field.

The Welsh national anthem begins. It's a crowdfunded moment – everyone gives what they've got to it.

Danielle laughs and presses her forehead to yours. You stop singing for a moment and tell her what you tell yourself every day: life's on an upward trajectory. And that's the truth of it.

Chapter 46

Harriet met Carwyn at Shelley Gardens in Plasnewydd, not far from her flat. The Gardens, once a hangout for gangs, had received council investment, which had transformed it with a basketball court, community garden and kiddies' playpark.

Harriet had brought two apple and cinnamon teas in keep-cups from home. Waiting on a bench, Carwyn sat cross-legged, reading the collected poems of Dylan Thomas.

A solitary father in a flat cap sent his pink-clad toddler down the slide, doing their best to ignore the spring morning wind.

Thanking Harriet, Carwyn took the mug and wrapped his long fingers around it.

'Are you alright?' she asked. 'How's the poetry? Congratulations by the way.'

The Silence of Pauses, having at last found a home, had won two poetry prize awards. The pulping of *Swimming with Sharks*, rather than ruining Carwyn's literary career, earned him a subversive, bad-boy notoriety that garnered the interest of publishers with whom his submissions had long been languishing at the bottom of their slush piles.

'I haven't written much of late,' Carwyn said, prising the lid from the cup and winding the string of the cinnamon and apple teabag around his finger.

The toddler on the slide let out a harrowing play-scream as she glided to the bottom.

'What's up?' Harriet said.

'I don't know,' he replied, his gaze downcast. This was Carwyn's way of getting into a difficult subject. 'I started at this insurance firm in town.'

'You're working?'

'Yeah, I was working part-time for this small press, but they went bust. I got this call centre gig. Didn't have much choice. Cost of living crisis and all that.'

It was difficult for Harriet to imagine Carwyn taking calls about road traffic accidents and no-claim bonuses.

'How long have you been there?'

'Three months,' he sighed and then swore under his breath.

It was his story to tell, but Harriet guessed what was next.

'And?'

'My boss is an absolute arsehole,' Carwyn said. 'Some perma-tanned twat from the Valleys with tattooed eyebrows who thinks he knows it all. I can't do anything right. If I go to the toilet, he accuses me of vaping. He times my breaks and records all my calls. Then he plays them back, criticising every fucking word I say, even though, most of the time, I'm reading off a crib sheet. He's all over me. I tried to transfer to another team, but he blocked it. You'd think he'd be pleased to see me go. What's wrong with this guy?'

'Do you want a pair of listening ears or advice?' Harriet asked him.

'Advice,' he said.

'The only way to change someone else's behaviour is to change your own. That means you'll either have to leave or make a stand, and then accept the consequences. Those consequences might result in you leaving anyway.'

'But it's so fucking unfair,' he said.

'I agree. It is.'

Harriet explained if she'd learned anything it was that you couldn't count on changing a toxic workplace culture by complaining, writing poetry or selling Shakespeare quotes on corporate mugs.

'I'm sorry. I didn't understand how it gets to you,' he said, tapping a finger to his temple. 'This fucking guy is in my head all the time.'

Carwyn put his cup down and took Harriet's hand. The heat lingered in his fingers. Harriet didn't read anything more into the gesture than he needed comfort, a little understanding.

'What are you doing now, workwise?' he asked.

'Phoebe, who runs this recruitment agency, says she's got the perfect job lined up for me, working as a PA in the employment department of a law firm. She knows the two partners I'd be working for. She says they're lovely people.'

'Employment law, huh?' he broke into a reluctant smile.

'Tell me about it,' I said. 'The irony. They won't know about any of this. I'm keeping a low profile.'

'But I thought you were going to work for that private investigator guy.'

'That was the plan, but we're dating. And I have a rule not to date anyone I work with. Always have.'

Carwyn grinned and jogged Harriet with his elbow. 'Oh, it's like that, is it?' he teased.

The truth was more complicated. While Harriet liked Gethin, she couldn't escape the feeling that circumstances had forced them together. The minute she'd trusted him in the centre of the storm, his very presence brought comfort. The awful fear that Marc Munday had caught Gethin in his house and hurt him gave rise to desperate emotions in Harriet. She'd never felt more alone and more in need of Gethin's presence. But was that genuine love or situational dependence? Only a clear run of normal life would let her know for sure.

Right now, they were still caught up in the drama, giving statements, sharing recollections, awaiting the criminal trials of Augusta Hertz, Dr Philip Stockton, the now-disgraced MP Nicholas Etheridge and Marc Munday.

Harriet had listened, astonished, as Gethin had relayed how Munday had indeed arrived back at his house and, out of time to escape, Gethin had taken a seat on the sofa as though calm confrontation had been his plan all along.

Munday, initially furious at the home invasion, calmed down when he recognised his old colleague. A pragmatic man, he explained how he'd resented Gethin's acquittal at first, but had later accepted the wrongness of his own actions at Occupy and during the legal process. After his release from prison, he'd bumped into Nigel who said he'd employed Gethin and had an American friend looking for a security consultant.

The first task for Munday was to provide Augusta with a portfolio of UK-wide human-interest stories that had the potential to be manipulated. She'd asked him to think in 'what-ifs' and outcomes.

Two weeks' later, Munday gave her a list that included a doctor in Bath vehemently speaking out about sub-standard palliative care – and Kennedy Jones.

This was the kind of work he enjoyed, but within weeks he realised Augusta Hertz wanted a whole lot more. The woman was more ruthless, he told Gethin, than any of the guys he'd met in prison.

Munday had come back to the house before dawn to collect a grab bag, intending to hop across to Penarth Marina, jump on his pal's boat and sail off into the sunset. Gethin had let him go. One look at the grim weather forecast told him Marc Munday wouldn't get far.

'I said I'll give Gethin a hand with research if anything interesting comes along,' Harriet said to Carwyn.

'Your resilience is something to behold, Harriet. I'm sorry about *Sharks*,' he said. 'I'm sorry if I made things harder.'

Carwyn sighed and winced, skyward.

'It's so weird,' he said. 'When my supervisor's given me nothing but shit in the morning, how I can't listen to another colleague sitting there, eating crisps morning and afternoon. I have a hard time not ripping the snacks from his hand and throwing them out the window. I hate that fucking guy. Chomp, chomp, chomp. Crunch, crunch, crunch. All day long. I want to bully him.'

'Maybe they're comfort eating because they're stressed. It doesn't sound like a good work environment.'

'Right.' Carwyn thought for a moment. 'Never thought of that.'

'Try and be nice. Kennedy Jones will tell you all about it. His take on all this is that life itself is the biggest contact sport. A smashes into B, who punishes C for the hurt, who makes himself feel better by taking down D. The trick is to resolve things without passing our pain onto others. I think that's good advice.'

Harriet finished her tea and stood. She had to get to the station if she and Gethin were to meet the Bangor train. From her pocket, she drew out a black, velvet box and raised the hinged lid, revealing the precious nurse's brooch. The police had given her permission to return Boyd's property to his mum and dad.

'I'll never forget you', she whispered, as diamonds danced in the light.